William Shakespeare

The Tragedy of
KING RICHARD
the Second

Edited by Kenneth Muir

The Signet Classic Shakespeare
GENERAL EDITOR: SYLVAN BARNET

*Revised and Updated
Bibliography*

A SIGNET CLASSIC
NEW AMERICAN LIBRARY
TIMES MIRROR
NEW YORK AND SCARBOROUGH, ONTARIO
THE NEW ENGLISH LIBRARY LIMITED, LONDON

SIGNET CLASSIC TRADEMARK REG. U.S. PAT. OFF. AND FOREIGN COUNTRIES
REGISTERED TRADEMARK—MARCA REGISTRADA
HECHO EN CHICAGO, U.S.A.

SIGNET, SIGNET CLASSICS, MENTOR, PLUME AND MERIDIAN BOOKS
are published in the United States by
The New American Library, Inc.,
1301 Avenue of the Americas, New York, New York 10019,
in Canada by The New American Library of Canada Limited,
81 Mack Avenue, Scarborough, Ontario M1L 1M8,
in the United Kingdom by The New English Library Limited,
Barnard's Inn, Holborn, London, EC1N 2JR, England.

11   12   13   14   15   16   17   18   19

Contents

Shakespeare: Prefatory Remarks

Between the record of his baptism in Stratford on 26 April 1564 and the record of his burial in Stratford on 25 April 1616, some forty documents name Shakespeare, and many others name his parents, his children, and his grandchildren. More facts are known about William Shakespeare than about any other playwright of the period except Ben Jonson. The facts should, however, be distinguished from the legends. The latter, inevitably more engaging and better known, tell us that the Stratford boy killed a calf in high style, poached deer and rabbits, and was forced to flee to London, where he held horses outside a playhouse. These traditions are only traditions; they may be true, but no evidence supports them, and it is well to stick to the facts.

Mary Arden, the dramatist's mother, was the daughter of a substantial landowner; about 1557 she married John Shakespeare, who was a glove-maker and trader in various farm commodities. In 1557 John Shakespeare was a member of the Council (the governing body of Stratford), in 1558 a constable of the borough, in 1561 one of the two town chamberlains, in 1565 an alderman (entitling him to the appellation "Mr."), in 1568 high bailiff —the town's highest political office, equivalent to mayor. After 1577, for an unknown reason he drops out of local politics. The birthday of William Shakespeare, the eldest son of this locally prominent man, is unrecorded; but the Stratford parish register records that the infant was baptized on 26 April 1564. (It is quite possible that he was born on 23 April, but this date has probably been assigned by tradition because it is the date on which, fifty-two years later, he died.) The attendance records of the Stratford grammar school of the period are not extant, but it is reasonable to assume that the son of a local official attended the school and received substantial training in Latin. The masters of the school from Shakespeare's seventh to fifteenth years held Oxford degrees; the Elizabethan curriculum excluded mathematics and the natural sciences but taught a good deal of Latin rhetoric, logic, and literature. On 27 November 1582 a marriage license was issued to Shakespeare and Anne Hathaway, eight years his senior. The couple had a child in May, 1583. Perhaps the marriage was necessary, but perhaps the couple had earlier engaged in a formal "troth-plight," which would render their children legitimate even if no further ceremony were performed. In 1585 Anne Hathaway bore Shakespeare twins.

That Shakespeare was born is excellent; that he married and had children is pleasant; but that we know nothing about his departure from Stratford to London, or about the beginning of his theatrical career, is lamentable and must be admitted. We would gladly sacrifice details about his children's baptism for details about his earliest days on the stage. Perhaps the poaching episode is true (but it is first reported almost a century after Shakespeare's death), or perhaps he first left Stratford to be a schoolteacher, as another tradition holds; perhaps he was moved by

> Such wind as scatters young men through the world,
> To seek their fortunes further than at home
> Where small experience grows.

In 1592, thanks to the cantankerousness of Robert Greene, a rival playwright and a pamphleteer, we have our first reference, a snarling one, to Shakespeare as an actor and playwright. Greene warns those of his own educated friends who wrote for the theater against an actor who has presumed to turn playwright:

> There is an upstart crow, beautified with our feathers, that with his *tiger's heart wrapped in a player's hide* supposes he is as well able to bombast out a blank verse as the best of you, and being an absolute Johannes-factotum is in his own conceit the only Shake-scene in a country.

The reference to the player, as well as the allusion to Aesop's crow (who strutted in borrowed plumage, as an actor struts in fine words not his own) makes it clear that by this date Shakespeare had both acted and written. That Shakespeare is meant is indicated not only by "Shake-scene" but by the parody of a line from one of Shakespeare's plays, *3 Henry VI*: "O, tiger's heart wrapped in a woman's hide." If Shakespeare in 1592 was prominent enough to be attacked by an envious dramatist, he probably had served an apprenticeship in the theater for at least a few years.

In any case, by 1592 Shakespeare had acted and written, and there are a number of subsequent references to him as an actor: documents indicate that in 1598 he is a "principal comedian," in 1603 a "principal tragedian," in 1608 he is one of the "men players." The profession of actor was not for a gentleman, and it occasionally drew the scorn of university men who resented writing speeches for persons less educated than themselves, but it was respectable enough: players, if prosperous, were in effect members of the bourgeoisie, and there is nothing to suggest that Stratford considered William Shakespeare less than a solid citizen. When, in 1596, the Shakespeares were granted a coat of arms, the grant was made to Shakespeare's father, but probably William Shakespeare (who the next year bought the second-largest house in town) had arranged the matter on his own behalf. In subsequent transactions he is occasionally styled a gentleman.

Although in 1593 and 1594 Shakespeare published

two narrative poems dedicated to the Earl òf Southampton, *Venus and Adonis* and *The Rape of Lucrece,* and may well have written most or all of his sonnets in the middle nineties, Shakespeare's literary activity seems to have been almost entirely devoted to the theater. (It may be significant that the two narrative poems were written in years when the plague closed the theaters for several months.) In 1594 he was a charter member of a theatrical company called the Chamberlain's Men (which in 1603 changed its name to the King's Men); until he retired to Stratford (about 1611, apparently), he was with this remarkably stable company. From 1599 the company acted primarily at the Globe Theatre, in which Shakespeare held a one-tenth interest. Other Elizabethan dramatists are known to have acted, but no other is known also to have been entitled to a share in the profits of the playhouse.

Shakespeare's first eight published plays did not have his name on them, but this is not remarkable; the most popular play of the sixteenth century, Thomas Kyd's *The Spanish Tragedy,* went through many editions without naming Kyd, and Kyd's authorship is known only because a book on the profession of acting happens to quote (and attribute to Kyd) some lines on the interest of Roman emperors in the drama. What is remarkable is that after 1598 Shakespeare's name commonly appears on printed plays—some of which are not his. Another indication of his popularity comes from Francis Meres, author of *Palladis Tamia: Wit's Treasury* (1598): in this anthology of snippets accompanied by an essay on literature, many playwrights are mentioned, but Shakespeare's name occurs more often than any other, and Shakespeare is the only playwright whose plays are listed.

From his acting, playwriting, and share in a theater, Shakespeare seems to have made considerable money. He put it to work, making substantial investments in Stratford real estate. When he made his will (less than a month before he died), he sought to leave his property intact to his descendants. Of small bequests to relatives and to friends (including three actors, Richard Burbage,

John Heminges, and Henry Condell), that to his wife of
the second-best bed has provoked the most comment;
perhaps it was the bed the couple had slept in, the best
being reserved for visitors. In any case, had Shakespeare
not excepted it, the bed would have gone (with the rest
of his household possessions) to his daughter and her
husband. On 25 April 1616 he was buried within the
chancel of the church at Stratford. An unattractive monument to his memory, placed on a wall near the grave,
says he died on 23 April. Over the grave itself are the
lines, perhaps by Shakespeare, that (more than his literary fame) have kept his bones undisturbed in the crowded
burial ground where old bones were often dislodged to
make way for new:

> Good friend, for Jesus' sake forbear
> To dig the dust enclosèd here.
> Blessed be the man that spares these stones
> And cursed be he that moves my bones.

Thirty-seven plays, as well as some nondramatic
poems, are held to constitute the Shakespeare canon.
The dates of composition of most of the works are
highly uncertain, but there is often evidence of a *terminus
a quo* (starting point) and/or a *terminus ad quem*
(terminal point) that provides a framework for intelli-
gent guessing. For example, *Richard II* cannot be
earlier than 1595, the publication date of some material
to which it is indebted; *The Merchant of Venice* cannot
be later than 1598, the year Francis Meres mentioned
it. Sometimes arguments for a date hang on an alleged
topical allusion, such as the lines about the unseasonable weather in *A Midsummer Night's Dream*, II.i.81-117,
but such an allusion (if indeed it is an allusion) can be
variously interpreted, and in any case there is always
the possibility that a topical allusion was inserted during a revision, years after the composition of a play.
Dates are often attributed on the basis of style, and although conjectures about style usually rest on other conjectures, sooner or later one must rely on one's literary

sense. There is no real proof, for example, that *Othello* is not as early as *Romeo and Juliet,* but one feels *Othello* is later, and because the first record of its performance is 1604, one is glad enough to set its composition at that date and not push it back into Shakespeare's early years. The following chronology, then, is as much indebted to informed guesswork and sensitivity as it is to fact. The dates, necessarily imprecise, indicate something like a scholarly consensus.

PLAYS

1588–93	*The Comedy of Errors*
1588–94	*Love's Labor's Lost*
1590–91	*2 Henry VI*
1590–91	*3 Henry VI*
1591–92	*1 Henry VI*
1592–93	*Richard III*
1592–94	*Titus Andronicus*
1593–94	*The Taming of the Shrew*
1593–95	*The Two Gentlemen of Verona*
1594–96	*Romeo and Juliet*
1595	*Richard II*
1594–96	*A Midsummer Night's Dream*
1596–97	*King John*
1596–97	*The Merchant of Venice*
1597	*1 Henry IV*
1597–98	*2 Henry IV*
1598–1600	*Much Ado About Nothing*
1598–99	*Henry V*
1599–1600	*Julius Caesar*
1599–1600	*As You Like It*
1599–1600	*Twelfth Night*
1600–01	*Hamlet*
1597–1601	*The Merry Wives of Windsor*
1601–02	*Troilus and Cressida*
1602–04	*All's Well That Ends Well*
1603–04	*Othello*
1604–05	*Measure for Measure*

1604–06	*King Lear*
1605–06	*Macbeth*
1606–07	*Antony and Cleopatra*
1605–08	*Timon of Athens*
1607–09	*Coriolanus*
1608–09	*Pericles*
1609–10	*Cymbeline*
1610–11	*The Winter's Tale*
1611–12	*The Tempest*
1612–13	*Henry VIII*

POEMS

1592	*Venus and Adonis*
1593–94	*The Rape of Lucrece*
1593–1600	*Sonnets*
1600–01	*The Phoenix and the Turtle*

Shakespeare's Theater

In Shakespeare's infancy, Elizabethan actors performed wherever they could—in great halls, at court, in the courtyards of inns. The innyards must have made rather unsatisfactory theaters: on some days they were unavailable because carters bringing goods to London used them as depots; when available, they had to be rented from the innkeeper; perhaps most important, London inns were subject to the Common Council of London, which was not well disposed toward theatricals. In 1574 the Common Council required that plays and playing places in London be licensed. It asserted that

sundry great disorders and inconveniences have been found to ensue to this city by the inordinate haunting of great multitudes of people, specially youth, to plays, interludes, and shows, namely occasion of frays and quarrels, evil practices of incontinency in great inns

having chambers and secret places adjoining to their
open stages and galleries,

and ordered that innkeepers who wished licenses to hold
performances put up a bond and make contributions to
the poor.

The requirement that plays and innyard theaters be
licensed, along with the other drawbacks of playing at
inns, probably drove James Burbage (a carpenter-turned-
actor) to rent in 1576 a plot of land northeast of the
city walls and to build here—on property outside the
jurisdiction of the city—England's first permanent construction designed for plays. He called it simply the
Theatre. About all that is known of its construction is
that it was wood. It soon had imitators, the most famous
being the Globe (1599), built across the Thames (again
outside the city's jurisdiction), out of timbers of the
Theatre, which had been dismantled when Burbage's
lease ran out.

There are three important sources of information
about the structure of Elizabethan playhouses—drawings,
a contract, and stage directions in plays. Of drawings,
only the so-called De Witt drawing (c. 1596) of the
Swan—really a friend's copy of De Witt's drawing—is
of much significance. It shows a building of three tiers,
with a stage jutting from a wall into the yard or center
of the building. The tiers are roofed, and part of the
stage is covered by a roof that projects from the rear
and is supported at its front on two posts, but the
groundlings, who paid a penny to stand in front of the
stage, were exposed to the sky. (Performances in such a
playhouse were held only in the daytime; artificial il-
lumination was not used.) At the rear of the stage are
two doors; above the stage is a gallery. The second
major source of information, the contract for the Fortune, specifies that although the Globe is to be the model,
the Fortune is to be square, eighty feet outside and
fifty-five inside. The stage is to be forty-three feet broad,
and is to extend into the middle of the yard (i.e., it is
twenty-seven and a half feet deep). For patrons willing

to pay more than the general admission charged of the groundlings, there were to be three galleries provided with seats. From the third chief source, stage directions, one learns that entrance to the stage was by doors, presumably spaced widely apart at the rear ("Enter one citizen at one door, and another at the other"), and that in addition to the platform stage there was occasionally some sort of curtained booth or alcove allowing for "discovery" scenes, and some sort of playing space "aloft" or "above" to represent (for example) the top of a city's walls or a room above the street. Doubtless each theater had its own peculiarities, but perhaps we can talk about a "typical" Elizabethan theater if we realize that no theater need exactly have fit the description, just as no father is the typical father with 3.7 children. This hypothetical theater is wooden, round or polygonal (in *Henry V* Shakespeare calls it a "wooden *O*"), capable of holding some eight hundred spectators standing in the yard around the projecting elevated stage and some fifteen hundred additional spectators seated in the three roofed galleries. The stage, protected by a "shadow" or "heavens" or roof, is entered by two doors; behind the doors is the "tiring house" (attiring house, i.e., dressing room), and above the doors is some sort of gallery that may sometimes hold spectators but that can be used (for example) as the bedroom from which Romeo—according to a stage direction in one text—"goeth down." Some evidence suggests that a throne can be lowered onto the platform stage, perhaps from the "shadow"; certainly characters can descend from the stage through a trap or traps into the cellar or "hell." Sometimes this space beneath the platform accommodates a sound-effects man or musician (in *Antony and Cleopatra* "music of the hautboys is under the stage") or an actor (in *Hamlet* the "Ghost cries under the stage"). Most characters simply walk on and off, but because there is no curtain in front of the platform, corpses will have to be carried off (Hamlet must lug Polonius' guts into the neighbor room), or will have to fall at the rear, where the curtain on the alcove or booth can be drawn to conceal them.

Such may have been the so-called "public theater." Another kind of theater, called the "private theater" because its much greater admission charge limited its audience to the wealthy or the prodigal, must be briefly mentioned. The private theater was basically a large room, entirely roofed, and therefore artificially illuminated, with a stage at one end. In 1576 one such theater was established in Blackfriars, a Dominican priory in London that had been suppressed in 1538 and confiscated by the Crown and thus was not under the city's jurisdiction. All the actors in the Blackfriars theater were boys about eight to thirteen years old (in the public theaters similar boys played female parts; a boy Lady Macbeth played to a man Macbeth). This private theater had a precarious existence, and ceased operations in 1584. In 1596 James Burbage, who had already made theatrical history by building the Theatre, began to construct a second Blackfriars theater. He died in 1597, and for several years this second Blackfriars theater was used by a troupe of boys, but in 1608 two of Burbage's sons and five other actors (including Shakespeare) became joint operators of the theater, using it in the winter when the open-air Globe was unsuitable. Perhaps such a smaller theater, roofed, artificially illuminated, and with a tradition of a courtly audience, exerted an influence on Shakespeare's late plays.

Performances in the private theaters may well have had intermissions during which music was played, but in the public theaters the action was probably uninterrupted, flowing from scene to scene almost without a break. Actors would enter, speak, exit, and others would immediately enter and establish (if necessary) the new locale by a few properties and by words and gestures. Here are some samples of Shakespeare's scene painting:

This is Illyria, lady.

Well, this is the Forest of Arden.

> This castle hath a pleasant seat; the air
> Nimbly and sweetly recommends itself
> Unto our gentle senses.

On the other hand, it is a mistake to conceive of the Elizabethan stage as bare. Although Shakespeare's Chorus in *Henry V* calls the stage an "unworthy scaffold" and urges the spectators to "eke out our performance with your mind," there was considerable spectacle. The last act of *Macbeth,* for example, has five stage directions calling for "drum and colors," and another sort of appeal to the eye is indicated by the stage direction "Enter Macduff, with Macbeth's head." Some scenery and properties may have been substantial; doubtless a throne was used, and in one play of the period we encounter this direction: "Hector takes up a great piece of rock and casts at Ajax, who tears up a young tree by the roots and assails Hector." The matter is of some importance, and will be glanced at again in the next section.

The Texts of Shakespeare

Though eighteen of his plays were published during his lifetime, Shakespeare seems never to have supervised their publication. There is nothing unusual here; when a playwright sold a play to a theatrical company, he surrendered his ownership of it. Normally a company would not publish the play, because to publish it meant to allow competitors to acquire the piece. Some plays, however, did get published: apparently treacherous actors sometimes pieced together a play for a publisher, sometimes a company in need of money sold a play, and sometimes a company allowed a play to be published that no longer drew audiences. That Shakespeare did not concern himself with publication, then, is scarcely remarkable; of his contemporaries only Ben Jonson carefully supervised the publication of his own plays. In 1623, seven years after Shakespeare's death, John Heminges and Henry Condell (two senior members of Shakespeare's company, who had performed with him for about twenty years) collected his plays—published and unpublished—into a large volume, commonly called the First Folio. (A folio is a volume consisting of sheets that have been folded once, each sheet thus making two leaves, or four pages. The eighteen plays published during Shakespeare's lifetime had been issued one play per volume in small books called quartos. Each sheet in a quarto has been folded twice, making four leaves, or eight pages.) The First Folio contains thirty-six plays; a thirty-seventh, *Pericles,* though not in the Folio is regarded as canonical. Heminges and Condell suggest in an address "To the great variety of readers" that the republished plays are presented in better form than in the quartos: "Before you were abused with diverse stolen and surreptitious copies, maimed and deformed by the frauds and stealths of injurious impostors that exposed them; even those, are now offered to your view cured and perfect of their limbs, and all the rest absolute in their numbers, as he [i.e., Shakespeare] conceived them."

Whoever was assigned to prepare the texts for publication in the First Folio seems to have taken his job seriously and yet not to have performed it with uniform care. The sources of the texts seem to have been, in general, good unpublished copies or the best published copies. The first play in the collection, *The Tempest,* is divided into acts and scenes, has unusually full stage directions and descriptions of spectacle, and concludes with a list of the characters, but the editor was not able (or willing) to present all of the succeeding texts so fully dressed. Later texts occasionally show signs of carelessness: in one scene of *Much Ado About Nothing* the names of actors, instead of characters, appear as speech prefixes (presumably evidence that the printer's copy for this play was a prompt copy); proofreading throughout the Folio is spotty and apparently was done without reference to the printer's copy; the pagination of *Hamlet* jumps from 156 to 257.

A modern editor of Shakespeare must first select his

copy; no problem if the play exists only in the Folio, but a considerable problem if the relationship between a quarto and the Folio—or an early quarto and a later one—is unclear. When an editor has chosen what seems to him to be the most authoritative text or texts for his copy, he has not done with making decisions. First of all, he must reckon with Elizabethan spelling. If he is not producing a facsimile, he probably modernizes it, but ought he to preserve the old form of words that apparently were pronounced quite unlike their modern forms—"lanthorn," "alablaster"? If he preserves these forms, is he really preserving Shakespeare's forms or perhaps those of a compositor in the printing house? What is one to do when one finds "lanthorn" and "lantern" in adjacent lines? (The editors of this series in general, but not invariably, assume that words should be spelled in their modern form.) Elizabethan punctuation, too, presents problems. For example, in the First Folio, the only text for the play, Macbeth rejects his wife's idea that he can wash the blood from his hand:

> no: this my Hand will rather
> The multitudinous Seas incarnardine,
> Making the Greene one, Red.

Obviously an editor will remove the superfluous capitals, and he will probably alter the spelling to "incarnadine," but will he leave the comma before "red," letting Macbeth speak of the sea as "the green one," or will he (like most modern editors) remove the comma and thus have Macbeth say that his hand will make the ocean *uniformly* red?

An editor will sometimes have to change more than spelling or punctuation. Macbeth says to his wife:

> I dare do all that may become a man,
> Who dares no more, is none.

For two centuries editors have agreed that the second

line is unsatisfactory, and have emended "no" to "do": "Who dares do more is none." But when in the same play Ross says that fearful persons

> floate vpon a wilde and violent Sea
> Each way, and moue,

need "move" be emended to "none," as it often is, on the hunch that the compositor misread the manuscript? The editors of the Signet Classic Shakespeare have restrained themselves from making abundant emendations. In their minds they hear Dr. Johnson on the dangers of emending: "I have adopted the Roman sentiment, that it is more honorable to save a citizen than to kill an enemy." Some departures (in addition to spelling, punctuation, and lineation) from the copy text have of course been made, but the original readings are listed in a note following the play, so that the reader can evaluate them for himself.

The editors of the Signet Classic Shakespeare, following tradition, have added line numbers and in many cases act and scene divisions as well as indications of locale at the beginning of scenes. The Folio divided most of the plays into acts and some into scenes. Early eighteenth-century editors increased the divisions. These divisions, which provide a convenient way of referring to passages in the plays, have been retained, but when not in the text chosen as the basis for the Signet Classic text they are enclosed in square brackets [ ] to indicate that they are editorial additions. Similarly, although no play of Shakespeare's published during his lifetime was equipped with indications of locale at the heads of scene divisions, locales have here been added in square brackets for the convenience of the reader, who lacks the information afforded to spectators by costumes, properties, and gestures. The spectator can tell at a glance he is in the throne room, but without an editorial indication the reader may be puzzled for a while. It should be mentioned, incidentally, that there are a few authentic stage directions—perhaps Shakespeare's, perhaps a prompter's—that suggest locales: for example, "Enter Brutus in his orchard," and "They go up into the Senate house." It is hoped that the bracketed additions provide the reader with the sort of help provided in these two authentic directions, but it is equally hoped that the reader will remember that the stage was not loaded with scenery.

No editor during the course of his work can fail to recollect some words Heminges and Condell prefixed to the Folio:

It had been a thing, we confess, worthy to have been wished, that the author himself had lived to have set forth and overseen his own writings. But since it hath been ordained otherwise, and he by death departed from that right, we pray you do not envy his friends the office of their care and pain to have collected and published them.

Nor can an editor, after he has done his best, forget Heminges and Condell's final words: "And so we leave you to other of his friends, whom if you need can be your guides. If you need them not, you can lead yourselves, and others. And such readers we wish him."

SYLVAN BARNET
Tufts University

Introduction

Richard II, at least in its present form, was written and performed in 1595, after the publication of Samuel Daniel's *Civil Wars* (which was registered in October 1594) and before December 9, when there was a private performance before Sir Edward Hoby and his friends. The play was a popular one. According to Elizabeth I, by 1601 it had been played "forty" times; but when the Essex conspirators asked Shakespeare's company to put on a special performance on the eve of the rebellion, because they thought that the deposition of Richard would be good propaganda, the players protested that it was "so old and so long out of use" that it would attract only a small audience. The conspirators therefore subsidized the performance.

Shakespeare had already dealt with the remote effects of Bolingbroke's usurpation in *Henry VI* and *Richard III*, and his obvious model in the present play was *Edward II*, a play in which Christopher Marlowe had brilliantly dramatized the deposition and murder of Richard of Bordeaux's great-grandfather. There were already at least two plays on the reign of Richard II, *Jack Straw* and *Woodstock,* and it has been argued by Professor John Dover Wilson (in his edition of *Richard II*) that Shakespeare's tragedy was based on a lost play by the author of *The Troublesome Reign of King John*, the source of Shakespeare's *King John*. The main arguments that have been advanced in support of this theory are (1) the presence of various details in the play that presuppose knowledge on the part of the audience; (2) the presence of "fossil" rhymes in blank verse speeches, which seem to indicate that the speeches were originally in rhymed verse; (3) the badness of certain scenes (e.g., V.iii) which, it is supposed, Shakespeare borrowed from the source play; (4) the use by Shakespeare, either directly or indirectly, of facts available only in two or three French chronicles that were still in manuscript. The last of these points is discussed in the appendix on sources. On the other three, I agree with most scholars that the existence of the source play has not been proved. I can see no resemblance between the style of *The Troublesome Reign* and that of the suspected scenes of *Richard II;* Shakespeare himself may have revised his own play, turning some rhymed verse into blank verse; the obscurities, which in any case are unnoticed in performance, may be explained by sheer carelessness in introducing facts that Shakespeare remembered from his reading; and it is not positively necessary to find a scapegoat for the feeble passages of rhymed verse in Act V. It will be remembered that in the other plays written about this time—*A Midsummer Night's Dream* and *Romeo and Juliet*—there is a considerable amount of rhyme, more than there had been in previous plays. These three plays have another characteristic in common—they are the first in which Shakespeare uses patterns of imagery for dramatic purposes.[1] The reasons for the rhymed verse are not far to seek. Shakespeare completed his second narrative poem in 1594, and he was still writing sonnets in 1595. Blank verse, moreover, was still a comparatively new medium for drama. Marlowe had led his audiences away from "jigging veins of rhyming mother wits" only seven years previously. The academic dramatists—Daniel and Greville—still used rhyme in their plays. Peele had used it in some scenes of *The Arraign-*

---

[1] See Richard D. Altick's analysis (printed below) of the play from this point of view. The imagery of the play has also been discussed by Mark Van Doren, W. H. Clemen, and Brents Stirling in the works listed in the Suggested References.

ment of Paris and Kyd, though he had used blank verse for *The Spanish Tragedy*, reverted to rhyme in his *Cornelia*. The Countess of Pembroke was known to favor it. Apart from Marlowe's, very little good blank verse had been written, and the best nondramatic poets—Spenser, Sidney, Daniel, Drayton—all stuck to rhyme. Looking back, we can see that Wilton, where the Countess lived, was the home of lost causes; but to Shakespeare, to whom rhyme came easily, the matter was not so obvious. After all, his early blank verse was comparatively artificial and certainly rhetorical. He did not suffer from Mr. Eliot's fear that the audience would realize that it was listening to poetry. The acting, too, in these early years, had a strong element of formality: the delivery of the verse was more important than the realistic portrayal of character. Shakespeare was only just beginning to portray character by varying the verse. He did this brilliantly with Juliet's Nurse and in the contrast between Richard and Bolingbroke in the abdication scene. But his touch was still uncertain. The Gardener scene (III.iv) was admirably conceived as a commentary by the common man on the state of England, and as a parabolic statement, which links up with Gaunt's description of England as "this other Eden." But the execution of the scene falls far short of the conception. The Gardener, speaking in formal blank verse, indistinguishable from that used by royal and aristocratic characters, never really emerges from his role as a chorus. It would have been better, perhaps, to have written the scene in prose; but, for some reason, Shakespeare avoided prose altogether. Perhaps he was trying to please his new aristocratic friends.

Whatever the reasons, Shakespeare introduced a considerable amount of rhymed verse into *Richard II*. Some of it is successful, as in Bolingbroke's couplets in the third scene of the play (144–47). But one scene (V.iii.73–134) is so bad that critics would like to believe that Shakespeare did not write it; or that, if he wrote it at all, it must belong to a much earlier version of the play, left inadvertently or ill-advisedly unrevised. As we have seen, however, Shakespeare hardly used rhyme at all in some of his early plays, so that the scene was probably written at the same period as the rest of the play. Swinburne, in *A Study of Shakespeare,* called the scene "the last hysterical struggle of rhyme to maintain its place in tragedy." The situation is farcical, with York, the Duchess, and Aumerle on their knees at once, and York actually urging the execution of his son. Shakespeare must have been aware of the absurdity, but he seems to have miscalculated the effect of the scene.

Richard II can be regarded either as a history play, the first of the tetralogy that includes the two parts of *Henry IV* and *Henry V*, or as a tragedy complete in itself. There are several indications in the play that Shakespeare had already planned to continue the story—e.g., the Bishop of Carlisle's prophecy, Richard's own prophecy about Northumberland, the references to Prince Hal and Glendower, and the introduction of Hotspur—but when the play was first printed it was entitled *The Tragedy of Richard II*. Although it is a political tragedy, since we are as much concerned with the fate of England as with the fate of the hero, Richard has a more central role than Henry VI in three earlier histories or Henry IV in the next two histories.

The critics have been very much divided on the amount of sympathy we should extend to Richard. Some find him wholly admirable, and others regard him as wholly contemptible. To Kreyssig,

> he affords us the shocking spectacle of an absolute bankruptcy, mental and spiritual no less than in the world of outward affairs, caused by one condition only: that nature has given him the character of a Dilettante, and called him to a position which, more than any other, demands the Artist.[2]

To Walter Pater, writing a few years later, Richard

---

[2] Quoted by A. P. Rossiter, *Angel with Horns and Other Shakespeare Lectures,* ed. Graham Storey. New York: Theatre Arts Books; London: Longmans, Green & Company, Ltd., 1961, p. 39.

seemed to be "an exquisite poet." Swinburne, in *Three Plays of Shakespeare*, declared that the third scene

> reveals the protagonist of the play as so pitifully mean and cruel a weakling that no future action or suffering can lift him above the level which divides and purifies pity from contempt.

Later in his essay, Swinburne accused Richard of "callous cruelty" and "heartless hypocrisy," remarking that "the histrionic young tyrant" was removed

> once for all beyond reach of manly sympathy or compassion unqualified by scorn. If we can ever be sorry for anything that befalls so vile a sample of royalty, our sorrow must be so diluted and adulterated by recollection of his wickedness and baseness that the tribute could hardly be acceptable to any but the most pitiable example or exception of mankind.

Walter Raleigh, however, remarked in *Shakespeare* that "It is difficult to condemn Richard without taking sides against poetry"; and two recent poets have sprung to Richard's defense, as they would have defended a minor poet of our own day, whose life had been a failure in the eyes of the world. W. B. Yeats, in *Ideas of Good and Evil*, passed lightly over the King's faults and declared that Shakespeare

> made his king fail, a little because he lacked some qualities that were doubtless common among his scullions, but more because he had certain qualities that are uncommon in all ages. To suppose that Shakespeare preferred the man who deposed his king is to suppose that Shakespeare judged men with the eyes of a Municipal Councilor weighing the merits of a Town Clerk; and that had he been by when Verlaine cried out from his bed, "Sir, you have been made by the stroke of a pen, but I have been made by the

breath of God," he would have thought the Hospital Superintendent the better man.

John Masefield, obviously much influenced by Yeats's essay, declares in *William Shakespeare* that Richard fails because he is not common:

> The tragedy of the sensitive soul, always acute, becomes terrible when that soul is made king here by one of the accidents of life.

John Bailey, irritated by Yeats and Masefield, retorted tartly in *The Continuity of Letters*:

> Fools such critics are. . . . For their own choice Mr. Yeats and Mr. Masefield are free. Only they must not father it upon Shakespeare. No man has ever known the theater better than he; and if he had meant us to admire Richard and despise Henry [Henry V, not Henry IV] we should most assuredly not have escaped doing it; but there is no audience from his day to ours which has not instantly and instinctively worshiped Henry and pitied Richard.

We may note in passing that many good critics have had reservations about Henry V, and modern audiences (except in time of war) have been less enthusiastic about him than Bailey appears to be, and more sympathetic to Richard, especially when the part was played by Sir John Gielgud. But the debate continues. A. P. Rossiter, to give a last example, unkindly suggests that there is "something in Richard which calls out the latent homosexuality of critics"; and to Pater's claim that Richard's nature is "that of a poet," he replies: "If so, surely a very *bad* poet."

Some of Richard's sympathetic critics seem to forget that he is depicted as a murderer; and those who find no redeeming features in his character ignore or misinterpret the changes brought about by suffering. Shakespeare's model for his play (as we have seen) was *Edward II*.

Marlowe's method was to concentrate on Edward's misgovernment in the opening acts of the play and to arouse sympathy for him after his deposition, partly by stressing the unscrupulousness of his opponents, partly by showing that Edward was beloved by his favorites, and partly by a detailed presentation of his sufferings. Shakespeare's method is similar. In the first two acts he gives a vivid portrayal of Richard's misgovernment, which is brought home to us particularly by the patriotic indignation of Gaunt's dying speeches. In the later acts, although we are shown again and again Richard's weaknesses of character, Shakespeare arouses sympathy for him by the poetic beauty of his long arias, by his tragic isolation, by the pathos of his leave-taking from his Queen, by the account of his entry into London, and by the episode of the loyal groom. Yet Shakespeare's method differs in several respects from Marlowe's. Richard's initial guilt is greater than Edward's, his suffering is mental rather than physical, and his character is purged by it. Although some critics believe that his scene with the Queen and his soliloquy in prison reveal that he is still an incorrigible sentimentalist, turning everything, like Ophelia, to favor and to prettiness, there are signs that he has acquired a greater self-awareness and a recognition of his faults:

> I wasted time, and now doth Time waste me.

But the greatest difference between the attitudes of the two dramatists is that Marlowe never mentions, while Shakespeare continually stresses, the divine right of kings. We are warned over and over again that Richard's deposition is a sin which will be punished by the horrors of civil war. It was to stress this point that Shakespeare deviated from his sources in giving the Bishop of Carlisle his eloquent prophecy just before the deposition scene.

Professor J. Dover Wilson has called *Richard II* "a Tudor passion play," a description which fits in with the frequent references to Scripture by which Shakespeare achieves its particular tone and atmosphere. Some

of Richard's speeches are lamentations on the fall of
princes, a recognition of the mortality of man and of the
peculiar vulnerability of those called to high estate,
which read like transmutations of Lydgate's *Fall of Princes*
or of *The Mirror for Magistrates*. These link up with the
medieval conception of tragedy as a fall from greatness
into misery. But the Scriptural references are mainly designed to emphasize the sin of rebellion against an
anointed king, and they show that Shakespeare was
steeped in the teaching of the Homilies, with whatever reservations he may have had about it. Richard compares
his treacherous friends to Judas and those who show an
outward pity at his fall to Pilate. He imagines that Bolingbroke will tremble at his sin; he boasts that the deputy
elected by the Lord cannot be deposed by the breath of
worldly men, that angels will fight on his side, and that
the unborn children of the rebels will be struck by pestilence. Bolingbroke, for having broken his oath of allegiance, is damned in the book of heaven. England, rent
by civil war, will be called Golgotha. The Bishop of
Carlisle warns Bolingbroke not to set house against house;
and Bolingbroke himself compares Richard's murderer to
Cain. In prison Richard meditates on two Gospel texts.

Richard's own Biblical references are an appeal for
Christian compassion. It is possible, indeed, that Shakespeare had in mind the whole problem of charity and
pity; but Professor Peter Alexander, who makes this
suggestion in *Shakespeare's Life and Art,* goes on to complain that

> the fallen king's insistence on his own position . . . is
> incompatible with the self-forgetfulness which is as es-
> sential to the tragic as to the Christian hero. For this
> is not the waking as from a dream of some disinter-
> ested heart to the self-seeking of society, but the
> long lament of one who gave short shrift to a dying
> Gaunt; and this contrast between Richard's indiffer-
> ence to others and exquisite sensibility for himself
> makes tragedy impossible.

Even if we could believe in the self-forgetfulness of Hamlet, Lear, or Othello, we may well feel that Professor Alexander does not make allowances for the development of Richard's character in the course of the play, nor for the Elizabethan convention by which a character comments on his own situation. When Lear talks of his own pitiful state, or when Othello or Antony makes his final apologia, these characters are not meant to be indulging in self-pity or vanity: they are used by the dramatist to guide the feelings of the audience. In the mature tragedies, it is true, we do not get the self-comparison of a character to Christ; but the method is largely justified in Richard's case by the central importance in the play of the concept of Divine Right. The same consideration justifies the strong element of ritual in the play.

We are presented throughout the play with the contrast between Richard and his successor. Richard, the anointed King, is unfit to rule, in spite of his good qualities, and in spite of his belated acquisition of self-knowledge. Henry Bolingbroke is a born ruler, but his reign is doomed to misery because he is a usurper. The contrast is brought out in other ways. Richard is frivolous, witty, eloquent, and poetic, a man of words who wears his heart upon his sleeve, one who is continually playing a part, to whom, as John Palmer says in *Political Characters,* "nothing has interest or significance but what concerns himself." He loses his crown not because he stops the duel at Coventry—an action which he takes with the approval of his council, and which can hardly be regarded as an example of his love of play acting—but because of his murder of Gloucester before the beginning of the play, because of his confiscation of Gaunt's estates, because his return from Ireland is delayed by contrary winds, and because he despairs on his arrival in England. This last point, which is usually taken as a prime example of his refusal to face realities, could as plausibly be used to prove that he was more realistic than his supporters. He is brought to his ruin, as all Shakespeare's tragic heroes are, by a combination of fate and faults of character.

Henry is a contrast in every respect. He is generally taci-

turn, although he can turn on his charm like a tap, as is
apparent from the way even Northumberland is capti-
vated by it. The account given in I.iv of his triumphant
journey into exile, although put into the mouth of an
enemy, is corroborated by what he himself admits in *1
Henry IV*:

> And then I stole all courtesy from heaven,
> And dressed myself in such humility
> That I did pluck allegiance from men's hearts,
> Loud shouts and salutations from their mouths,
> Even in the presence of the crownèd King.
>
> > (III.ii.50-54)

The same calculated behavior is described in Hotspur's
account of their first meeting. Bolingbroke, like Clau-
dius, is a "king of smiles," a "fawning greyhound" who
proffered Hotspur "a candy deal of courtesy." We do not
see Henry in any personal relationship, except with his father in the first act, and in his complaints about his son
in the last. We see him as a politician (in the Elizabethan sense of the term, "unscrupulous self-seeker")
who subordinates everything to his ambition. He obtains
the crown, as he confesses on his deathbed, by "bypaths
and indirect crook'd ways." Shakespeare presents the
character with a masterly ambiguity. As John Palmer
points out:

> Bolingbroke gives no sign of his purpose—and for an
> excellent reason. He is that most dangerous of climb-
> ing politicians, the man who will go further than his
> rivals because he never allows himself to know where
> he is going. Every step in his progress toward the throne
> is dictated by circumstances, and he never permits
> himself to have a purpose till it is more than half ful-
> filled.

The same point is made by Brents Stirling:

> Three times—at the end of III.iii, at the end of the dep-

osition scene, and in the Exton scenes at the end of the play—Henry has taken, if it may be so called, a decisive step. Each time the move he has made has been embodied in a terse statement, and each time someone else has either evoked it from him or stated its implications for him.

The characterization, apart from that of Richard and Bolingbroke, is less effective than that of the minor characters in *Richard III*. But it is not so bad as is sometimes pretended. Swinburne, with customary exaggeration, attacked what he regarded as Shakespeare's incompetence:

The poet was not yet dramatist enough to feel for each of his characters an equal or proportionate regard; to divide and disperse his interest among the various crowd of figures which claim each in its place . . . a fair and adequate share of their creator's attention and sympathy. His present interest was wholly concentrated on the single figure of Richard; . . . the subordinate figures became to him but heavy and vexatious encumbrances, to be shifted on and off the stage with as much haste and as little of labor as might be possible to an impatient and uncertain hand. . . . Even after a lifelong study of this as of all other plays of Shakespeare, it is for me at least impossible to determine what I doubt the poet could himself have clearly defined—the main principle, the motive and the meaning of such characters as York, Norfolk, and Aumerle. The Gaveston and the Mortimer of Marlowe are far more solid and definite figures than these; yet none after Richard is more important to the scheme of Shakespeare. They are fitful, shifting, vaporous; their outlines change, withdraw, dissolve, and leave not a rack behind.

Swinburne's views were influenced by his assumption that the play was one of Shakespeare's earliest. If he had realized that the poet was not a novice when he wrote it, but the author of nine or ten other plays, he might have been less anxious to complain of its immaturity. Even in Shakespeare's greatest plays, the minor characters are little more than sketches; and it must be said that York, Mowbray, and Aumerle are not really as important to the scheme of the play as Gaveston and Mortimer are in *Edward II*. The three characters, moreover, are not really as indeterminate and vague as Swinburne pretends. York, for example, whom Swinburne described as

> an incomparable, an incredible, an unintelligible and a monstrous nullity . . . a living and driveling picture of hysterical impotence on the downward grade to dotage and distraction,

is, in fact, a perfectly credible portrait of a man torn between conflicting loyalties. He deplores Richard's behavior but he is chosen to be Lord Governor because the King realizes that his criticisms were disinterested:

> For he is just, and always loved us well.

York tries to be faithful to his trust; but it is clear from II.ii that he is muddled, incompetent, and powerless. Both here, and in later scenes, Shakespeare extracts some humor from York's bumbling inefficiency. In II.iii his loyalty to the King, his sympathy with Bolingbroke's wrongs, and his shortage of troops combine to paralyze him. He begins by calling Bolingbroke a traitor; before long he admits:

> I have had feeling of my cousin's wrongs.

He confesses that his forces are too weak for him to arrest the traitor, and follows a declaration of neutrality by extending an invitation to the rebels to spend the night in the castle. Before the end of the scene he has half agreed to go with the rebels to Bristol, where Bolingbroke intends to execute the King's favorites. York has become a traitor almost without knowing it. Far from being incredible, the character is very shrewdly drawn.

Once Richard's downfall is assured, York becomes a wholehearted supporter of the new regime. Characteristically, York is full of pity for Richard; he remonstrates with Northumberland for leaving out his title (III.iii.8), and, although he is chosen to escort the King to his deposition, he movingly describes the entrance of Bolingbroke and Richard into London. His new loyalty is soon tested. When he finds that Aumerle has plotted to kill Bolingbroke, it never enters his head to be ashamed of his own coat-turning: he rushes off to Windsor to beg for his son's death. This is partly prudence—he has agreed to be pledge for Aumerle's "lasting fealty to the new-made king"—but partly the genuine zeal of a convert. The scene in which he goes on his knees to Bolingbroke, absurd as it is, is not out of character.

A similar defense could be made of Aumerle, who is deeply attached to Richard and loyal to him after his fall. He submits to Bolingbroke only when his carelessness has put his life in danger. Shakespeare tells us enough about him for the purposes of the play—his dislike of Bolingbroke revealed in his account of his leave-taking and in the accusations leveled against him in IV.i, his love for Richard shown by his tears in III.iii, and by his conspiracy against the usurper. There are some indications of irresponsibility in his character, but Shakespeare deliberately leaves unsettled whether or not he was implicated in Gloucester's murder. The scene at the beginning of Act IV where he is accused was described by Swinburne as "a morally chaotic introduction of incongruous causes, inexplicable plaintiffs, and incomprehensible defendants." But the question of which side is telling the truth is irrelevant to the effect which Shakespeare wished to give. Aumerle has to be attacked, not because of his guilt, but because he is an opponent of the usurper.

The third character of whom Swinburne complains, Thomas Mowbray, Duke of Norfolk, appears only in two scenes of the first act. Shakespeare could rely on most of his audience knowing that Richard himself was ultimately responsible for Gloucester's murder—and those who did not know were plainly informed by Gaunt in the second scene—and they would therefore appreciate that Bolingbroke's attack on Mowbray was aimed at the King, or at least at his favorites. Richard can only banish Bolingbroke if he consents to the perpetual banishment of Mowbray. If these facts are understood, Mowbray's conduct becomes intelligible. He tries to defend himself without betraying Richard, and he is bitterly surprised at his sentence of banishment. Some critics have thought that a character with such a doubtful past should not have been given the sympathetic lines in which he expresses his patriotism, and that he should not have been given so fine an epitaph as Carlisle's speech (IV.i.91 ff.). But there are no black and no white characters in *Richard II*. We need be no more surprised at Mowbray fighting

> For Jesu Christ in glorious Christian field

than that Bolingbroke should intend to expiate his responsibility for Richard's death by making a pilgrimage to the Holy Land.

Sometimes, it must be admitted, Shakespeare does not fully succeed in making his characters live. In the second scene of the play, for example, he tries to give reality to the portrait of the Duchess of Gloucester by making her forget what she was going to say:

> Commend me to thy brother, Edmund York.
> Lo, this is all—nay, yet depart not so;
> Though this be all, do not so quickly go;
> I shall remember more. Bid him—ah, what?—
> With all good speed at Plashy visit me.

Here the effect is blurred by the rigidity of the verse and the intrusive rhyme.

It has been necessary to defend the reality of the minor characters in the play because the conflict between Richard and Bolingbroke does not take place in a dramatic and political vacuum. The background is filled in economically and well: and the patriotism of Gaunt, the loyalty of Aumerle, the oscillation of York, the prophetic fervor of the Bishop of Carlisle are all essential to the effect of the tragedy.

In *Titus Andronicus* and *Richard III* Shakespeare had submerged tragedy in melodrama; in *Romeo and Juliet* the tragedy is brought about by accident rather than by defect of character; in *Richard II* the tragedy is firmly based on character and, as in *King Lear,* the character of the hero acquires greater depth as his fortunes decline. It may therefore be said that, in spite of its obvious weaknesses, and in spite of its inferiority in some respects to *Richard III*—it contains finer poetry and greater complexity but is usually less effective in the theater— it is closer to mature Shakespearean tragedy than any of the previous plays had been.

KENNETH MUIR
University of Liverpool

The Tragedy of
King Richard the Second

King Richard the Second
Edmund, Duke of York ⎫
John of Gaunt, Duke of Lancaster ⎬ his uncles
Henry Bolingbroke, Gaunt's son
The Duke of Aumerle, York's son
Thomas Mowbray, Duke of Norfolk
The Earl of Salisbury
The Earl of Berkeley
Sir John Bushy
Sir William Bagot ⎫ Richard's favorites
Sir Henry Green ⎭
The Earl of Northumberland
Harry Percy, his son
Lord Ross
Lord Willoughby
The Bishop of Carlisle
Sir Stephen Scroop
Lord Fitzwater
The Duke of Surrey
The Abbot of Westminster
Sir Pierce of Exton
Lord Marshal
Welsh Captain
Queen Isabel, Richard's second wife
Duchess of Gloucester, Gaunt's sister-in-law
Duchess of York
Ladies, attending on the Queen; Gardeners; a
    Keeper; a Groom; Lords, Heralds, Officers, Sol-
    diers, Attendants, Servants.

Scene: England and Wales]

The Tragedy of
King Richard the Second

[ACT I

Scene I.   *Windsor Castle.*]

*Enter King Richard, John of Gaunt, with other
Nobles and Attendants.*

*apparent veneration
for uncle, only
public*

Richard. Old John of Gaunt, time-honored Lancaster,
Hast thou according to thy oath and band° ¹ *bond display*
Brought hither Henry Hereford,° thy bold son,
Here to make good the boist'rous late appeal,°
Which then our° leisure would not let us hear,   5
Against the Duke of Norfolk, Thomas Mowbray?

Gaunt. I have, my liege.

Richard. Tell me, moreover, hast thou sounded him,
If he appeal° the Duke on ancient malice,
Or worthily,° as a good subject should,   10
On some known ground of treachery in him?

Gaunt. As near as I could sift° him on that
argument,°
On some apparent° danger seen in him
Aimed at your Highness, no inveterate malice.

---

¹ The degree sign (°) indicates a footnote, which is keyed to the
text by line number. Text references are printed in *italic* type; the annotation follows in roman type.

I.i. ² *band* bond   ³*Hereford* (pronounced "Herford")   ⁴ *appeal* accusation of treason   ⁵ *our* (the royal plural)   ⁹ *appeal* accuse   ¹⁰ *worthily* according to desert   ¹² *sift* examine thoroughly   ¹² *argument* subject   ¹³ *apparent* obvious

15 *Richard*. Then call them to our presence: face to face,
    And frowning brow to brow, ourselves will hear
    The accuser and the accusèd freely speak.
    High-stomached° are they both, and full of ire,
    In rage, deaf as the sea, hasty as fire.

Enter Bolingbroke and Mowbray.

20 *Bolingbroke*.° Many years of happy days befall
    My gracious sovereign, my most loving liege!

Mowbray. Each day still better other's happiness,
    Until the heavens envying earth's good hap,
    Add an immortal title to your crown!

25 *Richard*. We thank you both; yet one but flatters us,
    As well appeareth by the cause you come,
    Namely to appeal each other of high treason.
    Cousin of Hereford, what dost thou object
    Against the Duke of Norfolk, Thomas Mowbray?

Bolingbroke. First—heaven be the record to my
30   speech!—
    In the devotion of a subject's love,
    Tend'ring° the precious safety of my prince,
    And free from other misbegotten hate,
    Come I appellant° to this princely presence.
35 Now, Thomas Mowbray, do I turn to thee,
    And mark my greeting° well: for what I speak,
    My body shall make good upon this earth,
    Or my divine soul answer it in heaven.
    Thou art a traitor and a miscreant,°
40 Too good to be so, and too bad to live;
    Since the more fair and crystal is the sky,
    The uglier seem the clouds that in it fly.
    Once more, the more to aggravate the note,°
    With a foul traitor's name stuff I thy throat,
45 And wish—so please my sovereign—ere I move,

---

18 *High-stomached* high-spirited   20 *Bolingbroke* (pronounced and spelled "Bullingbrooke" in Shakespeare's time)   32 *Tend'ring* cherishing   34 *appellant* accuser   36 *greeting* address   39 *miscreant* unbeliever, villain   43 *note* reproach

What my tongue speaks my right-drawn° sword
    may prove.

Mowbray. Let not my cold words here accuse my
    zeal:°
'Tis not the trial of a woman's war,
The bitter clamor of two eager° tongues,
Can arbitrate this cause betwixt us twain;   *50*
The blood is hot that must be cooled for this.
Yet can I not of such tame patience boast,
As to be hushed, and naught at all to say.
First, the fair reverence of° your Highness
    curbs me
From giving reins and spurs to my free speech,   *55*
Which else would post° until it had returned
These terms of treason doubled down his throat.
Setting aside his high blood's royalty,
And let him be° no kinsman to my liege,
I do defy him, and I spit at him,   *60*
Call him a slanderous coward and a villain;
Which to maintain, I would allow him odds,
And meet him were I tied° to run afoot
Even to the frozen ridges of the Alps,
Or any other ground inhabitable,°   *65*
Where ever Englishman durst set his foot.
Meantime, let this° defend my loyalty:
By all my hopes° most falsely doth he lie.

Bolingbroke. Pale trembling coward, there I throw
    my gage,
Disclaiming here the kindred of the King,°   *70*
And lay aside my high blood's royalty,
Which fear, not reverence, makes thee to except.°
If guilty dread have left thee so much strength
As to take up mine honor's pawn,° then stoop.

---

46 *right-drawn* drawn to defend the right   47 *accuse my zeal* make me
seem unzealous   49 *eager* sharp   54 *fair reverence of* respect due to
56 *post* speed   59 *let him be* suppose him to be   63 *tied* obliged
65 *inhabitable* uninhabitable   67 *this* (his sword)   68 *hopes* i.e., of
heaven   70 *Disclaiming . . . King* (referring to Mowbray's words, lines
58–59)   72 *except* use as excuse   74 *pawn* pledge (his glove or hood,
which he throws down)

75 By that, and all the rites of knighthood else,
Will I make good against thee, arm to arm,
What I have spoke, or thou canst worse devise.

Mowbray. I take it up; and by that sword I swear,
Which gently laid my knighthood on my shoulder,
80 I'll answer thee in any fair degree°
Or chivalrous design of knightly trial;
And when I mount, alive may I not light,°
If I be traitor or unjustly fight.

Richard. What doth our cousin lay to Mowbray's
charge?
85 It must be great that can inherit us°
So much as of a thought of ill in him.

Bolingbroke. Look what I speak, my life shall prove
it true:
That Mowbray hath received eight thousand nobles°
In name of lendings° for your Highness' soldiers,
90 The which he hath detained for lewd° employments,
Like a false traitor and injurious villain.
Besides, I say, and will in battle prove,
Or° here, or elsewhere to the furthest verge
That ever was surveyed by English eye,
95 That all the treasons for these eighteen years
Complotted and contrivèd in this land
Fetch° from false Mowbray, their first head and
spring.
Further, I say and further will maintain
Upon his bad life to make all this good,
100 That he did plot the Duke of Gloucester's° death,
Suggest° his soon-believing adversaries,
And, consequently,° like a traitor coward,
Sluiced out his innocent soul through streams of
blood;
Which blood, like sacrificing Abel's, cries

---

80 *degree* manner 82 *light* dismount 85 *inherit us* make us have
88 *nobles* gold coins 89 *lendings* money on trust 90 *lewd* base 93 *Or*
either 97 *Fetch* derive 100 *Gloucester* Thomas of Woodstock, who had
been murdered at Richard's orders 101 *Suggest* incite 102 *consequently* afterward

Even from the tongueless caverns of the earth   105
To me for justice and rough chastisement:
And, by the glorious worth of my descent,
This arm shall do it, or° this life be spent.

Richard. How high a pitch° his resolution soars!
Thomas of Norfolk, what say'st thou to this?   110

Mowbray. O! let my sovereign turn away his face,
And bid his ears a little while be deaf,
Till I have told this slander of his blood
How God and good men hate so foul a liar.

Richard. Mowbray, impartial are our eyes and ears.   115
Were he my brother, nay, my kingdom's heir,
As he is but my father's brother's son,
Now by my scepter's awe I make a vow,
Such neighbor nearness to our sacred blood
Should nothing privilege him, nor partialize°   120
The unstooping firmness of my upright soul.
He is our subject, Mowbray, so art thou:
Free speech and fearless I to thee allow.

Mowbray. Then, Bolingbroke, as low as to thy heart,
Through the false passage of thy throat, thou
liest.   125
Three parts of that receipt I had° for Calais
Disbursed I duly to his Highness' soldiers;
The other part reserved I by consent,
For that my sovereign liege was in my debt
Upon remainder of a dear account,°   130
Since last I went to France to fetch his Queen.
Now swallow down that lie. For Gloucester's death,
I slew him not; but, to my own disgrace,
Neglected my sworn duty° in that case.
For you, my noble Lord of Lancaster,   135
The honorable father to my foe,
Once did I lay an ambush for your life,

---

108 *or* before   109 *pitch* peak of a falcon's flight (the King is uneasy
that his own guilt will come to light)   120 *partialize* make partial
126 *that receipt I had* what I received   130 *dear account* private or ex-
pensive debt   134 *duty* (either to kill Gloucester, or to reveal the
murder)

A trespass that doth vex my grievèd soul;
But, ere I last received the sacrament,
140　I did confess it, and exactly begged
Your grace's pardon, and I hope I had it.
This is my fault: as for the rest appealed,
It issues from the rancor of a villain,
A recreant° and most degenerate traitor;
145　Which in myself I boldly will defend,
And interchangeably° hurl down my gage
Upon this overweening traitor's foot,
To prove myself a loyal gentleman
Even in the best blood chambered in his bosom.
150　In haste whereof, most heartily I pray
Your Highness to assign our trial day.

Richard. Wrath-kindled gentlemen, be ruled by me.
Let's purge this choler° without letting blood:°
This we prescribe, though no physician;
155　Deep malice makes too deep incision;
Forget, forgive, conclude, and be agreed;
Our doctors say this is no month to bleed.
Good uncle, let this end where it begun:
We'll calm the Duke of Norfolk, you your son.

160　*Gaunt.* To be a make-peace shall become my age:
Throw down, my son, the Duke of Norfolk's gage.

Richard. And Norfolk, throw down his.

Gaunt.　　　　　　　　　When,° Harry, when?
Obedience bids I should not bid again.

Richard. Norfolk, throw down; we bid—there is no
boot.°

Mowbray. Myself I throw, dread sovereign, at thy
165　foot.
My life thou shalt command, but not my shame:
The one my duty owes; but my fair name

---

144 *recreant* renegade　146 *interchangeably* in exchange　153 *choler* anger
153 *letting blood* (pun on bleeding medicinally and bloodshed)
162 *When* (exclamation of impatience)　164 *boot* remedy

Despite of death that lives upon my grave,
To dark dishonor's use thou shalt not have.
I am disgraced, impeached,° and baffled° here,   *170*
Pierced to the soul with slander's venomed spear,
The which no balm can cure but his heart-blood
Which breathed this poison.

Richard.   Rage must be withstood.
Give me his gage; lions make leopards° tame.

Mowbray. Yea, but not change his spots.° Take but
    my shame,   *175*
And I resign my gage. My dear dear lord,
The purest treasure mortal times afford
Is spotless reputation—that away,
Men are but gilded loam, or painted clay.
A jewel in a ten-times-barred-up chest   *180*
Is a bold spirit in a loyal breast;
Mine honor is my life, both grow in one;
Take honor from me, and my life is done;
Then, dear my liege, mine honor let me try;
In that I live, and for that will I die.   *185*

Richard. Cousin, throw up° your gage; do you begin.

Bolingbroke. O, God defend my soul from such deep
    sin!
Shall I seem crestfallen in my father's sight?
Or with pale beggar-fear° impeach my height°
Before this out-dared dastard? Ere my tongue   *190*
Shall wound my honor with such feeble wrong,°
Or sound so base a parle,° my teeth shall tear
The slavish motive° of recanting fear,
And spit it bleeding in his high disgrace,

---

170 *impeached* accused   170 *baffled* treated with infamy   174 *lions make leopards* tame (alluding to the rampant lion in the King's royal arms and the standing beast in Mowbray's)   175 *spots* (alluding to the proverb and punning on spots, meaning stains)   186 *throw up* (perhaps to the upper stage on which Richard sits)   189 *beggar-*fear appropriate to a beggar   189 *height* rank   191 *feeble wrong* a wrong so grave that the man who submits to it exhibits himself as feeble   192 *parle* parley, truce   193 *motive* moving organ, i.e., tongue

195   Where shame doth harbor, even in Mowbray's face.

                              [*Exit Gaunt.*°]

Richard. We were not born to sue, but to command:
        Which since we cannot do to make you friends,
        Be ready, as your lives shall answer it,
        At Coventry upon Saint Lambert's day.°
200   There shall your swords and lances arbitrate
        The swelling difference of your settled hate:
        Since we cannot atone° you, we shall see
        Justice design the victor's chivalry.°
        Lord Marshal, command our officers-at-arms
205   Be ready to direct these home alarms.

                              Exit [Richard with others].

[Scene II.   *London. Gaunt's house.*]

*Enter John of Gaunt with the Duchess of
                Gloucester.*

Gaunt. Alas, the part I had in Woodstock's° blood
        Doth more solicit me than your exclaims°
        To stir against the butchers of his life;
        But since correction lieth in those hands°
5   Which made the fault that we cannot correct,
        Put we our quarrel to the will of heaven,
        Who, when they° see the hours° ripe on earth,
        Will rain hot vengeance on offenders' heads.

Duchess. Finds brotherhood in thee no sharper spur?
10   Hath love in thy old blood no living fire?

195 *s.d. Exit Gaunt* (Gaunt begins Scene II, and therefore according to
stage convention must leave the stage before the end of Scene i)
199 *Saint Lambert's day* (Sept. 17)   202 *atone* reconcile   203 *design the
victor's chivalry* indicate whose prowess will win the victory (i.e., the
victor will be vindicated)   I.ii. 1 *Woodstock* Gloucester, Gaunt's brother   2 *exclaims* outcries   4 *those hands* i.e., the King's   7 *they* God and
his angels   7 *hours* (two syllables)

Edward's seven sons, whereof thyself art one,
Were as seven vials of his sacred blood,
Or seven fair branches springing from one root.
Some of those seven are dried by nature's course,
Some of those branches by the destinies cut;   15
But Thomas, my dear lord, my life, my Gloucester,
One vial full of Edward's sacred blood,
One flourishing branch of his most royal root,
Is cracked, and all the precious liquor spilt,
Is hacked down, and his summer leaves all faded   20
By Envy's hand and Murder's bloody ax.
Ah! Gaunt, his blood was thine; that bed,
    that womb,
That metal,° that self° mold that fashioned thee,
Made him a man: and though thou livest and
    breathest,
Yet art thou slain in him; thou dost consent   25
In some large measure to thy father's death,
In that thou seest thy wretched brother die,
Who was the model° of thy father's life.
Call it not patience, Gaunt, it is despair:
In suff'ring° thus thy brother to be slaught'red,   30
Thou showest the naked pathway° to thy life,
Teaching stern Murder how to butcher thee.
That which in mean men we entitle patience
Is pale cold cowardice in noble breasts.
What shall I say? To safeguard thine own life,   35
The best way is to venge my Gloucester's death.

Gaunt. God's is the quarrel; for God's substitute,
His deputy° anointed in His sight,
Hath caused his death, the which if wrongfully,
Let heaven revenge, for I may never lift   40
An angry arm against His minister.

Duchess. Where, then, alas, may I complain myself?°

---

23 *metal* stuff 23 *self* same 28 *model* copy 30 *suff'ring* allowing
31 *naked pathway* open road (for his murderers) 38 *deputy* (the idea
that the King, however unworthy, is God's deputy is stressed throughout the play) 42 *Where . . . myself* to whom shall I complain

Gaunt. To God, the widow's champion and defense.

Duchess. Why, then, I will. Farewell, old Gaunt,
45   Thou goest to Coventry, there to behold
Our cousin° Hereford and fell° Mowbray fight.
O! sit my husband's wrongs on Hereford's spear,
That it may enter butcher Mowbray's breast;
Or if misfortune° miss the first career,°
50   Be Mowbray's sins so heavy in his bosom,
That they may break his foaming courser's back,
And throw the rider headlong in the lists,
A caitiff recreant° to my cousin Hereford.
Farewell, old Gaunt; thy sometimes° brother's wife
55   With her companion, Grief, must end her life.

Gaunt. Sister, farewell, I must to Coventry:
As much good stay with thee, as go with me.

Duchess. Yet one word more: grief boundeth where it
falls,
Not with the empty hollowness, but weight.°
60   I take my leave before I have begun,
For sorrow ends not when it seemeth done.
Commend me to thy brother, Edmund York.°
Lo! this is all: nay, yet depart not so;
Though this be all, do not so quickly go.
65   I shall remember more. Bid him . . . Ah! what?
With all good speed at Plashy° visit me.
Alack! and what shall good old York there see
But empty lodgings and unfurnished walls,
Unpeopled offices,° untrodden stones,
70   And what hear there for welcome but my groans?
Therefore commend me, let him not come there,
To seek out sorrow that dwells everywhere.
Desolate, desolate will I hence and die!
The last leave of thee takes my weeping eye.
                                        Exeunt.

---

⁴⁶ *cousin* kinsman ⁴⁶ *fell* ruthless ⁴⁹ *misfortune* disaster (to Mowbray) ⁴⁹ *career* encounter ⁵³ *caitiff recreant* captive coward ⁵⁴ *sometimes* sometime, former ⁵⁸⁻⁵⁹ *grief . . . weight* i.e., my grief returns because it is heavy, not like a ball ⁶² *York* Duke of York ⁶⁶ *Plashy* (in
Essex) ⁶⁹ *offices* kitchens, servants' quarters, etc.

[Scene III.   *The lists at Coventry.*]

Enter Lord Marshal and the Duke Aumerle.

Marshal. My Lord Aumerle, is Harry Hereford armed?

Aumerle. Yea, at all points, and longs to enter in.

Marshal. The Duke of Norfolk, sprightfully° and bold,
   Stays but the summons of the appellant's trumpet.

Aumerle. Why, then, the champions are prepared, and
      stay   *5*
   For nothing but his Majesty's approach.

*The trumpets sound, and the King enters with his
nobles, [including Gaunt, Bushy, Bagot, Green].
When they are set, enter [Mowbray,] the Duke
of Norfolk, in arms, defendant, [and a Herald].*

Richard. Marshal, demand of yonder champion
   The cause of his arrival here in arms;
   Ask him his name; and orderly proceed
   To swear him in the justice of his cause.   *10*

Marshal. In God's name and the King's, say who thou
      art
   And why thou comest thus knightly clad in arms,
   Against what man thou com'st, and what thy
      quarrel.
   Speak truly on thy knighthood and thy oath,
   As so defend thee heaven and thy valor.   *15*

Mowbray. My name is Thomas Mowbray, Duke of
      Norfolk,

I.iii. ³ *sprightfully* full of spirit

Who hither come engagèd by my oath—
Which God defend° a knight should violate!
Both to defend my loyalty and truth
20   To God, my king, and my succeeding issue,
Against the Duke of Hereford that appeals° me;
And by the grace of God, and this mine arm,
To prove him in defending of myself
A traitor to my God, my king, and me;
25   And as I truly° fight, defend me, heaven!

*The trumpets sound. Enter [Bolingbroke,] Duke
of Hereford, appellant, in armor.*

Richard. Marshal, demand of yonder knight in arms,
Both who he is, and why he cometh hither
Thus plated° in habiliments of war,
And formally, according to our law,
30   Depose° him in the justice of his cause.

Marshal. What is thy name? And wherefore com'st
thou hither
Before King Richard in his royal lists?
Against whom comest thou? And what's thy
quarrel?
Speak like a true knight, so defend thee heaven.

35 *Bolingbroke.* Harry of Hereford, Lancaster and Derby
Am I, who ready here do stand in arms
To prove by God's grace, and my body's valor
In lists, on Thomas Mowbray, Duke of Norfolk,
That he is a traitor, foul and dangerous,
40   To God of heaven, King Richard and to me:
And as I truly fight, defend me, heaven!

Marshal. On pain of death, no person be so bold
Or daring-hardy° as to touch the lists,
Except the Marshal and such officers
45   Appointed to direct these fair designs.

---

18 *defend* forbid 21 *appeals* accuses 25 *truly* with truth on my side
28 *plated* in plate armor 30 *Depose* examine on oath 43 *daring-hardy*
reckless

Bolingbroke. Lord Marshal, let me kiss my Sovereign's
        hand,
    And bow my knee before his Majesty;
    For Mowbray and myself are like two men
    That vow a long and weary pilgrimage:
    Then let us take a ceremonious leave   50
    And loving farewell of our several friends.

Marshal. The appellant in all duty greets your
        Highness,
    And craves to kiss your hand and take his leave.

Richard. We will descend and fold him in our arms.
    Cousin of Hereford, as thy cause is right,   55
    So be thy fortune in this royal fight:
    Farewell, my blood, which if today thou shed,
    Lament we may, but not revenge thee dead.

Bolingbroke. O, let no noble eye profane a tear
    For me, if I be gored with Mowbray's spear: 60
    As confident as is the falcon's flight
    Against a bird, do I with Mowbray fight.
    My loving lord, I take my leave of you;
    Of you, my noble cousin, Lord Aumerle,
    Not sick, although I have to do with death,   65
    But lusty, young, and cheerly° drawing breath.
    Lo! as at English feasts, so I regreet°
    The daintiest last, to make the end most sweet.
    O thou, the earthly author of my blood,
    Whose youthful spirit in me regenerate°   70
    Doth with a twofold vigor lift me up
    To reach at victory above my head,
    Add proof° unto mine armor with thy prayers,
    And with thy blessings steel my lance's point,
    That it may enter Mowbray's waxen° coat   75
    And furbish new the name of John a° Gaunt
    Even in the lusty havior° of his son.

Gaunt. God in thy good cause make thee prosperous;

66 *cheerly* cheerfully   67 *regreet* greet again   70 *regenerate* reborn
73 *proof* invulnerability   75 *waxen* i.e., soft   76 *a o',* of   77 *havior* behavior

Be swift like lightning in the execution,
80   And let thy blows doubly redoubled
Fall like amazing° thunder on the casque
Of thy adverse° pernicious enemy:
Rouse up thy youthful blood, be valiant and live.

Bolingbroke. Mine innocency and St. George to
thrive!

85 *Mowbray.* However God or fortune cast my lot,
There lives or dies, true to King Richard's throne,
A loyal, just and upright gentleman.
Never did captive with a freer heart
Cast off his chains of bondage, and embrace
90   His golden, uncontrolled enfranchisement°
More than my dancing soul doth celebrate
This feast of battle with mine adversary.
Most mighty liege, and my companion peers,
Take from my mouth the wish of happy years;
95   As gentle and as jocund as to jest°
Go I to fight: truth hath a quiet breast.

Richard. Farewell, my lord; securely° I espy
Virtue with valor couchèd° in thine eye.
Order the trial, Marshal, and begin.

100 *Marshal.* Harry of Hereford, Lancaster and Derby,
Receive thy lance, and God defend the right.

Bolingbroke. Strong as a tower in hope,° I cry Amen.

Marshal. Go bear this lance to Thomas, Duke of
Norfolk.

First Herald. Harry of Hereford, Lancaster and Derby,
105   Stands here for God, his Sovereign and himself,
On pain to be° found false and recreant,
To prove the Duke of Norfolk, Thomas Mowbray,
A traitor to his God, his king, and him,

---

81 *amazing* stupefying   82 *adverse* placed opposite   90 *enfranchisement*
liberation   95 *jest* sport   97 *securely* confidently   98 *couchèd* lying hidden
102 *Strong as a tower in hope* (cf. Psalms 61:3)   106 *On pain to be* at
the risk of being

And dares him to set forward to the fight.

Second Herald. Here standeth Thomas Mowbray,
     Duke of Norfolk,   *110*
     On pain to be found false and recreant,
     Both to defend himself, and to approve°
     Henry of Hereford, Lancaster and Derby,
     To God, his sovereign, and to him disloyal,
     Courageously and with a free desire   *113*
     Attending but the signal to begin.

Marshal. Sound trumpets; and set forward
     combatants!
            [*A charge sounded.*]
     Stay, the King hath thrown his warder° down.

Richard. Let them lay by their helmets and their spears
     And both return back to their chairs° again.   *120*
     Withdraw with us, and let the trumpets sound,
     While we return these dukes what we decree.
            [*A long flourish.°*]
     Draw near,
     And list° what with our council we have done.
     For that our kingdom's earth should not be soiled   *125*
     With that dear blood which it hath fosterèd;
     And for our eyes do hate the dire aspect
     Of civil wounds plowed up with neighbor's sword,
     And for we think the eagle-wingèd pride
     Of sky-aspiring and ambitious thoughts   *130*
     With rival-hating envy set on you
     To wake our peace, which in our country's cradle
     Draws the sweet infant breath of gentle sleep,
     Which so roused up with boist'rous untuned
         drums,
     With harsh resounding trumpets' dreadful bray,   *135*
     And grating shock of wrathful iron arms,
     Might from our quiet confines fright fair Peace,
     And make us wade even in our kindred's blood;

---

112 *approve* prove   118 *warder* truncheon (a signal to stop the combat)
120 *chairs* (on which the combatants sat before mounting)   122 s.d.
flourish trumpet call   124 *list* hear

Therefore we banish you our territories:
140 You, cousin Hereford, upon pain of life,
Till twice five summers have enriched our fields,
Shall not regreet° our fair dominions,
But tread the stranger° paths of banishment.

Bolingbroke. Your will be done: this must my
    comfort be,
145 That sun that warms you here shall shine on me,
And those his golden beams to you here lent
Shall point on me, and gild my banishment.

Richard. Norfolk, for thee remains a heavier doom
Which I with some unwillingness pronounce:
150 The sly slow hours shall not determinate°
The dateless° limit of thy dear° exile;
The hopeless word° of "Never to return"
Breathe I against thee, upon pain of life.

Mowbray. A heavy sentence,° my most sovereign
    liege,
155 And all unlooked for from your Highness' mouth:
A dearer merit,° not so deep a maim
As to be cast forth in the common air
Have I deservèd at your Highness' hands!
The language I have learnt these forty years,
160 My native English, now I must forgo,
And now my tongue's use is to me no more
Than an unstringèd viol or a harp,
Or like a cunning° instrument cased up,
Or being open, put into his hands
165 That knows no touch to tune the harmony.
Within my mouth you have enjailed my tongue,
Doubly portcullised° with my teeth and lips,
And dull unfeeling barren ignorance

---

142 *regreet* greet again   143 *stranger* foreign   150 *determinate* put a limit
to   151 *dateless* endless   151 *dear* severe   152 *word* utterance   154 *sentence* (punning on "word")   156 *dearer merit* better reward   163 *cunning* ingenious and requiring skill in the playing   167 *portcullised* (a portcullis was a grating which could be let down in the gateway of a castle to block it)

Is made my jailer to attend on me.
I am too old to fawn upon a nurse,   *170*
Too far in years to be a pupil now;
What is thy sentence then but speechless death,
Which robs my tongue from breathing native
    breath?

Richard. It boots° thee not to be compassionate:°
After our sentence, plaining comes too late.   *175*

Mowbray. Then thus I turn me from my country's
    light,
To dwell in solemn shades of endless night.

[*Turns to go.*]

Richard. Return again, and take an oath with thee.
Lay on our royal sword your banished hands;
Swear by the duty that you owe to God—   *180*
Our part therein we banish with yourselves—°
To keep the oath that we administer:
You never shall—so help you truth and God!—
Embrace each other's love in banishment,
Nor never look upon each other's face,   *185*
Nor never write, regreet, nor reconcile
This louring tempest of your home-bred hate,
Nor never by advisèd° purpose meet
To plot, contrive, or complot° any ill
'Gainst us, our state, our subjects, or our land.   *190*

Bolingbroke. I swear.

Mowbray.   And I, to keep all this.

Bolingbroke. Norfolk, so far as to mine enemy—
By this time, had the King permitted us,
One of our souls had wandered in the air,
Banished this frail sepulcher° of our flesh,   *195*
As now our flesh is banished from this land:

---

¹⁷⁴ *boots* avails   ¹⁷⁴ *compassionate* expressing passionate feeling
¹⁸¹ *Our . . . yourselves* i.e., we absolve you from allegiance to us
¹⁸⁸ *advisèd* deliberate   ¹⁸⁹ *complot* plot with others   ¹⁹⁵ *sepulcher* (here accented on second syllable)

Confess thy treasons ere thou fly the realm;
Since thou hast far to go, bear not along
The clogging burden of a guilty soul.

200 *Mowbray*. No, Bolingbroke, if ever I were traitor,
My name be blotted from the book of life,
And I from heaven banished as from hence!
But what thou art, God, thou, and I, do know,
And all too soon, I fear, the King shall rue.
205 Farewell, my liege, now no way can I stray:
Save back to England all the world's my way.

Exit.

Richard. Uncle, even in the glasses° of thine eyes
I see thy grievèd heart: thy sad aspect°
Hath from the number of his banished years
Plucked four away. [*To Bolingbroke*] Six frozen
210   winters spent,
Return with welcome home from banishment.

Bolingbroke. How long a time lies in one little word.
Four lagging winters and four wanton° springs
End in a word—such is the breath of kings.

215 *Gaunt*. I thank my liege that in regard of me
He shortens four years of my son's exile,
But little vantage° shall I reap thereby:
For ere the six years that he hath to spend
Can change their moons and bring their times°
        about,
220 My oil-dried lamp and time-bewasted light
Shall be extinct with age and endless night;
My inch of taper will be burnt and done,
And blindfold Death° not let me see my son.

Richard. Why! uncle, thou hast many years to live.

225 *Gaunt*. But not a minute, King, that thou canst give;

---

207 *glasses* (eyes were thought to reflect the heart)   208 *aspect* (accent
on second syllable)   213 *wanton* luxuriant   217 *vantage* advantage
219 *times* seasons   223 *blindfold Death* (Death is thought of as eyeless,
like a skull, and also as Atropos, Milton's "blind fury with the abhorred
shears," cutting short human lives)

Shorten my days thou canst with sullen sorrow
And pluck nights from me, but not lend a morrow;
Thou canst help time to furrow me with age,
But stop no wrinkle in his pilgrimage:
Thy word is current° with him for my death,   230
But dead, thy kingdom cannot buy my breath.

Richard. Thy son is banished upon good advice,
Whereto thy tongue a party-verdict° gave:
Why at our justice seem'st thou then to lour?

Gaunt. Things sweet to taste prove in digestion sour.   235
You urged me as a judge, but I had rather
You would have bid me argue like a father.
O, had it been a stranger, not my child,
To smooth his fault I should have been more mild:
A partial slander° sought I to avoid,   240
And in the sentence my own life destroyed.
Alas! I looked when some of you should say
I was too strict to make mine own away;
But you gave leave to my unwilling tongue
Against my will to do myself this wrong.   245

Richard. Cousin, farewell, and uncle, bid him so;
Six years we banish him, and he shall go.

    [*Flourish.*] *Exit* [*King Richard with his train*].

Aumerle. Cousin, farewell; what presence must not know,°
From where you do remain let paper show.

Marshal. My lord, no leave take I, for I will ride   250
As far as land will let me by your side.

Gaunt. O, to what purpose dost thou hoard thy words,
That thou returnest no greeting to thy friends?

Bolingbroke. I have too few to take my leave of you,
When the tongue's office should be prodigal°   255

---

230 *current* valid   233 *party-verdict* one person's share of a joint verdict
240 *partial slander* imputation of partiality   248 *what presence must not
know* (perhaps "as I cannot have your news from you in person," or
"what you cannot say in present company." Aumerle is anxious to
know Bolingbroke's intentions)   255 *prodigal* lavish

      To breathe the abundant dolor of the heart.

Gaunt. Thy grief° is but thy absence for a time.

Bolingbroke. Joy absent, grief is present for that time.

Gaunt. What is six winters? They are quickly gone.

Bolingbroke. To men in joy; but grief makes one hour
260   ten.

Gaunt. Call it a travel that thou tak'st for pleasure.

Bolingbroke. My heart will sigh when I miscall it so,
     Which finds it an enforcèd pilgrimage.

Gaunt. The sullen passage of thy weary steps
265   Esteem as foil° wherein thou art to set
     The precious jewel of thy home return.

Bolingbroke. Nay, rather, every tedious stride I make
     Will but remember° me what a deal of world
     I wander from the jewels that I love.
270   Must I not serve a long apprenticehood
     To foreign passages,° and in the end,
     Having my freedom,° boast of nothing else
     But that I was a journeyman° to grief?°

Gaunt. All places that the eye of heaven° visits
275   Are to a wise man ports and happy havens.
     Teach thy necessity to reason thus:
     There is no virtue° like necessity.
     Think not the King did banish thee,
     But thou the King. Woe doth the heavier sit
280   Where it perceives it is but faintly° borne.
     Go, say I sent thee forth to purchase honor,
     And not the King exiled thee; or suppose
     Devouring pestilence hangs in our air,
     And thou art flying to a fresher clime.

---

257 *grief* (1) grievance (2) sorrow   265 *foil* setting (metal leaf serving
as a background)   268 *remember* remind   271 *passages* experiences
272 *Having my freedom* at the end of his apprenticeship and of his exile
273 *a journeyman to grief* an employee of Grief (instead of his own
master)   273 *journeyman* (1) artisan (2) traveler   274 *eye of heaven* sun
(as in Ovid)   277 *virtue* efficacy   280 *faintly* faintheartedly

Look what° thy soul holds dear, imagine it 285
To lie that way thou goest, not whence thou com'st.
Suppose the singing birds musicians,
The grass whereon thou tread'st the presence
    strewed,°
The flowers fair ladies, and thy steps no more
Than a delightful measure or a dance; 290
For gnarling° sorrow hath less power to bite
The man that mocks at it and sets it light.

Bolingbroke. O, who can hold a fire in his hand
By thinking on the frosty Caucasus?
Or cloy the hungry edge of appetite 295
By bare imagination of a feast?
Or wallow naked in December snow
By thinking on fantastic° summer's heat?
O, no! the apprehension of the good
Gives but the greater feeling to the worse. 300
Fell° Sorrow's tooth doth never rankle° more
Than when he bites, but lanceth° not the sore.

Gaunt. Come, come, my son, I'll bring thee on thy way.
Had I thy youth and cause, I would not stay.°

Bolingbroke. Then England's ground, farewell; sweet
    soil, adieu; 305
My mother and my nurse that bears° me yet!
Where'er I wander, boast of this I can:
Though banished, yet a true-born Englishman.

                                        Exeunt.

---

285 *Look what* whatever   288 *presence strewed* royal presence chamber
strewn with rushes   291 *gnarling* snarling (with perhaps a suggestion of
the twisting effects of sorrow)   298 *fantastic* imaginary   301 *Fell* fierce
301 *rankle* fester   302 *lanceth* cuts with a surgeon's knife   304 *I would
not stay* i.e., away from England   306 *bears* (1) gives birth to (2)
supports me (for a discussion of these speeches see K. Muir, *Review
of English Studies*, X, 1959, 283-86.)

[Scene IV.   *The Court*.]

Enter the King, with Bagot, [Green], etc.
at one door, and the Lord Aumerle at another.

Richard. We did observe.° Cousin Aumerle,
   How far brought you high Hereford on his way?

Aumerle. I brought high Hereford, if you call him so,
   But to the next high way, and there I left him.

Richard. And say, what store of parting tears were
   shed?

Aumerle. Faith, none for me,° except the northeast
   wind,
   Which then blew bitterly against our faces,
   Awaked the sleeping rheum, and so by chance
   Did grace our hollow parting with a tear.

Richard. What said our cousin when you parted with
   him?

Aumerle. "Farewell."
   And for my heart disdainèd that my tongue
   Should so profane the word, that taught me craft
   To counterfeit oppression of such grief
   That words seemed buried in my sorrow's grave.
   Marry, would the word "Farewell" have length'nèd
   hours
   And added years to his short banishment,
   He should have had a volume of farewells;
   But since it would not, he had none of me.

Richard. He is our cousin,° cousin, but 'tis doubt,
   When time shall call him home from banishment,

I.iv.   1 *We did observe* (continuing a conversation)   6 *for me* for my
part   20 *cousin* (Richard, Aumerle, and Bolingbroke were cousins)

Whether our kinsman come to see his friends.
Ourself and Bushy, Bagot here and Green,
Observed his courtship to the common people,
How he did seem to dive into their hearts   25
With humble and familiar courtesy,
What reverence he did throw away on slaves,
Wooing poor craftsmen with the craft of smiles
And patient underbearing of his fortune,
As 'twere to banish their affects with him.   30
Off goes his bonnet to an oyster-wench;
A brace of draymen bid God speed him well,
And had the tribute of his supple knee,
With "Thanks, my countrymen, my loving
    friends";
As were our England in reversion his,   35
And he our subjects' next degree in hope.

Green. Well, he is gone, and with him go these
    thoughts.
Now for the rebels which stand out in Ireland;
Expedient manage° must be made, my liege,
Ere further leisure yield them further means   40
For their advantage and your Highness' loss.

Richard. We will ourself in person to this war,
And for our coffers with too great a court
And liberal largess are grown somewhat light,
We are enforced to farm° our royal realm,   45
The revenue whereof shall furnish us
For our affairs in hand. If that come short,
Our substitutes at home shall have blank charters;°
Whereto, when they shall know what men are rich,
They shall subscribe them for large sums of gold,   50
And send them after to supply our wants,
For we will make for Ireland presently.
                Enter Bushy.
Bushy, what news?

39 *manage* management   45 *farm* lease (Richard leased the crown lands
and customs dues to his favorites for £7000 a month)   48 *blank char-*
ters (documents given to Richard's agents, with power to insert what
sums they pleased for the rich to pay)

Bushy. Old John of Gaunt is grievous sick, my Lord,
55   Suddenly taken, and hath sent posthaste
         To intreat your Majesty to visit him.

Richard. Where lies he?

Bushy. At Ely House.

Richard. Now put it, God, in the physician's mind
60   To help him to his grave immediately!
         The lining° of his coffers shall make coats
         To deck our soldiers for these Irish wars.
         Come, gentlemen, let's all go visit him;
         Pray God we may make haste and come too late!

65   *All.* Amen!   *Exeunt.*

*reveals
deceitfulness
of Richard
Who said he likc
Gaunt earlier
publically "*

61 *lining* contents (with pun on *coats*)

[ACT II

Scene I.   *London. Ely House.*]

Enter John of Gaunt, sick, with the Duke of York,
[the Earl of Northumberland, Attendants], etc.

Gaunt. Will the King come, that I may breathe my last
  In wholesome counsel to his unstaid° youth?

York. Vex not yourself, nor strive not with your
    breath,
  For all in vain comes counsel to his ear.

Gaunt. O, but they say the tongues of dying men   5
  Enforce attention like deep harmony:
  Where words are scarce they are seldom spent
    in vain,
  For they breathe truth that breathe their words
    in pain;
  He that no more must say is listened more
  Than they whom youth and ease have taught to
    glose;°   10
  More are men's ends marked than their lives before;
  The setting sun, and music at the close,°
  As the last taste of sweets is sweetest last,°
  Writ in remembrance more than things long
    past:

II.i.   2 *unstaid* unrestrained   10 *glose* utter pleasing words   12 *close* conclusion of a musical phrase   13 *last* (because it comes last)

15   Though Richard my life's counsel would not hear,
      My death's sad tale° may yet undeaf his ear.

      York. No, it is stopped with other flattering sounds:
      As praises—of whose taste the wise° are fond—
      Lascivious meters, to whose venom° sound
20   The open ear of youth doth always listen;
      Report of fashions in proud Italy
      Whose manners still° our tardy-apish° nation
      Limps after in base imitation.°
      Where doth the world thrust forth a vanity—
25   So it be new, there's no respect how vile—
      That is not quickly buzzed into his ears?
      Then all too late comes counsel to be heard,
      Where will° doth mutiny with wit's regard.°
      Direct not him whose way himself will choose:
      'Tis breath thou lack'st, and that breath wilt
30   thou lose.

      Gaunt. Methinks I am a prophet new inspired,
      And thus expiring° do foretell of him:
      His rash fierce blaze of riot° cannot last,
      For violent fires soon burn out themselves.
      Small showers last long, but sudden storms are
35   short;
      He tires betimes that spurs too fast betimes;°
      With eager feeding, food doth choke the feeder.
      Light vanity, insatiate cormorant,°
      Consuming means, soon preys upon itself.
40   This royal throne of kings, this scept'red isle,
      This earth of majesty, this seat of Mars,
      This other Eden, demi-paradise,
      This fortress built by Nature for herself

16 *My death's sad tale* my solemn dying words   18 *the wise* even the
wise (see Textual Note)   19 *venom* venomous   22 *still* always   22 *tardy-
apish* imitative, but behind the fashion   23 *imitation* (five syllables. Complaints of the aping of foreign fashions were common in Elizabethan
England. For this speech and the next see K. Muir, *Review of English
Studies*, X, 1959, pp. 286-89.)   28 *will* desire   28 *wit's regard* what intelligence ought to regard   31-32 *inspired . . . expiring* (pun)   33 *riot* pro-
fligacy   36 *betimes* (1) soon (2) early   38 *cormorant* glutton (from the
bird)

Syntax used to underline power of indictment

verb

Against infection° and the hand of war,
This happy breed° of men, this little world,°   45
This precious stone set in the silver sea
Which serves it in the office of a wall,
Or as a moat defensive to a house,
Against the envy of less happier lands,
This blessed plot, this earth, this realm, this
    England,   50
This nurse, this teeming womb of royal kings,
Feared by their breed, and famous by their
    birth,
Renownèd for their deeds as far from home,
For Christian service° and true chivalry,
As is the sepulcher in stubborn° Jewry   55
Of the world's ransom, blessed Mary's son,
This land of such dear souls, this dear dear land—
Dear for her reputation through the world—
Is now leased out—I die pronouncing it—
Like to a tenement° or pelting° farm.°   60
England, bound in with the triumphant sea,
Whose rocky shore beats back the envious siege°
Of wat'ry Neptune, is now bound in with shame,
With inky blots, and rotten parchment bonds.
That England that was wont to conquer others   65
Hath made a shameful conquest of itself.
Ah! would the scandal vanish with my life,
How happy then were my ensuing death!

   Enter King and Queen, etc. [Aumerle, Bushy,
     Green, Bagot, Ross, and Willoughby.]

York. The King is come; deal mildly with his youth,
  For young hot colts being raged° do rage the more.   70

Queen. How fares our noble uncle, Lancaster?

Richard. What comfort, man? How is't with aged
    Gaunt?

---

44 *infection* moral infection **45** *happy breed* fortunate race **45** *little
world* i.e., a world by itself **54** *Christian service* i.e., the Crusades
55 *stubborn* (because they rejected Christ) **60** *tenement* leased land or
property **60** *pelting* paltry **40-60** *This . . . farm* (the verb comes in line
59) **62** *siege* (perhaps a partial pun on "surge") **70** *raged* enraged

Gaunt. O, how that name befits my composition!
　　Old Gaunt indeed, and gaunt in being old!
75　Within me Grief hath kept a tedious fast;
　　And who abstains from meat that is not gaunt?
　　For sleeping England long time have I watched:
　　Watching breeds leanness, leanness is all gaunt.
　　The pleasure that some fathers feed upon
80　Is my strict fast°—I mean my children's looks—
　　And therein fasting hast thou made me gaunt;
　　Gaunt am I for the grave, gaunt as a grave°
　　Whose hollow womb inherits° naught but bones.

Richard. Can sick men play so nicely° with their
　　names?

85　*Gaunt.* No, misery makes sport to mock itself:
　　Since thou dost seek to kill my name in me,°
　　I mock my name, great King, to flatter thee.

Richard. Should dying men flatter with those that
　　live?

Gaunt. No, no, men living flatter those that die.

90　*Richard.* Thou, now a-dying, sayest thou flatterest me.

Gaunt. O no, thou diest, though I the sicker be.

Richard. I am in health, I breathe, and see thee ill.

Gaunt. Now he that made me knows I see thee ill;
　　Ill in myself to see, and in thee seeing ill.°
95　Thy deathbed is no lesser than thy land,
　　Wherein thou liest in reputation sick;
　　And thou, too careless patient° as thou art,
　　Commit'st thy anointed body to the cure
　　Of those physicians that first wounded thee.
100　A thousand flatterers sit within thy crown,
　　Whose compass is no bigger than thy head,

---

80 *Is my strict fast* I must go without   73-82 *name . . . grave* (Coleridge defended the psychological truth of these puns)   83 *inherits* (the grave will get only bones because Gaunt is wasted away)   84 *nicely* subtly and prettily   86 *kill my name in me* i.e., by banishing my son and heir   94 *Ill . . . ill* (1) bad eyesight (2) evil   97 *careless patient* one who does not take proper steps to cure himself

And yet incagèd in so small a verge°
The waste° is no whit lesser than thy land.
O, had thy grandsire° with a prophet's eye
Seen how his son's son should destroy his sons,°   105
From forth thy reach he would have laid thy
   shame,
Deposing thee before thou wert possessed,
Which art possessed° now to depose thyself.
Why, cousin,° wert thou regent of the world,
It were a shame to let this land by lease;   110
But for thy world° enjoying but this land
Is it not more than shame to shame it so?
Landlord of England art thou now, not king;
Thy state of law° is bondslave to the law,
And thou——

Richard. [*Interrupting*] A lunatic, lean-witted fool,   115
   Presuming on an ague's privilege,
   Darest with thy frozen° admonition
   Make pale our cheek, chasing the royal blood
   With fury from his native residence.°
   Now, by my seat's° right-royal majesty   120
   Wert thou not brother to great Edward's son,
   This tongue that runs so roundly° in thy head
   Should run thy head from thy unreverent
      shoulders.

Gaunt. O, spare me not, my brother Edward's son,
   For that I was his father Edward's son,   125
   That blood already like the pelican°

---

¹⁰² *verge* limit (and possibly area within a radius of twelve miles around
the court)   ¹⁰³ *waste* (1) destruction of landlord's property by tenant
(2) useless expense (3) wide space   ¹⁰⁴ *grandsire* i.e., Edward III
¹⁰⁵ *sons* i.e., Gloucester and Gaunt   ¹⁰⁷⁻¹⁰⁸ *possessed . . . possessed* (1)
possessed of the crown (2) possessed with devils   ¹⁰⁹ *cousin* kinsman
¹¹¹ *world* cf. line 45   ¹¹⁴ *state of law* legal status   ¹¹⁷ *frozen* (1) frigid
in style (2) prompted by ague (3) cold, and so cooling me   ¹¹⁹ *residence* i.e., his cheek   ¹²⁰ *seat's* throne's   ¹²² *roundly* bluntly   ¹²⁶ *pel-
ican* (thought to wound its breast to feed its young with its blood
—a symbol both of parental self-sacrifice and filial ingratitude)

Hast thou tapped out and drunkenly caroused:
My brother Gloucester, plain well-meaning soul—
Whom fair befall in heaven 'mongst happy souls!—
130   May be a precedent and witness good
That thou respect'st not spilling Edward's blood.
Join with the present sickness that I have,
And thy unkindness be like crooked° age
To crop at once a too-long-withered flower.
135   Live in thy shame, but die not shame with thee;
These words hereafter thy tormentors be.
Convey me to my bed, then to my grave;
Love they to live that love and honor have.

> Exit [*Gaunt, borne by Attendants,
> and Northumberland*].

Richard. And let them die that age and sullens° have,
140   For both hast thou, and both become the grave.

York. I do beseech your Majesty, impute his words
To wayward sickliness and age in him:
He loves you, on my life, and holds you dear
As Harry, Duke of Hereford, were he here.

Richard. Right, you say true, as Hereford's love, so
145   his,
As theirs, so mine; and all be as it is.°

> [*Enter Northumberland.*]

Northumberland. My liege, old Gaunt commends him
to your Majesty.

Richard. What says he?

Northumberland.   Nay, nothing, all is said;
His tongue is now a stringless instrument;
150   Words, life and all, old Lancaster hath spent.

York. Be York the next that must be bankrout° so!
Though death be poor, it ends a mortal woe.

Richard. The ripest fruit first falls, and so doth he;

133 *crooked* bent (and suggesting Time with a scythe; cf. line 134)
139 *sullens* sulks   146 *and all be as it is* let what will be, be   151 *bankrout* bankrupt

His time is spent, our pilgrimage must be;
So much for that.° Now for our Irish wars.   155
We must supplant those rough rug-headed kernes°
Which live like venom, where no venom° else,
But only they, have privilege to live.
And for these great affairs do ask some charge,
Towards our assistance we do seize to us   160
The plate, coin, revenues, and movables
Whereof our uncle Gaunt did stand possessed.

York. How long shall I be patient? Ah, how long
    Shall tender duty make me suffer wrong?
    Not Gloucester's death, nor Hereford's banishment,   165
    Nor Gaunt's rebukes,° nor England's private
       wrongs,°
    Nor the prevention of poor Bolingbroke
    About his marriage,° nor my own disgrace,°
    Have ever made me sour° my patient cheek,
    Or bend one wrinkle° on my Sovereign's face.   170
    I am the last of noble Edward's sons,
    Of whom thy father, Prince of Wales, was first:
    In war was never lion raged more fierce,
    In peace was never gentle lamb more mild,
    Than was that young and princely gentleman.   175
    His face thou hast, for even so looked he,
    Accomplished with the number of thy hours;°
    But when he frowned it was against the French,
    And not against his friends; his noble hand
    Did win what he did spend, and spent not that   180
    Which his triumphant father's hand had won;

153-55 *The . . . that* (cf. Bolingbroke's equally callous reception of
Mowbray's death, IV.i. 103-04. He also changes the subject in the
middle of a line)   156 *rug-headed kernes* shag-haired light-armed Irish
foot soldiers   157 *venom* reptiles (alluding to the tradition that St. Pat-
rick expelled snakes from Ireland)   166 *Gaunt's rebukes* rebukes suffered by Gaunt   166 *private wrongs* wrongs suffered by private citizens
167-68 *prevention . . . marriage* (Richard prevented Bolingbroke's marriage in exile to the French King's cousin)   168 *my own disgrace* (un-
explained; possibly we should accept the equally difficult original reading of Q1, "his own disgrace," corrected in all copies save one)
169 *sour* make sour   170 *wrinkle* frown   177 *Accomplished . . . hours*
when he was your age

His hands were guilty of no kindred blood,
But bloody with the enemies of his kin.
O, Richard, York is too far gone with grief,
185 Or else he never would compare between——

Richard. Why, uncle, what's the matter?

York.   O my liege,
Pardon me, if you please; if not, I pleased
Not to be pardoned, am content withal.
Seek you to seize and gripe° into your hands
190 The royalties° and rights of banished Hereford?
Is not Gaunt dead? and doth not Hereford live?
Was not Gaunt just? and is not Harry true?
Did not the one deserve to have an heir?
Is not his heir a well-deserving son?
195 Take° Hereford's rights away, and take from time
His charters and his customary rights,
Let not tomorrow then ensue° today;
Be not thyself. For how art thou a king
But by fair sequence and succession?°
200 Now afore God—God forbid I say true—
If you do wrongfully seize Hereford's rights,
Call in the letters patents that he hath
By his attorneys-general to sue
His livery,° and deny° his off'red homage,
205 You pluck a thousand dangers on your head,
You lose a thousand well-disposèd hearts,
And prick my tender patience to those thoughts
Which honor and allegiance cannot think.

Richard. Think what you will, we seize into our
        hands
210 His plate, his goods, his money, and his lands.

York. I'll not be by° the while. My liege, farewell.
What will ensue hereof there's none can tell:

Right margin handwritten annotation: Richard Breaks law + tradition + that make him king

189 *gripe* clutch   190 *royalties* gifts from the King   195 *Take* if you take
197 *ensue* follow upon   199 *succession* (four syllables)   202-04 *Call . . .
livery* if you revoke the royal letters-patent that enable his attorneys to
obtain for him his father's lands   204 *deny* refuse   211 *by* near

But by° bad courses may be understood
That their events° can never fall out good.   *Exit.*

Richard. Go, Bushy, to the Earl of Wiltshire°
    straight;   215
Bid him repair to us to Ely House,
To see this business. Tomorrow next
We will for Ireland—and 'tis time, I trow;
And we create in absence of ourself
Our uncle York Lord Governor of England,   220
For he is just, and always loved us well.°
Come on, our queen, tomorrow must we part;
Be merry, for our time of stay is short.

    [*Flourish.*] *Exeunt King and Queen. Manet°*
        Northumberland, [with Willoughby, and Ross].

Northumberland. Well, lords, the Duke of Lancaster is
    dead.

Ross. And living too, for now his son is duke.   225

Willoughby. Barely in title, not in revenues.

Northumberland. Richly in both, if justice had her
    right.

Ross. My heart is great, but it must break with
    silence
Ere 't be disburdened with a liberal° tongue.

Northumberland. Nay, speak thy mind, and let him
    ne'er speak more   230
That speaks thy words again to do thee harm.

Willoughby. Tends that that thou would'st speak to
    the Duke of Hereford?
If it be so, out with it boldly, man;
Quick is mine ear to hear of good towards him.

Ross. No good at all that I can do for him,   235

213 *by* concerning 214 *events* outcomes 215 *Wiltshire* William le Scrope,
treasurer of England 221 *For . . . well* (in spite of York's criticisms of
his conduct, Richard apparently appreciates his honesty) 223 s.d. *Manet*
remains 229 *liberal* free

Unless you call it good to pity him,
Bereft, and gelded of his patrimony.

Northumberland. Now, afore God, 'tis shame such
    wrongs are borne
    In him a royal prince and many moe°
240   Of noble blood in this declining land!
    The King is not himself, but basely led
    By flatterers; and what they will inform
    Merely in hate 'gainst any of us all,
    That will the King severely prosecute
245   'Gainst us, our lives, our children, and our heirs.

Ross. The commons hath he pilled° with grievous
    taxes
    And quite lost their hearts. The nobles hath
    he fined
    For ancient quarrels and quite lost their hearts.

Willoughby. And daily new exactions are devised,
250   As blanks,° benevolences,° and I wot not what:
    But what, a° God's name, doth become of this?

Northumberland. Wars hath not wasted it, for warred
    he hath not,
    But basely yielded upon compromise
    That which his noble ancestors achieved with blows:
255   More hath he spent in peace than they in wars.

Ross. The Earl of Wiltshire hath the realm in farm.

Willoughby. The King's grown bankrout like a broken
    man.

Northumberland. Reproach and dissolution hangeth
    over him.

Ross. He hath not money for these Irish wars,
260   His burdenous taxations notwithstanding,
    But by the robbing of the banished Duke.

---

239 *moe* more   246 *pilled* plundered   250 *blanks* cf. I.iv.48.   250 *benevolences* forced loans (an anachronism, as they were introduced in 1473) 251 *a* in

Northumberland. His noble kinsman—most degen-
    erate king!
  But, lords, we hear this fearful tempest sing,
  Yet seek no shelter to avoid the storm:
  We see the wind sit sore upon our sails,   265
  And yet we strike° not, but securely perish.

Ross. We see the very wrack° that we must suffer,
  And unavoided is the danger now,
  For suffering so the causes of our wrack.

Northumberland. Not so; even through the hollow
    eyes of death   270
  I spy life peering, but I dare not say
  How near the tidings of our comfort is.

Willoughby. Nay, let us share thy thoughts, as thou
    dost ours.

Ross. Be confident to speak, Northumberland;
  We three are but thyself, and speaking so   275
  Thy words are but as thoughts: therefore be bold.

Northumberland. Then thus: I have from le Port
    Blanc, a bay
  In Brittaine,° received intelligence
  That Harry, Duke of Hereford, Rainold, Lord
    Cobham,
  [The son of Richard, Earl of Arundel,]°   280
  That late broke° from the Duke of Exeter,
  His brother, Archbishop, late of Canterbury,
  Sir Thomas Erpingham, Sir Thomas Ramston,
  Sir John Norbery, Sir Robert Waterton, and Francis
    Quoint—
  All these well furnished by the Duke of Brittaine   285
  With eight tall ships, three thousand men of war,°
  Are making hither with all due expedience,°

266 *strike* (a pun on striking sails and striking blows)   267 *wrack* wreck
278 *Brittaine* Brittany   280 *The . . . Arundel* (some such line, necessary
for the sense, is lacking, possibly because an Earl of Arundel was executed in October 1595)   281 *broke* escaped   286 *men of war* soldiers
287 *expedience* speed

And shortly mean to touch our northern shore.
Perhaps they had ere this, but that they stay
290 The first departing of the King for Ireland.
If then we shall shake off our slavish yoke,
Imp out° our drooping country's broken wing,
Redeem from broking pawn° the blemished
    crown,
Wipe off the dust that hides our scepter's gilt,°
295 And make high majesty look like itself,
Away with me in post° to Ravenspurgh;
But if you faint, as fearing to do so,
Stay, and be secret, and myself will go.

Ross. To horse, to horse, urge doubts to them that
    fear.

Willoughby. Hold out my horse,° and I will first be
300   there.   *Exeunt.*

[Scene II.   *Windsor Castle.*]

Enter the Queen, Bushy, Bagot.

Bushy. Madam, your Majesty is too much sad.
You promised, when you parted with the King,
To lay aside life-harming heaviness,
And entertain a cheerful disposition.

5 *Queen.* To please the King I did: to please myself
I cannot do it; yet I know no cause
Why I should welcome such a guest as Grief,
Save bidding farewell to so sweet a guest

---

292 *Imp out* engraft new feathers   293 *broking pawn* lending money
upon pawns, which was fraudulent (cf. II.i.113)   294 *gilt* (pun on
"guilt")   296 *in post* with speed, with relays of horses   300 *Hold out
my horse* if my horse holds out

As my sweet Richard. Yet again methinks
Some unborn sorrow ripe in Fortune's womb   10
Is coming towards me; and my inward soul
With nothing trembles—at something it grieves
More than with parting from my lord the King.

Bushy. Each substance of a grief hath twenty
        shadows,°
  Which shows like grief itself, but is not so;   15
  For Sorrow's eye, glazèd with blinding tears,
  Divides one thing entire to many objects,
  Like perspectives° which, rightly gazed upon,
  Show nothing but confusion; eyed awry,
  Distinguish form. So your sweet Majesty,   20
  Looking awry upon your lord's departure,
  Find° shapes of grief more than himself to wail,°
  Which looked on as it is, is nought but shadows
  Of what it is not; then, thrice-gracious Queen,
  More than your lord's departure weep not:
        more's not seen,   25
  Or if it be, 'tis with false Sorrow's eye,
  Which for things true weeps° things imaginary.

Queen. It may be so; but yet my inward soul
  Persuades me it is otherwise. Howe'er it be,
  I cannot but be sad—so heavy sad,   30
  As, though on thinking on no thought I think,°
  Makes me with heavy nothing faint and shrink.

Bushy. 'Tis nothing but conceit,° my gracious lady.

Queen. 'Tis nothing less:° conceit is still derived
  From some forefather grief; mine is not so,   35
  For nothing hath begot my something grief,
  Or something hath the nothing that I grieve:°

II.ii. 14 *shadows* i.e., illusory griefs 18 *perspectives* pictures constructed
so that they look distorted when viewed directly ("rightly"), and intelligible when viewed from the side ("awry") 22 *Find* (the subject
"you" is understood from "Majesty") 22 *wail* bewail 27 *weeps* weeps
for 31 *though . . . think* though I try to think about nothing
33 *conceit* fancy 34 *'Tis nothing less* it's anything except mere fancy
37 *something . . . grieve* the nothing that I grieve hath something in it

'Tis in reversion that I do possess,°
But what it is that is not yet known what,
40 I cannot name; 'tis nameless woe I wot.°

[*Enter Green.*]

Green. God save your Majesty! and well met, gentlemen.
I hope the King is not yet shipped for Ireland.

Queen. Why hopest thou so? 'Tis better hope he is,
For his designs crave° haste, his haste good
hope:
45 Then wherefore dost thou hope he is not shipped?

Green. That he our hope might have retired his
power
And driven into despair an enemy's hope,
Who strongly° hath set footing in this land:
The banished Bolingbroke repeals° himself,
50 And with uplifted arms is safe arrived
At Ravenspurgh.

Queen.   Now God in heaven forbid!

Green. Ah, madam! 'tis too true; and that° is worse,
The Lord Northumberland, his son, young Henry
Percy,°
The lords of Ross, Beaumond, and Willoughby,
55 With all their powerful friends are fled to him.

Bushy. Why have you not proclaimed Northumberland
And all the rest° revolted faction, traitors?

Green. We have: whereupon the Earl of Worcester°
Hath broken his staff, resigned his stewardship,
60 And all the household servants fled with him
To Bolingbroke.

---

38 *'Tis . . . possess* I am heir to it, and I shall know what it is when
I experience it   40 *wot* know   44 *crave* demand   48 *strongly* with a strong
force   49 *repeals* recalls   52 *that* what   53 *young Henry Percy* (these
words are repeated in the next scene, and either "Henry" or "his son"
may be spurious here)   57 *rest* remaining   58 *Worcester* Northumberland's brother, and the Lord Steward of the King's household

Queen. So, Green, thou art the midwife to my woe,
  And Bolingbroke, my sorrow's dismal heir;°
  Now hath my soul brought forth her prodigy,°
  And I, a gasping, new-delivered mother,   65
  Have woe to woe, sorrow to sorrow, joined.

Bushy. Despair not, madam.

Queen.   Who shall hinder me?
  I will despair and be at enmity
  With cozening Hope: he is a flatterer,
  A parasite, a keeper-back of Death,   70
  Who gently would dissolve the bands° of life
  Which false Hope lingers° in extremity.

              [*Enter the Duke of York.*]

Green. Here comes the Duke of York.

Queen. With signs of war° about his aged neck.
  O, full of careful business° are his looks!   75
  Uncle, for God's sake, speak comfortable words.°

York. Should I do so, I should belie my thoughts.
  Comfort's in heaven, and we are on the earth,
  Where nothing lives but crosses, cares, and grief.
  Your husband, he is gone to save far off,   80
  Whilst others come to make him lose at home.
  Here am I left to underprop his land,
  Who, weak with age, cannot support myself.
  Now comes the sick hour that his surfeit° made;
  Now shall he try his friends that flattered him.   85

              [*Enter Servingman.*]

Servingman. My lord, your son was gone before I
    came.

York. He was? Why so, go all which way it will.
  The nobles, they are fled, the commons cold,

---

⁶³ *heir* offspring ⁶⁴ *prodigy* monster ⁷¹ *dissolve the bands* unloose the
bonds ⁷² *lingers* causes to linger ⁷⁴ *signs of war* (York is wearing
throat armor) ⁷⁵ *careful business* anxious preoccupation ⁷⁶ *comfortable* comforting (the phrase "comfortable words" is used in the Angli-
can communion service) ⁸⁴ *surfeit* overindulgence

And will, I fear, revolt on Hereford's side.
90 Sirrah, get thee to Plashy to my sister° Gloucester;
Bid her send me presently a thousand pound.
Hold, take my ring.

Servingman. My lord, I had forgot to tell your lord-
    ship:
Today as I came by I callèd there—
95 But I shall grieve you to report the rest.

York. What is't, knave?

Servingman. An hour before I came the Duchess
    died.°

York. God for his mercy, what a tide of woes
Comes rushing on this woeful land at once.
100 I know not what to do. I would to God—
So my untruth° had not provoked him to it—
The King had cut off my head with my brother's.
What! are there no posts dispatched for Ireland?
How shall we do for money for these wars?
Come, sister—cousin, I would say—pray pardon
105   me.
Go fellow, get thee home, provide some carts,
And bring away the armor that is there.

                            [*Exit Servingman.*]

Gentlemen, will you go muster men?
If I know how or which way to order these affairs,
110 Thus disorderly thrust into my hands,
Never believe me. Both are my kinsmen.
Th' one is my sovereign, whom both my oath
And duty bids defend; t'other again
Is my kinsman, whom the King hath wronged,
115 Whom conscience and my kindred bids to right.
Well, somewhat we must do. Come, cousin,
I'll dispose of° you. Gentlemen, go muster up
    your men,

---

90 *sister* sister-in-law   97 *died* (in fact she died later; but Shakespeare
wishes to give the effect of a succession of woes)   101 *untruth* disloyalty
117 *dispose of* make arrangements for

And meet me presently at Berkeley.
I should to Plashy too,
But time will not permit. All is uneven,   120
And everything is left at six and seven.°

Exeunt Duke, Queen. Manent Bushy,
[Bagot], Green.

Bushy. The wind sits° fair for news to go for Ire-
  land,
But none returns. For us to levy power
Proportionable° to the enemy
Is all unpossible.   125

Green. Besides, our nearness to the King in love
Is near the hate of those love not the King.

Bagot. And that is the wavering commons, for their
  love
Lies in their purses, and whoso empties them
By so much fills their hearts with deadly hate.   130

Bushy. Wherein the King stands generally
  condemned.

Bagot. If judgment lie in° them, then so do we,
Because we ever have been near the King.

Green. Well, I will for refuge straight to Bristow°
  Castle.
The Earl of Wiltshire is already there.   135

Bushy. Thither will I with you, for little office
The hateful commons will perform for us,
Except like curs to tear us all to pieces.
Will you go along with us?

Bagot. No, I will to Ireland to his Majesty.   140
Farewell; if heart's presages be not vain,
We three here part that ne'er shall meet again.

Bushy. That's as York thrives to beat back Bolingbroke.

---

[121] *six and seven* i.e., in confusion   [123] *sits* blows   [124] *Proportionable*
proportional   [133] *lie in* depends on   [134] *Bristow* (old form of Bristol)

Green. Alas, poor Duke, the task he undertakes
145   Is numb'ring sands, and drinking oceans dry:
       Where one on his side fights, thousands will
          fly.
       Farewell at once, for once, for all, and ever.

Bushy. Well, we may meet again.

Bagot.   I fear me, never.

                              [*Exeunt.*]

[Scene III.   *In Gloucestershire.*]

Enter [*Bolingbroke, Duke of*] *Hereford,* [*and*]
       Northumberland [*with soldiers*].

Bolingbroke. How far is it, my lord, to Berkeley now?

Northumberland. Believe me, noble lord,
       I am a stranger here in Gloucestershire.
       These high wild hills and rough uneven ways
5   Draws out our miles and makes them wearisome;
       And yet your fair discourse hath been as sugar,
       Making the hard way sweet and delectable.°
       But I bethink me what a weary way
       From Ravenspurgh to Cotshall° will be found
10   In Ross and Willoughby, wanting your company,
       Which I protest hath very much beguiled
       The tediousness and process° of my travel:
       But theirs is sweet'ned with the hope to have
       The present benefit which I possess;
15   And hope to joy is little less in joy
       Than hope enjoyed. By this the weary lords

II.iii.   7 *delectable* (accents on first and third syllables)   9 *Cotshall*
Cotswold   12 *tediousness and process* tedious process

Shall make their way seem short as mine hath done,
By sight of what I have, your noble company.

Bolingbroke. Of much less value is my company
  Than your good words. But who comes here?   20

Enter Harry Percy.

Northumberland. It is my son, young Harry Percy,
  Sent from my brother Worcester whencesoever.°
  Harry, how fares your uncle?

Percy. I had thought, my lord, to have learned his
  health of you.

Northumberland. Why, is he not with the Queen?   25

Percy. No, my good lord, he hath forsook the court,
  Broken his staff of office, and dispersed
  The household of the King.

Northumberland.   What was his reason?
  He was not so resolved when last we spake
  together.

Percy. Because your lordship was proclaimèd
  traitor;   30
  But he, my lord, is gone to Ravenspurgh
  To offer service to the Duke of Hereford,
  And sent me over by Berkeley to discover
  What power the Duke of York had levied there,
  Then with directions to repair to Ravenspurgh.   35

Northumberland. Have you forgot the Duke of
  Hereford, boy?

Percy. No, my good lord, for that is not forgot
  Which ne'er I did remember. To my knowledge
  I never in my life did look on him.

Northumberland. Then learn to know him now—this is
  the Duke.   40

Percy. My gracious lord, I tender you my service,
  Such as it is, being tender, raw, and young,

22 *whencesoever* from wherever he is

Which elder days shall ripen and confirm
To more approvèd service and desert.

45 *Bolingbroke.* I thank thee, gentle Percy, and be sure
I count myself in nothing else so happy
As in a soul rememb'ring my good friends;
And as my fortune ripens with thy love,
It shall be still thy true love's recompense:
My heart this covenant makes, my hand thus
50   seals it.

Northumberland. How far is it to Berkeley, and what
        stir
Keeps good old York there with his men of war?

Percy. There stands the castle by yon tuft of trees,
Manned with three hundred men, as I have heard,
And in it are the Lords of York, Berkeley, and
55   Seymour,
None else of name and noble estimate.

        [*Enter Ross and Willoughby.*]

Northumberland. Here come the Lords of Ross and
        Willoughby,
Bloody with spurring, fiery red with haste.

Bolingbroke. Welcome, my lords, I wot your love
        pursues
60   A banished traitor. All my treasury
Is yet but unfelt° thanks, which more enriched
Shall be your love° and labor's recompense.

Ross. Your presence makes us rich, most noble lord.

Willoughby. And far surmounts our labor to attain it.

Bolingbroke. Evermore thank's the exchequer of the
65   poor,
Which till my infant° fortune comes to years
Stands for my bounty. But who comes here?

        [*Enter Berkeley.*]

61 *unfelt* intangible   62 *love* love's   66 *infant* (and so unable to possess
property)

Northumberland. It is my Lord of Berkeley, as I
　　guess.

Berkeley. My Lord of Hereford, my message is to
　　you.

Bolingbroke. My lord, my answer is—to Lancaster;° 70
　　And I am come to seek that name in England;
　　And I must find that title in your tongue
　　Before I make reply to aught you say.

Berkeley. Mistake me not, my lord; 'tis not my
　　meaning
　　To race one title° of your honor out.　　　　　　 75
　　To you, my lord, I come—what lord you will—
　　From the most gracious regent of this land,
　　The Duke of York, to know what pricks you on
　　To take advantage of the absent time,°
　　And fright our native peace with self-borne° arms? 80

　　　　　　[*Enter York, attended.*]

Bolingbroke. I shall not need transport my words by
　　you:
　　Here comes his Grace in person. My noble uncle!

　　　　　　[*Kneels.*]

York. Show me thy humble heart, and not thy knee,
　　Whose duty is deceivable° and false.

Bolingbroke. My gracious uncle——　　　　　　 85

York. Tut, tut! Grace me no grace, nor uncle me no
　　uncle;
　　I am no traitor's uncle, and that word "grace"
　　In an ungracious mouth is but profane.
　　Why have those banished and forbidden legs
　　Dared once to touch a dust of England's ground? 90

---

70 *to Lancaster* (Bolingbroke is about to reply, but in the middle of
the sentence he changes his mind, to say that he will answer only in
the name of Lancaster) 75 *race one title* erase title (with pun on
"tittle") 79 *absent time* time of the King's absence 80 *self-borne* borne
for one's own cause 84 *deceivable* deceptive

But then, more "why?" Why have they dared to
    march
So many miles upon her peaceful bosom,
Frighting her pale-faced villages with war,
And ostentation of despisèd° arms?
95 Com'st thou because the anointed King is hence?
Why, foolish boy, the King is left behind,
And in my loyal bosom lies his power.
Were I but now the lord of such hot youth
As when brave Gaunt, thy father, and myself
100 Rescued the Black Prince, that young Mars of men,
From forth the ranks of many thousand French,
O, then, how quickly should this arm of mine,
Now prisoner to the palsy, chastise thee,
And minister correction to thy fault!

Bolingbroke. My gracious uncle, let me know my
105   fault:
On what condition stands it, and wherein?

York. Even in condition of the worst degree
In gross rebellion and detested treason.
Thou art a banished man, and here art come
110 Before the expiration of thy time,
In braving arms against thy sovereign.

Bolingbroke. As I was banished, I was banished
        Hereford,
But as I come, I come for Lancaster.
And, noble uncle, I beseech your Grace,
115 Look on my wrongs with an indifferent° eye.
You are my father, for methinks in you
I see old Gaunt alive. O, then, my father,
Will you permit that I shall stand condemned,
A wandering vagabond, my rights and royalties
120 Plucked from my arms perforce, and given away
To upstart unthrifts?° Wherefore was I born?
If that my cousin king be King in England,

94 *despisèd* despicable   115 *indifferent* impartial   121 *unthrifts* prodigals

It must be granted I am Duke of Lancaster.
You have a son, Aumerle, my noble cousin:
Had you first died, and he been thus trod down,   *125*
He should have found his uncle Gaunt a father,
To rouse his wrongs and chase them to the bay.°
I am denied to sue my livery here,
And yet my letters patents give me leave.
My father's goods are all distrained and sold,   *130*
And these, and all, are all amiss employed.
What would you have me do? I am a subject;
And° I challenge law, attorneys are denied me;
And therefore personally I lay my claim
To my inheritance of free descent.   *135*

Northumberland. The noble Duke hath been too much
    abused.

Ross. It stands your Grace upon° to do him right.

Willoughby. Base men by his endowments are made
    great.

York. My lords of England, let me tell you this:
I have had feeling of my cousin's wrongs,   *140*
And labored all I could to do him right;
But in this kind to come in braving arms,
Be his own carver,° and cut out his way,
To find out right with wrong—it may not be:
And you that do abet him in this kind   *145*
Cherish rebellion, and are rebels all.

Northumberland. The noble Duke hath sworn his
    coming is
But for his own; and for the right of that
We all have strongly sworn to give him aid:
And let him never see joy that breaks that oath.   *150*

York. Well, well, I see the issue of these arms.
I cannot mend it, I must needs confess,
Because my power is weak and all ill left:°

---

127 *bay* quarry's last stand   133 *And if*   137 *It stands your Grace upon*
it behooves your Grace   143 *Be his own carver* i.e., be a law to himself
153 *ill left* left inadequate (?) left in disorder (?)

But if I could, by Him that gave me life,
155   I would attach° you all, and make you stoop
Unto the sovereign mercy of the King.
But since I cannot, be it known unto you
I do remain as neuter.° So fare you well—
Unless you please to enter in the castle,
160   And there repose you for this night.

Bolingbroke. An offer, uncle, that we will accept.
But we must win your grace to go with us
To Bristow Castle, which they say is held
By Bushy, Bagot, and their complices,°
165   The caterpillars of the commonwealth,°
Which I have sworn to weed and pluck away.

York. It may be I will go with you, but yet I'll pause,
For I am loath to break our country's laws.
Nor friends, nor foes, to me welcome you are.
170   Things past redress are now with me past care.

Exeunt.

[Scene IV.   *In Wales.*]

Enter Earl of Salisbury, and a Welsh Captain.°

Captain. My Lord of Salisbury, we have stayed ten
      more days.
And hardly keep our countrymen together,
And yet° we hear no tidings from the King;
Therefore we will disperse ourselves. Farewell.

5   *Salisbury.* Stay yet another day, thou trusty Welshman;
The King reposeth all his confidence in thee.

---

¹⁵⁵ *attach* arrest ¹⁵⁸ *neuter* neutral ¹⁶⁴ *complices* accomplices ¹⁶⁵ *The
. . . commonwealth* (common Elizabethan expression, ultimately Biblical, for those who preyed on society) II.iv s.d. *Captain* (possibly Owen
Glendower, mentioned in III.i.43) ³ *yet* so far

Captain. 'Tis thought the King is dead: we will not
    stay.
  The bay trees in our country are all withered,
  And meteors fright the fixèd stars of heaven,
  The pale-faced moon looks bloody on the earth,   *10*
  And lean-looked° prophets whisper fearful change;
  Rich men look sad, and ruffians dance and leap,
  The one in fear to lose what they enjoy,°
  The other to enjoy by rage° and war.
  These signs forerun the death or fall of kings.   *15*
  Farewell; our countrymen are gone and fled,
  As well assured Richard their king is dead. [*Exit.*]
Salisbury. Ah, Richard! With the eyes of heavy mind
  I see thy glory like a shooting star
  Fall to the base earth from the firmament;   *20*
  Thy sun sets weeping in the lowly west,
  Witnessing storms to come, woe and unrest;°
  Thy friends are fled to wait upon thy foes,
  And crossly° to thy good all fortune goes.   [*Exit.*]

---

11 *lean-looked* lean-looking **13** *enjoy* possess **14** *to enjoy by rage* in
hope of enjoying by violent action **21-22** *sun . . . unrest* (Richard's
badge was a sun obscured by or breaking from clouds) **24** *crossly*
adversely

*Boll: decisive,
effecient, but
we begin to
question his
legitimacy*

[ACT III

Scene I.   *Bristol. Before the Castle.*]

*Enter [Bolingbroke] Duke of Hereford, York,
Northumberland, [other Lords, Soldiers,] Bushy
and Green prisoners.*

Bolingbroke. Bring forth these men.
    Bushy and Green, I will not vex your souls,
    Since presently° your souls must part° your bodies,
    With too much urging your pernicious lives,
5   For 'twere no charity; yet, to wash your blood
    From off my hands, here in the view of men,
    I will unfold some causes of your deaths.
    You have misled a prince, a royal king,
    A happy° gentleman in blood and lineaments,
10 By you unhappied and disfigured clean;
    You have in manner with your sinful hours
    Made a divorce° betwixt his queen and him,
    Broke the possession of a royal bed,
    And stained the beauty of a fair queen's cheeks
    With tears, drawn from her eyes by your foul
15   wrongs.°
    Myself a prince, by fortune of my birth,

III.i.   3 *presently* immediately   3 *part* part from   9 *happy* fortunate
11-12 *in manner . . . divorce* you have made a kind of divorce
11-15 *You . . . wrongs* (there is no suggestion elsewhere in the play that
Richard was estranged from his queen, though Holinshed does refer to his
adultery. If the accusation is one of homosexuality, it may echo Marlowe's *Edward II;* and in *Woodstock* Queen Ann complains of Richard's favorites. But Bolingbroke is making a propaganda speech)

Near to the King in blood, and near in love
Till you did make him misinterpret me,
Have stooped my neck under your injuries,
And sighed my English breath in foreign clouds,   20
Eating the bitter bread of banishment,
Whilst you have fed upon my signories,°
Disparked° my parks, and felled my forest woods,
From my own windows torn my household coat,°
Raced out my impresse,° leaving me no sign,   25
Save men's opinions and my living blood,
To show the world I am a gentleman.°
This and much more, much more than twice all this,
Condemns you to the death. See them delivered over
To execution and the hand of death.   30

Bushy. More welcome is the stroke of death to me
Than Bolingbroke to England. Lords, farewell.

Green. My comfort is that heaven will take our souls
And plague injustice with the pains of hell.

Bolingbroke. My Lord Northumberland, see them
dispatched.°   35

[*Exeunt Northumberland with Bushy and Green.*]

Uncle, you say the Queen is at your house;
For God's sake, fairly let her be intreated.°
Tell her I send to her my kind commends;°
Take special care my greetings be delivered.

York. A gentleman of mine I have dispatched   40
With letters of your love to her at large.°

Bolingbroke. Thanks, gentle uncle. Come, Lords, away
To fight with Glendower° and his complices;
A while to work, and after holiday.   *Exeunt.*

22 *signories* estates 23 *Disparked* thrown open 24 *From . . . coat*
broke the coat of arms in stained glass 25 *Raced out my impresse*
erased my impresa (emblem) 16-27 *Myself . . . gentleman* (Bolingbroke's real complaint. He does not mention the forced loans and the
farming of the land) 35 *dispatched* executed 37 *intreated* treated
38 *commends* commendations, greetings 41 *at large* in full 43 *Glendower* (cf. note in II.iv.s.d. Perhaps Bolingbroke does not know that
the Welsh army has disbanded)

[Scene II.   *The coast of Wales, near Barkloughly Castle.*]

Enter the King, Aumerle, [*the Bishop of*] *Carlisle, etc.* [*Drums, flourish, and colors.*]

Richard. Barkloughly Castle call they this at hand?

Aumerle. Yea, my lord. How brooks° your Grace the air
After your late tossing on the breaking seas?

Richard. Needs must I like it well. I weep for joy
5   To stand upon my kingdom once again.
Dear earth, I do salute° thee with my hand,
Though rebels wound thee with their horses' hoofs.
As a long-parted mother with her child
Plays fondly with her tears and smiles in meeting,
10   So weeping, smiling, greet I thee, my earth,
And do thee favors with my royal hands.
Feed not thy sovereign's foe, my gentle earth,
Nor with thy sweets comfort his ravenous sense;
But let thy spiders, that suck up thy venom,
15   And heavy-gaited toads lie in their way,
Doing annoyance to the treacherous feet
Which with usurping steps do trample thee;
Yield stinging nettles to mine enemies;
And when they from thy bosom pluck a flower,
20   Guard it, I pray thee, with a lurking adder
Whose double tongue may with a mortal° touch
Throw death upon thy sovereign's enemies.
Mock not my senseless° conjuration, lords:

III.ii.   2 *brooks* enjoys   6 *salute* greet with a gesture   21 *mortal* deadly
23 *senseless* addressed to senseless things

This earth shall have a feeling, and these stones
Prove armèd soldiers, ere her native king   25
Shall falter under foul rebellion's arms.

Carlisle. Fear not, my lord; that power that made
      you king
Hath power to keep you king in spite of all.
The means that heavens yield must be embraced
And not neglected. Else heaven would,   30
And we will not:° heaven's offer we refuse,
The proffered means of succor and redress.

Aumerle. He means, my lord, that we are too remiss,
Whilst Bolingbroke through our security
Grows strong and great in substance and in power.   35

Richard. Discomfortable° cousin, know'st thou not
That when the searching eye of heaven is hid
Behind the globe° and lights the lower world,°
Then thieves and robbers range abroad unseen
In murders and in outrage boldly here: 40
But when from under this terrestrial ball
He fires the proud tops of the eastern pines
And darts his light through every guilty hole,
Then murders, treasons, and detested sins,
The cloak of night being plucked from off their
      backs,   45
Stand bare and naked, trembling at themselves?
So when this thief, this traitor, Bolingbroke,
Who all this while hath reveled in the night
Whilst we were wand'ring with the Antipodes,
Shall see us rising in our throne, the east,   50
His treasons will sit blushing in his face,
Not able to endure the sight of day,
But self-affrighted tremble at his sin,
Not all the water in the rough rude sea
Can wash the balm° off from an anointed king;   55
The breath of worldly° men cannot depose

30-31 *Else . . . not* otherwise we go against the will of heaven   36 *Dis-comfortable* discomforting   38 *globe* earth   38 *lower world* antipodes
55 *balm* (cf. IV.i.206)   56 *worldly* earthly

The deputy elected by the Lord.
For every man that Bolingbroke hath pressed°
To lift shrewd° steel against our golden crown,
60   God for his Richard hath in heavenly pay
A glorious angel;° then, if angels fight,
Weak men must fall, for heaven still guards the
      right.

Enter Salisbury.

Welcome, my lord. How far off lies your power?°

Salisbury. Nor near, nor farther off, my gracious
      lord,
65   Than this weak arm. Discomfort guides my tongue,
And bids me speak of nothing but despair.
One day too late, I fear me, noble lord,
Hath clouded all thy happy days on earth.
O, call back yesterday, bid time return,
70   And thou shalt have twelve thousand fighting men.
Today, today, unhappy day too late,
O'erthrows thy joys, friends, fortune, and thy state;
For all the Welshmen, hearing thou wert dead,
Are gone to Bolingbroke, dispersed and fled.

Aumerle. Comfort, my liege, why looks your Grace
75   so pale?

Richard. But now the blood of twenty thousand men
Did triumph in my face, and they are fled;
And till so much blood thither come again,
Have I not reason to look pale and dead?
80   All souls that will be safe fly from my side,
For Time hath set a blot upon my pride.

Aumerle. Comfort, my liege, remember who you are.

Richard. I had forgot myself: am I not King?
Awake, thou coward majesty! Thou sleepest.
85   Is not the King's name twenty thousand names?
Arm, arm, my name! a puny subject strikes
At thy great glory. Look not to the ground,

58 *pressed* conscripted   59 *shrewd* sharp   59-61 *crown . . . angel* (possibly
a pun on these two coins)   63 *power* army

Ye favorites of a king, are we not high?
High° be our thoughts. I know my uncle York
Hath power enough to serve our turn. But who
  comes here?   90

Enter Scroop.

Scroop. More health and happiness betide my liege
  Than can my care-tuned° tongue deliver him.

Richard. Mine ear is open, and my heart prepared;
  The worst is worldly loss thou canst unfold.
  Say, is my kingdom lost? Why, 'twas my care,   95
  And what loss is it to be rid of care?
  Strives Bolingbroke to be as great as we?
  Greater he shall not be; if he serve God,
  We'll serve Him too, and be his fellow so.
  Revolt our subjects? That we cannot mend: 100
  They break their faith to God as well as us.
  Cry woe, destruction, ruin, and decay:
  The worst is death, and death will have his day.

Scroop. Glad am I that your Highness is so armed
  To bear the tidings of calamity.   105
  Like an unseasonable stormy day
  Which makes the silver rivers drown their shores
  As if the world were all dissolved to tears,
  So high above his limits swells the rage
  Of Bolingbroke, covering your fearful land   110
  With hard bright steel and hearts harder than steel.
  White beards have armed their thin and hairless
    scalps
  Against thy majesty; boys with women's voices
  Strive to speak big,° and clap their female° joints
  In stiff unwieldy arms against thy crown;   115
  Thy very beadsmen° learn to bend their bows
  Of double-fatal° yew against thy state;
  Yea, distaff-women manage° rusty bills°

---

89 *High* i.e., high in name and place   92 *care-tuned* tuned to the key of sorrow   114 *speak big* assume men's voices   114 *female* weak, effeminate   116 *beadsmen* pensioners who pray for their benefactors   117 *double-fatal* (the berry is poisonous and the wood used for bows)   118 *manage* wield   118 *bills* wooden shafts with spiked blades

Against thy seat: both young and old rebel,
120   And all goes worse than I have power to tell.

Richard. Too well, too well thou tell'st a tale so ill.
    Where is the Earl of Wiltshire? Where is Bagot?
    What is become of Bushy? Where is Green?
    That they have let the dangerous enemy
125   Measure our confines with such peaceful° steps?
    If we prevail, their heads shall pay for it.
    I warrant they have° made peace with Bolingbroke.

Scroop. Peace have they made with him indeed, my
    lord.

Richard. O, villains, vipers, damned without
    redemption!
130   Dogs easily won to fawn on any man!
    Snakes in my heart-blood warmed that sting my
    heart!
    Three Judases, each one thrice worse than Judas!
    Would they make peace? Terrible hell
    Make war upon their spotted° souls for this!

135 *Scroop.* Sweet love, I see, changing his property,°
    Turns to the sourest and most deadly hate.
    Again uncurse their souls: their peace is made
    With heads and not with hands; those whom you
    curse
    Have felt the worst of death's destroying wound,
140   And lie full low, graved in the hollow ground.

Aumerle. Is Bushy, Green, and the Earl of Wiltshire
    dead?

Scroop. Ay, all of them at Bristow lost their heads.

Aumerle. Where is the Duke, my father, with his
    power?°

Richard. No matter where—of comfort no man
    speak.

---

125 *peaceful* i.e., unopposed   127 *they have* (pronounced "they've")
134 *spotted* sinful   135 *property* distinctive quality   143 *power* army

Let's talk of graves, of worms, and epitaphs,   _145_
Make dust our paper, and with rainy eyes
Write sorrow on the bosom of the earth.
Let's choose executors and talk of wills:
And yet not so, for what can we bequeath
Save our deposèd bodies to the ground?   _150_
Our lands, our lives, and all are Bolingbroke's,
And nothing can we call our own, but death
And that small model° of the barren earth
Which serves as paste and cover° to our bones.
For God's sake let us sit upon the ground   _155_
And tell sad stories of the death of kings:
How some have been deposed, some slain in war,
Some haunted by the ghosts they have deposed,
Some poisoned by their wives, some sleeping killed,
All murdered—for within the hollow° crown   _160_
That rounds the mortal temples of a king
Keeps Death his court, and there the antic° sits,
Scoffing his state and grinning at his pomp,
Allowing him a breath, a little scene,
To monarchize,° be feared, and kill with looks,   _165_
Infusing him with self and vain conceit,°
As if this flesh which walls about our life
Were brass impregnable; and, humored° thus,
Comes at the last, and with a little pin
Bores thorough° his castle wall, and farewell king!   _170_
Cover your heads, and mock not flesh and blood
With solemn reverence; throw away respect,
Tradition, form, and ceremonious duty;
For you have but mistook me all this while:
I live with bread like you, feel want,   _175_
Taste grief, need friends—subjected° thus,
How can you say to me, I am a king?

153 _model_ (variously explained as mold, grave mound, and microcosm)
154 _paste and cover_ (an image taken from pie crust, since this was
sometimes called a coffin) 160 _hollow_ empty circle, vain, transitory
162 _antic_ clown   165 _monarchize_ play the monarch   166 _self and vain
conceit_ empty estimate of self   168 _humored_ (perhaps "Death thus
amused" or "the King thus indulged")   170 _thorough_ through   176 _sub-
jected_ made a subject and subject to the ordinary needs of man

Carlisle. My lord, wise men ne'er sit and wail their
    woes,
    But presently° prevent the ways to wail.
180   To fear the foe, since fear oppresseth strength,
    Gives in your weakness strength unto your foe;
    And so your follies fight against yourself.
    Fear and be slain, no worse can come to fight,°
    And fight and die is death destroying death,
185   Where fearing dying pays death servile breath.°

Aumerle. My father hath a power; inquire of him,
    And learn to make a body of a limb.°

Richard. Thou chid'st me well. Proud Bolingbroke, I
    come
    To change° blows with thee for our day of doom.
190   This ague fit of fear is overblown;°
    An easy task it is to win our own.
    Say, Scroop, where lies our uncle with his power?°
    Speak sweetly, man, although thy looks be sour.

Scroop. Men judge by the complexion of the sky
195   The state and inclination of the day;
    So may you by my dull and heavy eye.
    My tongue hath but a heavier tale to say.
    I play the torturer by small and small°
    To lengthen out the worst that must be spoken:
200   Your uncle York is joined with Bolingbroke,
    And all your northern castles yielded up,
    And all your southern gentlemen in arms
    Upon his party.°

Richard.   Thou hast said enough.
    Beshrew thee,° cousin, which° didst lead me
    forth
205   Of that sweet way° I was in to despair.

---

179 *presently* immediately   183 *to fight* by fighting   185 *pays . . . breath*
makes us slaves to death   187 *body of a limb* make a whole out of a part
189 *change* exchange   190 *overblown* blown over   192 *power* army
198 *small and small* little by little   203 *Upon his party* on his side
204 *Beshrew thee* ill befall you   204 *which* who   205 *way* path, habit

What say you now? What comfort have we now?
By heaven, I'll hate him everlastingly
That bids me be of comfort any more.
Go to Flint Castle: there I'll pine away;
A king, woe's slave, shall kingly woe obey.   210
That power I have, discharge, and let them go
To ear the land that hath some hope to grow,°
For I have none. Let no man speak again
To alter this, for counsel is but vain.

Aumerle. My liege, one word.

Richard.   He does me double wrong   215
That wounds me with the flatteries of his tongue.
Discharge my followers, let them hence away,
From Richard's night to Bolingbroke's fair day.

                                        [*Exeunt.*]

[*Scene III. Wales, before Flint Castle.*]

Enter [*with drum and colors*] *Bolingbroke,
York, Northumberland,* [*Attendants and
Soldiers*].

Bolingbroke. So that by this intelligence we learn
The Welshmen are dispersed, and Salisbury
Is gone to meet the King, who lately landed
With some few private friends upon this coast.

Northumberland. The news is very fair and good, my
      lord;   5
Richard not far from hence hath hid his head.

York. It would beseem the Lord Northumberland

---

212 *To . . . grow* to cultivate the fertile ground, i.e., desert to Bolingbroke

To say "King Richard." Alack, the heavy day
When such a sacred king should hide his head.

Northumberland. Your Grace mistakes; only to be
10   brief
Left I his title out.

York.   The time hath been
Would you have been so brief° with him, he would
Have been so brief with you to shorten you,
For taking so the head,° your whole head's length.

Bolingbroke. Mistake° not, uncle, further than you
13   should.

York. Take not, good cousin, further than you
      should,
Lest you mis-take:° the heavens are over our
      heads.

Bolingbroke. I know it, uncle, and oppose not myself
Against their will. But who comes here?

                Enter Percy.

20   Welcome, Harry. What, will not this castle yield?

Percy. The castle royally is manned, my lord,
Against thy entrance.

Bolingbroke.   Royally!
Why, it contains no king?

Percy.   Yes, my good lord,
It doth contain a king: King Richard lies
25   Within the limits of yon lime and stone;
And with him are the Lord Aumerle, Lord
      Salisbury,
Sir Stephen Scroop, besides a clergyman
Of holy reverence—who, I cannot learn.

Northumberland. O, belike it is the Bishop of Carlisle.

III.iii. 11-12 *The . . . brief* there was a time when if you had been
so curt 14 *taking so the head* (1) chopping off the title (2) acting
without restraint 15 *Mistake* take amiss 17 *mis-take* transgress, take
what is not yours, i.e., the crown

Bolingbroke. Noble lord,   30
   Go to the rude ribs° of that ancient castle,
   Through brazen trumpet send the breath of parley
   Into his ruined ears, and thus deliver:
   Henry Bolingbroke
   On both his knees doth kiss King Richard's hand,   35
   And sends allegiance and true faith of heart
   To his most royal person; hither come
   Even at his feet to lay my arms and power,
   Provided that my banishment repealed,
   And lands restored again be freely granted;   40
   If not, I'll use the advantage of my power,
   And lay the summer's dust with showers of blood
   Rained from the wounds of slaughtered
      Englishmen—
   The which,° how far off from the mind of
      Bolingbroke
   It is such crimson tempest should bedrench   45
   The fresh green lap of fair King Richard's land,
   My stooping duty tenderly° shall show.
   Go, signify as much, while here we march
   Upon the grassy carpet of this plain.
   Let's march without the noise of threat'ning drum,   50
   That from this castle's tattered° battlements
   Our fair appointments° may be well perused.
   Methinks King Richard and myself should meet
   With no less terror than the elements
   Of fire and water,° when their thund'ring shock   55
   At meeting tears the cloudy cheeks of heaven.
   Be he the fire, I'll be the yielding water;
   The rage be his, whilst on the earth I rain°
   My waters—on the earth, and not on him.
   March on, and mark King Richard how he looks.   60

*The trumpets sound [parle without, and answer
within; then a flourish]. Richard appeareth on*

---

³¹ *ribs* protecting walls   ⁴⁴ *The which* as to which   ⁴⁷ *tenderly* solicitously   ⁵¹ *tattered* crenelated, dilapidated   ⁵² *appointments* arms and equipment   ⁵⁵ *fire and water* lightning and rain clouds   ⁵⁸ *rain* (pun on "reign")

the walls [with the Bishop of Carlisle, Aumerle, Scroop, Salisbury].

See, see King Richard doth himself appear,
As doth the blushing discontented sun
From out the fiery portal of the East,
When he perceives the envious clouds are bent
65   To dim his glory, and to stain the track
Of his bright passage to the Occident.

York. Yet looks he like a king: behold his eye,
As bright as is the eagle's, lightens forth°
Controlling majesty. Alack, alack for woe,
70   That any harm should stain so fair a show.

Richard. [*To Northumberland*] We are amazed,
and thus long have we stood
To watch the fearful bending of thy knee,
Because we thought ourself thy lawful king:
And if we be, how dare thy joints forget
75   To pay their awful° duty to our presence?
If we be not, show us the hand of God
That hath dismissed us from our stewardship;
For well we know no hand of blood and bone
Can gripe the sacred handle of our scepter,
80   Unless he do profane, steal, or usurp;
And though you think that all, as you have done,
Have torn their souls by turning° them from us,
And we are barren and bereft of friends,
Yet know, my master, God omnipotent,
85   Is mustering in his clouds on our behalf
Armies of pestilence, and they shall strike
Your children yet unborn and unbegot
That lift your vassal hands against my head,
And threat the glory of my precious crown.
90   Tell Bolingbroke—for yon methinks he stands—
That every stride he makes upon my land
Is dangerous treason. He is come to open
The purple testament of bleeding war;

68 *lightens forth* flashes   75 *awful* reverential   82 *torn . . . turning* (pun)

But ere the crown he looks for live in peace
Ten thousand bloody crowns° of mothers' sons   95
Shall ill become the flower of England's face,
Change the complexion of her maid-pale peace
To scarlet indignation, and bedew
Her pastor's° grass with faithful English blood.

Northumberland. The King of heaven forbid our lord
     the King   100
Should so with civil and uncivil arms
Be rushed upon. Thy thrice-noble cousin,
Harry Bolingbroke, doth humbly kiss thy hand,
And by the honorable tomb he swears
That stands upon your royal grandshire's bones,   105
And by the royalties of both your bloods—
Currents that spring from one most gracious
     head—
And by the buried hand of warlike Gaunt,
And by the worth and honor of himself,
Comprising all that may be sworn or said,   110
His coming hither hath no further scope°
Than for his lineal royalties,° and to beg
Infranchisement° immediate on his knees;
Which on thy royal party° granted once,
His glittering arms he will commend to rust,   115
His barbèd° steeds to stables, and his heart
To faithful service of your Majesty.
This swears he, as he is a prince and just;
And, as I am a gentleman, I credit him.

Richard. Northumberland, say thus the King returns,° 120
His noble cousin is right welcome hither,
And all the number of his fair demands
Shall be accomplished without contradiction.
With all the gracious utterance thou hast
Speak to his gentle hearing kind commends.°   125

---

[95] *crowns* (punning on the *crown* of line 94)   [99] *pastor's* (the King was
the shepherd of his kingdom)   [111] *scope* aim   [112] *lineal royalties* hereditary rights   [113] *Infranchisement* recall from banishment and restitution
of his lands   [114] *party* side   [116] *barbèd* armored   [120] *returns* answers
[125] *commends* greetings

[*To Aumerle*] We° do debase ourselves, cousin,
   do we not,
To look so poorly° and to speak so fair?
Shall we call back Northumberland, and send
Defiance to the traitor and so die?

Aumerle. No, good my lord; let's fight with gentle
130   words,
   Till time lend friends, and friends their helpful
   swords.

Richard. O God! O God! that e'er this tongue of mine,
   That laid the sentence of dread banishment
   On yon proud man, should take it off again
135   With words of sooth!° O, that I were as great
   As is my grief, or lesser than my name!°
   Or that I could forget what I have been!
   Or not remember what I must be now!
   Swell'st thou, proud heart? I'll give thee scope to
   beat,
140   Since foes have scope to beat both thee and me.

Aumerle. Northumberland comes back from
   Bolingbroke.

Richard. What must the King do now? Must he
   submit?
   The King shall do it. Must he be deposed?
   The King shall be contented. Must he lose
145   The name of king? a° God's name, let it go.
   I'll give my jewels for a set of beads;°
   My gorgeous palace for a hermitage;
   My gay apparel for an almsman's gown;
   My figured° goblets for a dish of wood;
150   My scepter for a palmer's° walking-staff;
   My subjects for a pair of carvèd saints;
   And my large kingdom for a little grave,
   A little, little grave, an obscure grave;

---

126 *We* (the speech prefix is repeated in the quarto perhaps because a
line of Northumberland's has dropped out)   127 *poorly* abjectly
135 *sooth* flattery   136 *name* i.e., king   145 *a* in   146 *set of beads* rosary
149 *figured* ornamented   150 *palmer's* pilgrim's

Or I'll be buried in the King's highway,
Some way of common trade,° where subjects' feet   *155*
May hourly trample on their sovereign's head;
For on my heart they tread now whilst I live,
And buried once, why not upon my head?
Aumerle, thou weep'st, my tender-hearted cousin:
We'll make foul weather with despisèd tears;   *160*
Our sighs and they shall lodge° the summer corn,
And make a dearth in this revolting land:
Or shall we play the wantons° with our woes
And make some pretty match with shedding tears,
As thus, to drop them still° upon one place,   *165*
Till they have fretted° us a pair of graves
Within the earth; and, therein laid, "there lies
Two kinsmen digged their graves with weeping
    eyes":
Would not this ill do well? Well, well, I see
I talk but idly, and you laugh at me.   *170*
Most mighty prince, my Lord Northumberland,
What says King Bolingbroke? Will his Majesty
Give Richard leave to live till Richard die?
You make a leg,° and Bolingbroke says "Ay."

Northumberland. My lord, in the base court° he
    doth attend
To speak with you; may it please you to come   *175*
    down?

Richard.   Down, down I come, like glist'ring
    Phaethon,°
Wanting the manage° of unruly jades.
In the base court! Base court where kings grow
    base,
To come at traitors' calls, and do them grace: *180*
In the base court, come down: down court,
    down king,

---

155 *trade* coming and going   161 *lodge* beat down   163 *play the wantons*
be unrestrained   165 *still* always   166 *fretted* worn   174 *make a leg* curtsy
175 *base court* basse cour, the lower and outer courtyard   177 *Phaethon*
(he drove the sun chariot of his father, Apollo, and was struck by
Zeus's thunderbolt)   178 *manage* art of managing horses

For <u>night owls</u> shriek where <u>mounting larks</u> should
    sing.

Bolingbroke. What says his Majesty?

Northumberland.   Sorrow and grief of heart
    Makes him speak fondly° like a frantic man;
    Yet he is come.

> [*Enter King Richard and Attendants, below.*]

185   *Bolingbroke.*   Stand all apart,
    And show fair duty to his Majesty.

> *He kneels down.*

My gracious Lord.

Richard. Fair cousin, you debase your princely knee
    To make the base earth proud with kissing it.
190   Me rather° had my heart might feel your love,
    Than my unpleased eye see your courtesy.
    Up, cousin, up, your heart is up, I know,
    Thus high° at least, although your knee be low.

Bolingbroke. My gracious lord, I come but for mine
    own.

Richard. Your own is yours, and I am yours, and
195   all.

Bolingbroke. So far be mine, my most redoubted°
    lord,
    As my true service shall deserve your love.

Richard. Well you deserve: they well deserve to have
    That know the strong'st and surest way to get.
200   Uncle, give me your hands; nay, dry your eyes;
    Tears show their love, but want their remedies.°
    Cousin, I am too young to be your father,
    Though you are old enough to be my heir.
    What you will have, I'll give, and willing too,

---

184 *fondly* foolishly   190 *Me rather* I would sooner   193 *Thus high* (pointing to his crown)   196 *redoubted* dreaded   201 *want their remedies* i.e., cannot provide a cure for themselves or for the grief which causes them

For do we must what force will have us do.   205
Set on towards London, cousin, is it so?

Bolingbroke. Yea, my good Lord.

Richard.   Then I must not say no.

[*Flourish. Exeunt.*]

[Scene IV.   *The Duke of York's garden.*]

*Enter the Queen with [two Ladies,] her
Attendants.*

Queen. What sport shall we devise here in this garden,
To drive away the heavy thought of care?

Lady. Madame,° we'll play at bowls.

Queen. 'Twill make me think the world is full of rubs,°
And that my fortune runs against the bias.°   5

Lady. Madame, we'll dance.

Queen. My legs can keep no measure in delight,
When my poor heart no measure° keeps in grief:
Therefore no dancing, girl; some other sport.

Lady. Madame, we'll tell tales.   10

Queen. Of sorrow, or of joy?

Lady.   Of either, madame.

Queen. Of neither, girl.
For if of joy, being altogether wanting,

III.iv. ³ *Madame* (spelled thus in the quarto, possibly to suggest that
the ladies came with the Queen from France) ⁴ *rubs* obstacles by
which bowls were diverted from their proper course ⁵ *bias* the form
of the bowl which imparts an oblique motion ⁷⁻⁸ *measure . . . measure*
(1) time to music (2) a stately dance (3) moderation

It doth remember° me the more of sorrow;
15 Or if of grief, being altogether had,
It adds more sorrow to my want of joy:
For what I have I need not to repeat,
And what I want it boots° not to complain.

Lady. Madame, I'll sing.

Queen.   'Tis well that thou hast cause;
But thou should'st please me better, would'st thou
20   weep.

Lady. I could weep, madame, would it do you good.

Queen. And I could sing, would weeping do me good,
And never borrow any tear of thee.

> *Enter Gardeners, [one the master, the other
> two his men].*

But stay, here come the gardeners.
25 Let's step into the shadow of these trees.
My wretchedness unto a row of pins,
They will talk of state,° for every one doth so
Against a change;° woe is forerun with woe.

Gardener. [*To one Servant*] Go, bind thou up
      young dangling apricocks,°
30 Which like unruly children make their sire
Stoop with oppression° of their prodigal° weight;
Give some supportance° to the bending twigs.
[*To the other*] Go thou, and like an executioner
Cut off the heads of too fast growing sprays
35 That look too lofty in our commonwealth:
All must be even in our government.
You thus employed, I will go root away
The noisome weeds which without profit suck
The soil's fertility from wholesome flowers.

40 *Man.* Why should we, in the compass of a pale,°
Keep law and form and due proportion,

---

14 *remember* remind   18 *boots* avails   27 *state* the realm   28 *Against a change* when a change is expected   29 *apricocks* apricots   31 *oppression* weighing down   31 *prodigal* wasteful   32 *supportance* support   40 *pale* fenced-in land

Showing, as in a model,° our firm estate,
When our sea-wallèd garden, the whole land,
Is full of weeds, her fairest flowers choked up,
Her fruit trees all unpruned, her hedges ruined,   45
Her knots° disordered, and her wholesome herbs
Swarming with caterpillars?° — *rich's flatterers*

Gardener.   Hold thy peace.
He that hath suffered this disordered spring
Hath now himself met with the fall of leaf:
The weeds which his broad spreading leaves did
    shelter,   50
That seemed in eating him to hold him up,
Are plucked up root and all by Bolingbroke—
I mean the Earl of Wiltshire, Bushy, Green.

Man. What, are they dead?

Gardener.   They are; and Bolingbroke
Hath seized the wasteful King. O, what pity is it   55
That he had not so trimmed and dressed° his land
As we this garden! We at time of year
Do wound the bark, the skin of our fruit trees,
Lest being overproud in sap and blood
With too much riches it confound itself;   60
Had he done so to great and growing men,
They might have lived to bear, and he to taste
Their fruits of duty. Superfluous branches
We lop away, that bearing boughs may live:
Had he done so, himself had borne the crown,   65
Which waste of idle hours hath quite thrown down.

Man. What, think you the King shall be deposed?

Gardener. Depressed° he is already, and deposed
'Tis doubt he will be. Letters came last night
To a dear friend of the good Duke of York's,   70
That tell black tidings.

Queen.   O, I am pressed to death

⁴² *as in a model* in miniature   ⁴⁶ *knots* laid-out flower beds   ⁴⁷ *cater-pillars* (cf. II.iii.165)   ⁵⁶ *dressed* tended   ⁶⁸ *depressed* lowered in for-tune

Through want of speaking!°

[Comes forward.]

Thou, old Adam's likeness, set to dress this
        garden,
How dares thy harsh rude tongue sound this
        unpleasing news?
75   What Eve, what serpent hath suggested° thee
To make a second fall of cursèd man?
Why dost thou say King Richard is deposed?
Dar'st thou, thou little better thing than earth,
Divine his downfall? Say, where, when and how
80   Cam'st thou by this ill tidings? Speak, thou wretch.

Gardener. Pardon me, madam; little joy have I
To breathe this news, yet what I say is true:
King Richard he is in the mighty hold°
Of Bolingbroke. Their fortunes both are weighed:
85   In your lord's scale is nothing but himself
And some few vanities that make him light;
But in the balance of great Bolingbroke
Besides himself are all the English peers,
And with that odds he weighs King Richard down.
90   Post you to London, and you will find it so;
I speak no more than everyone doth know.

Queen. Nimble mischance, that art so light of foot,
Doth not thy embassage belong to me,
And am I last that knows it? O, thou thinkest
95   To serve me last that I may longest keep
Thy sorrow in my breast! Come, ladies, go
To meet at London London's king in woe.
What, was I born to this, that my sad look
Should grace the triumph of great Bolingbroke?
100   Gard'ner, for telling me these news of woe,
Pray God, the plants thou graft'st may never grow.

Exit [with Ladies].

71-72 *O . . . speaking* (referring to the torture of pressing to death ad-
ministered to prisoners who refused to speak)   75 *suggested* tempted
83 *hold* custody

Gardener. Poor queen, so that thy state might be no
        worse,
    I would my skill were subject to thy curse.
    Here did she fall a tear; here in this place
    I'll set a bank of rue, sour herb of grace;   105
    Rue even for ruth° here shortly shall be seen,
    In the remembrance of a weeping queen.

                                            Exeunt.

106 *ruth* pity

[ACT IV

Scene I. *Westminster Hall.*]

Enter Bolingbroke, with the Lords [Aumerle, Northumberland, Percy, Fitzwater, Surrey, the Bishop of Carlisle, the Abbot of Westminster, another Lord, Herald, and Officers] to Parliament.

Bolingbroke. Call forth Bagot.
         Enter Bagot [with Officers].
      Now, Bagot, freely speak thy mind,
      What thou dost know of noble Gloucester's death,
      Who wrought it with° the King, and who performed
5   The bloody office of his timeless° end.

Bagot. Then set before my face the Lord Aumerle.

Bolingbroke. Cousin, stand forth, and look upon that
      man.

Bagot. My Lord Aumerle, I know your daring tongue
      Scorns to unsay what once it hath delivered.
      In that dead time° when Gloucester's death was
10   plotted,
      I heard you say, "Is not my arm of length,
      That reacheth from the restful English court

IV.i.   4 *wrought it with* persuaded   5 *timeless* untimely (or everlasting)
10 *dead time* (variously interpreted: past time, deadly time, midnight hour)

112

As far as Callice° to mine uncle's head?"
Amongst much other talk that very time
I heard you say that you had rather refuse   *15*
The offer of an hundred thousand crowns
Than Bolingbroke's return to England;
Adding withal, how blest this land would be
In this your cousin's death.

Aumerle.   Princes and noble Lords,
What answer shall I make to this base man?   *20*
Shall I so much dishonor my fair stars
On equal terms° to give him chastisement?
Either I must, or have mine honor soiled
With the attainder° of his slanderous lips.
There is my gage, the manual° seal of death,   *25*
That marks thee out for hell: I say thou liest,
And will maintain what thou hast said is false
In thy heart-blood, though being all too base
To stain the temper° of my knightly sword.

Bolingbroke. Bagot, forbear, thou shalt not take it up.   *30*

Aumerle. Excepting one, I would he were the best
In all this presence that hath moved me so.°

Fitzwater. If that thy valor stand on sympathy,°
There is my gage, Aumerle, in gage° to thine;
By that fair sun which shows me where thou
      stand'st,   *35*
I heard thee say, and vauntingly thou spak'st it,
That thou wert cause of noble Gloucester's death.
If thou deniest it twenty times, thou liest,
And I will turn thy falsehood to thy heart,
Where it was forgèd, with my rapier's point.   *40*

Aumerle. Thou dar'st not, coward, live to see that day.

---

13 *Callice* Calais   22 *On equal terms* (Aumerle was Bagot's superior and
could therefore refuse to fight with him)   24 *attainder* accusation
25 *manual* by my own hand (punning on a seal fixed to a document and
his glove)   29 *temper* i.e., excellence   31-32 *Excepting . . . so* I wish I
had been angered by the highest in rank present, except Bolingbroke
33 *stand on sympathy* depends on correspondence of rank   34 *in gage*
in pledge

Fitzwater. Now, by my soul, I would it were this hour!

Aumerle. Fitzwater, thou art damned to hell for this.

Percy. Aumerle, thou liest, his honor is as true
45   In this appeal as thou art all unjust;
And that thou art so, there I throw my gage,
To prove it on thee to the extremest point
Of mortal breathing;° seize it if thou dar'st.

Aumerle. And if° I do not, may my hands rot off,
50   And never brandish more revengeful steel
Over the glittering helmet of my foe.

Another Lord. I task the earth to the like,° forsworn
Aumerle,
And spur thee on with full as many lies
As may be hollowed° in thy treacherous ear
55   From sun to sun:° there is my honor's pawn;
Engage° it to the trial if thou darest.

Aumerle. Who sets me else?° By heaven, I'll throw°
at all!
I have a thousand spirits in one breast
To answer twenty thousand such as you.

60   *Surrey.* My Lord Fitzwater, I do remember well
The very time Aumerle and you did talk.

Fitzwater. 'Tis very true; you were in presence° then,
And you can witness with me this is true.

Surrey. As false, by heaven, as heaven itself is true!

Fitzwater. Surrey, thou liest.

65   *Surrey.*   Dishonorable boy,
That lie shall lie so heavy on my sword,
That it shall render vengeance and revenge,
Till thou, the lie-giver, and that lie do lie
In earth as quiet as thy father's skull.

47-48 *extremest . . . breathing* to the death   49 *And if* if indeed   52 *task
. . . like* lay on the earth the task of bearing another gage   54 *hollowed*
shouted   55 *sun to sun* sunrise to sunset   56 *Engage* (pun on "gage" and
"engage")   57 *Who sets me else* who else puts up a stake against me
57 *throw* (metaphor from dicing)   62 *in presence* present (or in attendance at court)

In proof whereof, there is my honor's pawn;   70
Engage it to the trial if thou dar'st.

Fitzwater. How fondly° dost thou spur a forward°
    horse!
If I dare eat, or drink, or breathe, or live,
I dare meet Surrey in a wilderness,
And spit upon him, whilst I say he lies,   75
And lies, and lies. There is my bond of faith,
To tie thee to my strong correction.°
As I intend to thrive in this new world,°
Aumerle is guilty of my true appeal.
Besides, I heard the banished Norfolk say   80
That thou, Aumerle, did'st send two of thy men
To execute the noble Duke at Callice.

Aumerle. Some honest Christian trust me with a
    gage.°
That Norfolk lies, here do I throw down this,
If he may be repealed to try his honor.   85

Bolingbroke. These differences shall all rest under
    gage°
Till Norfolk be repealed; repealed he shall be,
And, though mine enemy, restored again
To all his lands and signories.° When he is
    returned,
Against Aumerle we will inforce his trial.   90

Carlisle. That honorable day shall never be seen.
Many a time hath banished Norfolk fought
For Jesu Christ in glorious Christian field,
Streaming° the ensign of the Christian cross
Against black pagans, Turks, and Saracens;   95
And, toiled° with works of war, retired himself
To Italy, and there at Venice gave
His body to that pleasant country's earth,
And his pure soul unto his captain, Christ,

72 *fondly* foolishly   72 *forward* willing   77 *correction* punishment
78 *new world* i.e., of the new reign   83 *Some . . . gage* (he has used both
his own gloves)   86 *under gage* i.e., prorogued   89 *signories* estates
94 *streaming* flying   96 *toiled* exhausted with toil

100   Under whose colors he had fought so long.

Bolingbroke. Why, Bishop, is Norfolk dead?

Carlisle. As surely as I live, my lord.

Bolingbroke. Sweet peace conduct his sweet soul to
          the bosom
          Of good old Abraham!° Lords appellants,°
105   Your differences shall all rest under gage,
          Till we assign you to your days of trial.

Enter York.

York. Great Duke of Lancaster, I come to thee
          From plume-plucked° Richard, who with willing
          soul
          Adopts thee heir, and his high scepter yields
110   To the possession of thy royal hand.
          Ascend his throne, descending now from him,
          And long live Henry, fourth of that name!

Bolingbroke. In God's name, I'll ascend the regal
          throne.

Carlisle. Marry,° God forbid!
115   Worst° in this royal presence may I speak,
          Yet best beseeming me to speak the truth.
          Would God that any in this noble presence
          Were enough noble to be upright judge
          Of noble Richard. Then true noblesse would
120   Learn° him forbearance from so foul a wrong.
          What subject can give sentence on his king?
          And who sits here that is not Richard's subject?
          Thieves are not judged, but they are by to hear,
          Although apparent° guilt be seen in them;
125   And shall the figure° of God's majesty,
          His captain, steward, deputy elect,°
          Anointed, crownèd, planted many years,

104 *Abraham* cf. Luke 16:22   104 *appellants* those who are appealing or
accusing each other   108 *plume-plucked* i.e., humbled   114 *Marry* (a
light oath, from "By the Virgin Mary")   115 *Worst* i.e., least in
rank or competence   120 *Learn* teach   124 *apparent* manifest   125 *figure*
image   126 *elect* chosen

Be judged by subject° and inferior breath,
And he himself not present? O, forfend° it, God,
That in a Christian climate souls refined°   *130*
Should show so heinous, black, obscene° a deed!
I speak to subjects and a subject speaks,
Stirred up by God thus boldly for his king.
My Lord of Hereford here, whom you call king,
Is a foul traitor to proud Hereford's king;   *135*
And if you crown him, let me prophesy
The blood of English shall manure the ground,
And future ages groan for this foul act;
Peace shall go sleep with Turks and infidels,
And, in this seat of peace, tumultuous wars   *140*
Shall kin with° kin, and kind° with kind, confound;
Disorder, horror, fear, and mutiny
Shall here inhabit, and this land be called
The field of Golgotha° and dead men's skulls.
O, if you raise this house against this house,°   *145*
It will the woefullest division prove
That ever fell upon this cursèd earth!°
Prevent it, resist it, let it not be so,
Lest child, child's children, cry against you woe.

Northumberland. Well have you argued, sir; and for
          your pains   *150*
Of capital treason we arrest you here.
My Lord of Westminster, be it your charge
To keep him safely till his day of trial.
May it please you, lords, to grant the Commons'
          suit?°

Bolingbroke. Fetch hither Richard, that in common
          view   *155*
He may surrender; so we shall proceed
Without suspicion.

---

128 *subject* of a subject   129 *forfend* avert   130 *refined* purified by the
Christian environment   131 *obscene* offensive   141 *with* by means of
141 *kind* race   144 *Golgotha* cf. Mark 15:22 "a place of dead mens
skulles" (Bishops' Bible)   145 *O . . . house* cf. Mark 3:25   147 *cursèd
earth* earth cursed by civil war   154 *suit* (that the charges against the
King should be published)

York.   I will be his conduct.°

                                                    Exit.

Bolingbroke. Lords, you that here are under our
      arrest,
      Procure your sureties for your days of answer.
160   Little are we beholding to your love,
      And little looked for at your helping hands.

                Enter Richard and York.

Richard. Alack, why am I sent for to a king,
      Before I have shook off the regal thoughts
      Wherewith I reigned? I hardly yet have learned
165   To insinuate,° flatter, bow, and bend my knee.
      Give Sorrow leave a while to tutor me
      To this submission. Yet I well remember
      The favors° of these men: were they not mine?
      Did they not sometime cry "All hail!" to me?
170   So Judas° did to Christ: but he in twelve°
      Found truth in all but one; I, in twelve thousand,
         none.
      God save the King! Will no man say "Amen"?
      Am I both priest and clerk?° Well, then, amen.
      God save the King, although I be not he;
175   And yet amen, if heaven do think him me.
      To do what service am I sent for hither?

York. To do that office° of thine own good will,
      Which tired majesty did make thee offer:
      The resignation of thy state and crown
      To Henry Bolingbroke.

180 *Richard.*   Give me the crown.
      Here, cousin, seize the crown. Here, cousin,
      On this side my hand, and on that side yours.
      Now is this golden crown like a deep well
      That owes° two buckets, filling one another,

---

157 *conduct* conductor 165 *insinuate* progress by devious ways 168 *fa-vors* (1) faces (2) benefits 170 *Judas* cf. Matthew 26:49 170 *twelve* i.e., the apostles 173 *clerk* (employed to utter responses to the priest's prayers) 177 *office* (York corrects Richard's "service") 184 *owes* owns

The emptier ever dancing in the air,   185
The other down, unseen, and full of water.
That bucket down and full of tears am I,
Drinking my griefs, whilst you mount up on high.

Bolingbroke. I thought you had been willing to resign.

Richard. My crown I am, but still my griefs are mine: 190
  You may my glories and my state depose,
  But not my griefs; still am I King of those.

Bolingbroke. Part of your cares you give me with
    your crown.

Richard. Your cares° set up, do not pluck my cares
    down.
  My care is loss of care, by old care done;   195
  Your care is gain of care, by new care won.°
  The cares I give, I have, though given away;
  They 'tend° the crown, yet still with me they stay.

Bolingbroke. Are you contented to resign the crown?

Richard. Ay, no; no, ay: for I must nothing be.   200
  Therefore no, no, for I resign to thee.
  Now, mark me how I will undo° myself.
  I give this heavy weight from off my head,
  And this unwieldy scepter from my hand,
  The pride of kingly sway from out my heart;   205
  With mine own tears I wash away my balm,°
  With mine own hands I give away my crown,
  With mine own tongue deny my sacred state,
  With mine own breath release all duteous oaths;
  All pomp and majesty I do forswear;   210
  My manors, rents, revenues,° I forgo;
  My acts, decrees, and statutes I deny:
  God pardon all oaths that are broke to me,

---

194 *cares* (the word is used in several different senses in lines
194-97—sorrows, responsibilities, diligence or carefulness, anxiety)
195-96 *My . . . won* my sorrow is loss of responsibility by failing to take
pains; your anxiety is gain of responsibility won by your new carefulness   198 *'tend* attend on   202 *undo* (1) strip (2) ruin   206 *balm* anointing ointment used at coronation   211 *revenues* (accent on second syllable)

God keep all vows unbroke are° made to thee.
215 Make me, that nothing have, with nothing grieved,
And thou with all pleased, that hast all achieved.
Long may'st thou live in Richard's seat to sit,
And soon lie Richard in an earthy pit.
God save King Henry, unkinged Richard says,
220 And send him many years of sunshine days.
What more remains?

Northumberland.   No more, but that you read
These accusations, and these grievous crimes,
Committed by your person and your followers,
Against the state and profit of this land:
225 That by confessing them, the souls of men
May deem that you are worthily° deposed.

Richard. Must I do so? and must I ravel out°
My weaved-up follies? Gentle Northumberland,
If thy offenses were upon record,°
230 Would it not shame thee, in so fair a troop,°
To read a lecture of them?° If thou would'st,
There should'st thou find one heinous article,
Containing the deposing of a king,
And cracking the strong warrant of an oath,
235 Marked with a blot, damned in the book of heaven.
Nay, all of you that stand and look upon me,
Whilst that my wretchedness doth bait myself,
Though some of you, with Pilate,° wash your
    hands,
Showing an outward pity: yet you Pilates
240 Have here delivered me to my sour° cross,
And water cannot wash away your sin.

Northumberland. My lord, dispatch,° read o'er these
    articles.

Richard. Mine eyes are full of tears, I cannot see:
And yet salt water blinds them not so much,

---

214 *are* that are   226 *worthily* deservedly   227 *ravel out* unweave   229 *record* (accent on second syllable)   230 *troop* assembly   231 *read a lecture of them* read them aloud   238 *Pilate* cf. Matthew 27:24.   240 *sour* bitter   242 *dispatch* hurry up

But they can see a sort° of traitors here.   245
Nay, if I turn mine eyes upon myself,
I find myself a traitor with the rest;
For I have given here my soul's consent
T' undeck the pompous° body of a king;
Made glory base, and sovereignty a slave,   250
Proud majesty a subject, state a peasant.

Northumberland. My lord——
Richard. No lord of thine, thou haught,° insulting
      man,
  Nor no man's lord: I have no name, no title,
  No, not that name was given me at the font   255
  But 'tis usurped.° Alack, the heavy day!
  That I have worn so many winters out,
  And know not now what name to call myself.
  O, that I were a mockery king of snow,
  Standing before the sun of Bolingbroke,   260
  To melt myself away in water drops!
  Good king, great king—and yet not greatly good—
  And if my word be sterling° yet in England,
  Let it command a mirror hither straight,
  That it may show me what a face I have,   265
  Since it is bankrout° of his majesty.

Bolingbroke. Go some of you, and fetch a looking
      glass.   [*Exit Attendant.*]

Northumberland. Read o'er this paper while the glass
      doth come.

Richard. Fiend, thou torments me, ere I come to hell.

Bolingbroke. Urge it no more, my Lord Northumber-
      land.   270

Northumberland. The Commons will not then be
      satisfied.

Richard. They shall be satisfied: I'll read enough,

---

245 *sort* group, pack   249 *pompous* splendid   253 *haught* haughty
255-56 *No . . . usurped* (Richard was rumored to be a bastard)   263 *sterl-
ing* current   266 *bankrout* bankrupt

When I do see the very book indeed,
Where all my sins are writ,° and that's myself.

Enter one with a glass.

275 Give me the glass, and therein will I read.
No deeper wrinkles yet? Hath Sorrow struck
So many blows upon this face of mine,
And made no deeper wounds? O, flatt'ring glass!
Like to my followers in prosperity,
280 Thou dost beguile me. Was this face the face
That every day under his household roof
Did keep ten thousand men? Was this the face
That, like the sun,° did make beholders wink?
Was this the face that faced° so many follies,
285 And was at last outfaced by Bolingbroke?
A brittle glory shineth in this face,
As brittle as the glory is the face,

[*Throws glass down.*]

For there it is, cracked in a hundred shivers.
Mark, silent king, the moral of this sport:
290 How soon my sorrow hath destroyed my face.

Bolingbroke. The shadow° of your sorrow hath
destroyed
The shadow° of your face.

Richard.   Say that again.
"The shadow of my sorrow"? Ha, let's see.
'Tis very true, my grief lies all within,
295 And these external manners of laments
Are merely shadows to the unseen grief
That swells with silence in the tortured soul.°
There lies the substance: and I thank thee, King,
For thy great bounty, that not only giv'st
300 Me cause to wail, but teachest me the way

273-74 *book . . . writ* (cf. Psalms 139:16)   283 *sun* (cf. III.ii.50)
284 *faced* brazened out, countenanced   291 *shadow* outward show
292 *shadow* reflection   294-97 *my . . . soul* (Bolingbroke had implied that
Richard was putting on an act; Richard replies that his visible grief
is a reflection of a deeper grief he is feeling)

How to lament the cause. I'll beg one boon,
And then be gone, and trouble you no more.
Shall I obtain it?

Bolingbroke.   Name it, fair cousin.

Richard. Fair cousin? I am greater than a king:
For when I was a king, my flatterers   305
Were then but subjects; being now a subject,
I have a king here to° my flatterer.
Being so great, I have no need to beg.

Bolingbroke. Yet ask.

Richard. And shall I have?   310

Bolingbroke. You shall.

Richard. Then give me leave to go.

Bolingbroke. Whither?

Richard. Whither you will, so I were from your
    sights.

Bolingbroke. Go some of you, convey him to the
    Tower.   315

Richard. O, good! "Convey"! Conveyers° are you
    all,
That rise thus nimbly by a true king's fall.

[*Exeunt Richard, some Lords, and Guards.*]

Bolingbroke. On Wednesday next we solemnly set
    down°
Our coronation: Lords, prepare yourselves.

    Exeunt. Manent [*the Abbot of*] *Westminster,*
        [*the Bishop of*] *Carlisle, Aumerle.*

Abbot. A woeful pageant have we here beheld.   320

Carlisle. The woe's to come; the children yet unborn
Shall feel this day as sharp to them as thorn.

307 *to* for 316 *Conveyers* thieves ("convey" was a euphemism for
"steal") 318 *set down* appoint

   Aumerle. You holy clergymen, is there no plot
      To rid the realm of this pernicious blot?

325 *Abbot.* My lord,
      Before I freely speak my mind herein,
      You shall not only take the sacrament
      To bury mine intents,° but also to effect
      Whatever I shall happen to devise.
330   I see your brows are full of discontent,
      Your hearts of sorrow, and your eyes of tears.
      Come home with me to supper: I will lay
      A plot shall show us all a merry day.   *Exeunt.*

---

328 *bury mine intents* conceal my plans

[ACT V

Scene I.   *London. A Street.*]

Enter the Queen with her Attendants.

Queen. This way the King will come, this is the way
  To Julius Caesar's ill-erected Tower,°
  To whose flint bosom my condemnèd lord
  Is doomed a prisoner by proud Bolingbroke.
  Here let us rest, if this rebellious earth   *5*
  Have any resting for her true king's queen.

Enter Richard [and Guard].

  But soft, but see, or rather do not see
  My fair rose wither; yet look up, behold,
  That you in pity may dissolve to dew,
  And wash him fresh again with true-love tears.   *10*
  Ah, thou the model where old Troy did stand!°
  Thou map of honor, thou King Richard's tomb,
  And not King Richard, thou most beauteous inn,
  Why should hard-favored grief be lodged in thee,
  When triumph is become an alehouse° guest?   *15*

Richard. Join not with grief, fair woman, do not so,
  To make my end too sudden; learn, good soul,

V.i.   2 *Tower* (the Tower of London was built, according to legend, by
Julius Caesar, *ill-erected* because it was used as a prison)   11 *model
where old Troy did stand* outline of the walls where Troy once stood,
i.e., ruined majesty—suggested by London's old name of Trinovantum,
New Troy   15 *alehouse* (Bolingbroke, contrasted with Richard, the
beauteous inn)

125

To think our former state a happy dream,
From which awaked, the truth of what we are
20 Shows us but this: I am sworn brother, sweet,
To grim Necessity, and he and I
Will keep a league till death. Hie thee to France,
And cloister thee in some religious house:°
Our holy lives must win a new world's crown,
Which our profane hours here have stricken
25   down.°

Queen. What! is my Richard both in shape and mind
Transformed and weakened? Hath Bolingbroke
Deposed thine intellect? Hath he been in thy heart?
The lion dying thrusteth forth his paw
30 And wounds the earth, if nothing else, with rage
To be o'erpow'red, and wilt thou, pupil-like,
Take the correction mildly, kiss the rod,
And fawn on Rage with base humility,
Which art a lion and the king of beasts?

35 Richard. A king of beasts indeed: if aught but beasts,
I had been still a happy king of men.
Good sometimes° queen, prepare thee hence for
France.
Think I am dead, and that even here thou takest
As from my deathbed thy last living leave.
40 In winter's tedious nights sit by the fire
With good old folks, and let them tell thee tales
Of woeful ages long ago betid;°
And ere thou bid good night, to quite their griefs°
Tell thou the lamentable tale of me,
45 And send the hearers weeping to their beds.
For why,° the senseless brands will sympathize°
The heavy accent of thy moving tongue,
And in compassion weep the fire out:
And some° will mourn in ashes, some coal-black,

23 *religious house* convent   25 *our profane . . . down* our careless lives
have endangered our hopes of heaven   37 *sometimes* sometime, former
42 *betid* happened   43 *quite their griefs* requite, or cap, their tragic
stories   46 *For why* because of this   46 *sympathize* correspond to
49 *some* (of the brands)

For the deposing of a rightful king.   50

Enter Northumberland.

Northumberland. My lord, the mind of Bolingbroke is
  changed:
  You must to Pomfret,° not unto the Tower.
  And, madam, there is order ta'en° for you:
  With all swift speed you must away to France.

Richard. Northumberland, thou ladder wherewithal   55
  The mounting Bolingbroke ascends my throne,
  The time shall not be many hours of age
  More than it is, ere foul sin, gathering head,°
  Shall break into corruption. Thou shalt think,
  Though he divide the realm and give thee half,   60
  It is too little, helping him° to all;
  He shall think that thou which knowest the way
  To plant unrightful kings, wilt know° again,
  Being ne'er so little urged another way,
  To pluck him headlong from the usurped throne.   65
  The love of wicked men converts° to fear,
  That fear to hate, and hate turns one or both
  To worthy° danger and deservèd death.

Northumberland. My guilt be on my head, and there
  an end.°
  Take leave and part, for you must part°
  forthwith.   70

Richard. Doubly divorced! Bad men, you violate
  A twofold marriage: 'twixt my crown and me,
  And then betwixt me and my married wife.
  Let me unkiss the oath 'twixt thee and me—
  And yet not so, for with a kiss 'twas made.   75
  Part us, Northumberland; I towards the north,
  Where shivering cold and sickness pines° the clime;

---

⁵²*Pomfret* Pontefract Castle, in Yorkshire   ⁵³ *there is order ta'en* arrangements have been made   ⁵⁸ *gathering head* (metaphor from a boil)
⁶¹ *helping him* seeing that you helped him   ⁶³ *know* know how   ⁶⁶ *converts* changes   ⁶⁸ *worthy* deserved   ⁶⁹ *there an end* i.e., that's all I have
to say   ⁷⁰ *part, for you must part* part from your queen, for you must
depart   ⁷⁷ *pines* causes to pine

My wife to France, from whence, set forth in
  pomp,
She came adornèd hither like sweet May,
80   Sent back like Hallowmas,° or short'st of day.°

Queen. And must we be divided? Must we part?

Richard. Ay, hand from hand, my love, and heart
    from heart.

Queen. Banish us both, and send the King with me.

Richard. That were some love, but little policy.

85 *Queen.* Then whither he goes, thither let me go.

Richard. So two together weeping make one woe.
    Weep thou for me in France, I for thee here;
    Better far off than, near, be ne'er the near.°
    Go count thy way with sighs, I mine with groans.

90 *Queen.* So longest way shall have the longest moans.

Richard. Twice for one step I'll groan, the way being
    short,
    And piece the way out° with a heavy heart.
    Come, come, in wooing sorrow, let's be brief,
    Since, wedding it, there is such length in grief.°
95   One kiss shall stop our mouths, and dumbly part:
    Thus give I mine, and thus take I thy heart.

Queen. Give me mine own again, 'twere no good part
    To take on me to keep and kill thy heart.
    So now I have mine own again, be gone,
100   That I may strive to kill it with a groan.

Richard. We make woe wanton° with this fond delay:
    Once more adieu, the rest let sorrow say.

Exeunt, [different ways].

---

80 *Hallowmas* Nov. 1   80 *short'st of day* Dec. 22   88 *ne'er the near*
never the nearer (proverbial)   92 *piece the way out* lengthen (with
possible pun on "pace")   94 *Since . . . grief* we are wedded to sorrow
till death and shall have plenty of time to grieve   101 *wanton* unrestrained (with secondary sense of promiscuous)

[Scene II.   *The Duke of York's palace.*]

Enter Duke of York and the Duchess.

Duchess. My lord, you told me you would tell the
        rest,
    When weeping made you break the story off,
    Of our two cousins' coming into London.

York. Where did I leave?

Duchess.   At that sad stop, my lord,
    Where rude misgoverned° hands from windows'
        tops   3
    Threw dust and rubbish on King Richard's head.

York. Then, as I said, the Duke, great Bolingbroke,
    Mounted upon a hot and fiery steed,
    Which his aspiring rider seemed to know,°
    With slow but stately pace kept on his course,   10
    Whilst all tongues cried "God save thee, Boling-
        broke!"
    You would have thought the very windows spake:
    So many greedy looks of young and old
    Through casements darted their desiring eyes
    Upon his visage; and that all the walls   15
    With painted imagery° had said at once,
    "Jesu preserve thee! Welcome, Bolingbroke!"
    Whilst he, from the one side to the other turning,
    Bareheaded, lower than his proud steed's neck,
    Bespake them thus: "I thank you, countrymen."   20
    And thus still doing, thus he passed along.

V.ii.   5 *rude misgoverned* uncivilized and wrongly directed   9 *rider
seemed to know* seemed to know his rider   16 *painted imagery* painted
cloths, resembling tapestry

Duchess. Alack, poor Richard! Where rode he the
    whilst?

York. As in a theater the eyes of men,
    After a well-graced° actor leaves the stage,
25   Are idly° bent on him that enters next,
    Thinking his prattle to be tedious;
    Even so, or with much more contempt, men's eyes
    Did scowl on gentle Richard; no man cried "God
      save him!"
    No joyful tongue gave him his welcome home,
30   But dust was thrown upon his sacred head;
    Which with such gentle° sorrow he shook off,
    His face still combating with tears and smiles,
    The badges° of his grief and patience,
    That had not God for some strong purpose steeled
    The hearts of men, they must perforce° have
35   melted,
    And barbarism itself have pitied him.
    But heaven hath a hand in these events,
    To whose high will we bound our calm contents.°
    To Bolingbroke are we sworn subjects now,
40   Whose state and honor I for aye° allow.

[Enter Aumerle.]

Duchess. Here comes my son, Aumerle.

York.   Aumerle that was,
    But that is lost for being Richard's friend;
    And, madam, you must call him Rutland now.
    I am in Parliament pledge for his truth°
45   And lasting fealty to the new-made king.

Duchess. Welcome, my son; who are the violets° now
    That strew the green lap of the new-come spring?

Aumerle. Madam, I know not, nor I greatly care not.

24 *well-graced* accomplished 25 *idly* without interest 31 *gentle* noble
33 *badges* signs 35 *perforce* inevitably 38 *bound our calm contents* limit
our wishes to calm content 40 *aye* ever 44 *truth* loyalty 46 *violets*
favorites in the new court

    God knows I had as lief° be none as one.

York. Well, bear you well in this new spring of time,   *50*
    Lest you be cropped before you come to prime.
    What news from Oxford?° Do these jousts and
      triumphs hold?°

Aumerle. For aught I know, my lord, they do.

York. You will be there, I know.

Aumerle. If God prevent me not, I purpose so.   *55*

York. What seal° is that that hangs without thy
      bosom?
    Yea, look'st thou pale? Let me see the writing.

Aumerle. My lord, 'tis nothing.

York.   No matter, then, who see it.
    I will be satisfied: let me see the writing.

Aumerle. I do beseech your Grace to pardon me: *60*
    It is a matter of small consequence,
    Which for some reasons I would not have seen.

York. Which for some reasons, sir, I mean to see.
    I fear, I fear——

Duchess.   What should you fear?
    'Tis nothing but some band° that he is ent'red
      into   *65*
    For gay apparel 'gainst° the triumph day.

York. Bound to himself? What doth he with a bond
    That he is bound to? Wife, thou art a fool.
    Boy, let me see the writing.

Aumerle. I do beseech you, pardon me. I may not
    show it.   *70*

York. I will be satisfied. Let me see it, I say!

49 *had as lief* would find it as pleasant   52 *Oxford* (cf. line 99) Aumerle
would give a start   52 *Do . . . hold* will these tournaments and trium-
phal celebrations be held   56 *seal* (which would be hanging from the
document on an attached strip of parchment)   65 *band* bond   66 *'gainst*
in preparation for

He plucks it out of his bosom and reads it.

Treason, foul treason, villain, traitor, slave!

Duchess. What is the matter, my lord?

York. Ho, who is within there? Saddle my horse.
75   God for his mercy!° What treachery is here!

Duchess. Why, what is it, my lord?

York. Give me my boots, I say! Saddle my horse!
Now, by mine honor, by my life, my troth,
I will appeach° the villain.

Duchess.   What is the matter?

80   *York.* Peace, foolish woman.

Duchess. I will not peace. What is the matter,
Aumerle?

Aumerle. Good mother, be content; it is no more
Than my poor life must answer.

Duchess.   Thy life answer?

York. Bring me my boots: I will unto the King.

His man enters with his boots.

Duchess. Strike him, Aumerle. Poor boy, thou art
85   amazed.°
Hence, villain, never more come in my sight.

York. Give me my boots, I say.

Duchess. Why, York, what wilt thou do?
Wilt thou not hide the trespass of thine own?
90   Have we more sons? Or are we like to have?
Is not my teeming date° drunk up with time?
And wilt thou pluck my fair son from mine age?
And rob me of a happy mother's name?
Is he not like thee? Is he not thine own?

95   *York.* Thou fond,° mad woman,
Wilt thou conceal this dark conspiracy?

75 *God for his mercy* Lord have mercy upon us   79 *appeach* peach,
inform against   85 *amazed* dazed   91 *teeming date* time of childbearing
95 *fond* foolish

A dozen of them here have ta'en the sacrament
And interchangeably° set down their hands
To kill the King at Oxford.

Duchess.   He shall be none;
 We'll keep him here. Then what is that to him?   *100*

York. Away, fond woman, were he twenty times my
    son,
 I would appeach him.

Duchess.   Had'st thou groaned for him
 As I have done, thou would'st be more pitiful.
 But now I know thy mind; thou dost suspect
 That I have been disloyal to thy bed,   *105*
 And that he is a bastard, not thy son:
 Sweet York, sweet husband, be not of that mind;
 He is as like thee as a man may be,
 Not like to me, or any of my kin,
 And yet I love him.

York.   Make way, unruly woman.   *110*

                                        Exit.

Duchess. After, Aumerle! Mount thee upon his horse;
 Spur, post,° and get before him to the King,
 And beg thy pardon ere he do accuse thee.
 I'll not be long behind; though I be old,
 I doubt not but to ride as fast as York;   *115*
 And never will I rise up from the ground
 Till Bolingbroke have pardoned thee. Away!
    Be gone!   *[Exeunt.]*

interchangeably reciprocally   112 *post* hasten

[Scene III.   *Windsor Castle.*]

*Enter [Bolingbroke, now] the King, with his
Nobles [Percy and others].*

sets up Henry IV play!

Bolingbroke. Can no man tell me of my unthrifty°
    son?°
'Tis full three months since I did see him last.
If any plague° hang over us, 'tis he.
I would to God, my lords, he might be found:
Inquire at London, 'mongst the taverns there,
For there, they say, he daily doth frequent
With unrestrainèd loose companions,
Even such, they say, as stand in narrow lanes,
And beat our watch° and rob our passengers;°
While he, young wanton and effeminate° boy,
Takes on the point of honor° to support
So dissolute a crew.

Inappropriate action for a Prince

Percy. My lord, some two days since I saw the Prince,
And told him of those triumphs held at Oxford.

15 *Bolingbroke.* And what said the gallant?

Percy. His answer was, he would unto the stews,°
And from the commonest creature pluck a glove,
And wear it as a favor, and with that
He would unhorse the lustiest challenger.

20 *Bolingbroke.* As dissolute as desperate; but yet
Through both° I see some sparks of better hope,
Which elder years may happily bring forth.

V.iii. 1 *unthrifty* prodigal   1 *son* (Prince Hal of *Henry IV*)   3 *plague*
(he is thinking of the prophecies of Richard and Carlisle)   9 *watch*
watchmen   9 *passengers* wayfarers   10 *effeminate* voluptuous   11 *Takes
on the point of honor* undertakes as a point of honor   16 *stews* brothels
21 *both* i.e., dissoluteness and desperateness

But who comes here?

Enter Aumerle, amazed.

Aumerle.   Where is the King?

Bolingbroke.   What means
Our cousin, that he stares and looks so wildly?

Aumerle. God save your Grace! I do beseech your
Majesty   25
To have some conference° with your Grace
alone.

Bolingbroke. Withdraw yourselves, and leave us here
alone.

                              [Exeunt Percy and Lords.]
What is the matter with our cousin now?

Aumerle. For ever may my knees grow to the earth,

                    [Kneels.]

My tongue cleave to my roof within my mouth,   30
Unless a pardon° ere I rise or speak.

Bolingbroke. Intended, or committed, was this fault?
If on the first,° how heinous e'er it be,
To win thy after-love I pardon thee.

Aumerle. Then give me leave that I may turn the key,   35
That no man enter till my tale be done.

Bolingbroke. Have thy desire.

      *[Aumerle locks the door.] The Duke of
         York knocks at the door and crieth.*

York. *[Within]* My liege, beware, look to thyself:
Thou hast a traitor in thy presence there.

Bolingbroke. Villain, I'll make thee safe.°   40

            [Draws his sword.]

Aumerle. Stay thy revengeful hand; thou hast no cause
to fear.

26 *conference* conversation 31 *Unless a pardon* unless I have a pardon
33 *on the first* of the former kind 40 *safe* harmless (by killing him)

York. Open the door, secure,° foolhardy King!
    Shall I for love speak treason° to thy face?
    Open the door, or I will break it open.

                      [*Bolingbroke opens.*]

             [*Enter York.*]

45 *Bolingbroke.* What is the matter, uncle? Speak.

              [*He relocks door.*]

    Recover breath. Tell us, how near is danger,
    That we may arm us to encounter it.

York. Peruse this writing here, and thou shalt know
    The treason that my haste forbids° me show.

Aumerle. Remember, as thou read'st, thy promise
50   passed.°
    I do repent me, read not my name there;
    My heart is not confederate with my hand.

York. It was, villain, ere thy hand did set it down.
    I tore it from the traitor's bosom, King:
55   Fear, and not love, begets his penitence.
    Forget° to pity him, lest thy pity prove
    A serpent that will sting thee to the heart.

Bolingbroke. O heinous, strong° and bold con-
      spiracy!
    O loyal father of a treacherous son!
60   Thou sheer immaculate and silver fountain,
    From whence this stream, through muddy passages,
    Hath held his° current, and defiled himself,°
    Thy overflow of good converts° to bad;
    And thy abundant goodness shall excuse
65   This deadly blot in thy digressing° son.

York. So shall my virtue be his vice's bawd,
    And he shall spend mine honor with his shame,

---

⁴² *secure* overconfident   ⁴³ *treason* (by calling him a fool)   ⁴⁹ *haste forbids* (because he is out of breath)   ⁵⁰ *passed* given   ⁵⁶ *Forget* forget your promise   ⁵⁸ *strong* dangerous   ⁶² *his* its   ⁶² *himself* itself   ⁶³ *converts* changes   ⁶⁵ *digressing* transgressing

As thriftless sons their scraping° fathers' gold.
Mine honor lives when his dishonor dies,
Or my shamed life in his dishonor lies.   70
Thou kill'st me in his life, giving him breath;
The traitor lives, the true man's put to death.

Duchess. [*Within*] What ho! My liege, for God's
    sake, let me in!

Bolingbroke. What shrill-voiced suppliant makes this
    eager cry?

Duchess. A woman, and thy aunt, great King—'tis I.   75
Speak with me, pity me, open the door;
A beggar begs that never begged before.

Bolingbroke. Our scene is alt'red from a serious thing,
And now changed to "The Beggar and the King."°
My dangerous cousin, let your mother in: 80
I know she is come to pray for your foul sin.

    [*Aumerle unlocks door during York's speech.*]

York. If thou do pardon, whosoever pray,°
More sins for this forgiveness prosper may.

    [*Enter Duchess.*]

This fest'red joint cut off, the rest rest° sound;
This let alone will all the rest confound.   85

Duchess. O King, believe not this hardhearted man:
Love loving not itself, none other can.°

York. Thou frantic woman, what dost thou make
    here?
Shall thy old dugs once more a traitor rear?°

Duchess. Sweet York, be patient. Hear me, gentle
    liege.   90

    [*Kneels.*]

---

⁶⁸ *scraping* parsimonious   ⁷⁹ *The Beggar and the King* (referring to the
title, but not to the contents, of the ballad about King Cophetua and
the Beggar Maid)   ⁸² *whosoever pray* whoever prays   ⁸⁴ *rest rest* those
that remain stay   ⁸⁷ *Love . . . can* i.e., if he does not love his son he
cannot love anyone, even you   ⁸⁹ *rear* raise him to life (with a pun
on the usual sense)

Bolingbroke. Rise up, good aunt.

Duchess.   Not yet, I thee beseech.
   For ever will I walk upon my knees,
   And never see day that the happy sees,
   Till thou give joy—until thou bid me joy—
95   By pardoning Rutland, my transgressing boy.

Aumerle. Unto my mother's prayers I bend my knee.

              [*Kneels.*]

York. Against them both my true joints bended be;

              [*Kneels.*]

   Ill may'st thou thrive, if thou grant any grace.

Duchess. Pleads he in earnest? Look upon his face.
100   His eyes do drop no tears, his prayers are in jest;
   His words come from his mouth, ours from our
      breast;
   He prays but faintly, and would be denied;
   We pray with heart and soul, and all beside;
105   His weary joints would gladly rise, I know;
   Our knees still kneel till to the ground they grow;
   His prayers are full of false hypocrisy,
   Ours of true zeal and deep integrity;
   Our prayers do outpray his—then let them have
   That mercy which true prayer ought to have.

Bolingbroke. Good aunt, stand up.

110 *Duchess.*   Nay, do not say "Stand up";
   Say "Pardon" first, and afterwards "Stand up";
   And if I were thy nurse thy tongue to teach,
   "Pardon" should be the first word of thy speech.
   I never longed to hear a word till now.
115   Say "Pardon," King; let pity teach thee how.
   The word is short, but not so short as sweet:
   No word like "pardon" for kings' mouths so meet.

York. Speak it in French, King; say "Pardonne
     moy."°

---

118 *Pardonne moy* pray excuse me, i.e., "No" (*moy* rhymes with *destroy*)

Duchess. Dost thou teach pardon pardon to destroy?
    Ah, my sour husband, my hardhearted lord!   120
    <u>That sets the word itself against the word.</u>
    Speak "Pardon" as 'tis current in our land:
    The chopping° French we do not understand.
    Thine eye begins to speak; set thy tongue there,
    Or in thy piteous heart plant thou thine ear,   125
    That hearing how our plaints and prayers do
       pierce,
    Pity may move thee "Pardon" to rehearse.°

Bolingbroke. Good aunt, stand up.

Duchess.   I do not sue to stand.
    Pardon is all the suit° I have in hand.

Bolingbroke. I pardon him as God shall pardon me.   130

Duchess. O, happy vantage of a kneeling knee!
    Yet° am I sick for fear; speak it again.
    Twice saying "Pardon" doth not pardon twain,°
    But makes one pardon strong.

Bolingbroke.   With all my heart
    I pardon him.

Duchess. [*Standing*]   A god on earth° thou art.   *135*

        [*York and Aumerle rise.*]

Bolingbroke. But for our trusty° brother-in-law,° and
      the abbot,
    With all the rest of that consorted crew,
    Destruction straight shall dog them at the heels.
    Good uncle, help to order several powers
    To Oxford, or where'er these traitors are;   140
    They shall not live within this world, I swear,
    But I will have them if I once know where.
    Uncle, farewell, and cousin, too, adieu.

123 *chopping* changing the meaning of words   127 *rehearse* repeat (a perfect rhyme with "pierce" in the 16th century)   129 *suit* (1) suit of cards (2) petition   132 *Yet* still   133 *twain* (1) two people (2) divide   135 *god on earth* (the Homilies taught this; and, as Portia says, "earthly power doth then show likest God's/When mercy seasons justice")   136 *trusty* (ironical)   136 *brother-in-law* (Duke of Exeter, Richard's half-brother, who had married Bolingbroke's sister)

Your mother well hath prayed, and prove you
     true.°

Duchess. Come, my old° son, I pray God make thee
145   new.   *Exeunt.*

[Scene IV.   *Windsor Castle.*]

Enter Sir Pierce Exton & [a Man].

Exton. Didst thou not mark the King, what words he
     spake?
"Have I no friend will rid me of this living fear?"
Was it not so?

Man.   These were his very words.

Exton. "Have I no friend?" quoth he: he spake it
     twice,
5   And urged it twice together, did he not?

Man. He did.

Exton. And speaking it, he wishtly° looked on me,
As who should say, "I would thou wert the man
That would divorce this terror from my heart"—
10   Meaning the King at Pomfret. Come, let's go:
I am the King's friend, and will rid his foe.

                              [*Exeunt.*]

144 *true* loyal   145 *old* unregenerate   V.iv.   7 *wishtly* (probably "wish-fully," with an undertone of "wistly," i.e., intently)

[Scene V.   *Pomfret Castle.*]

preserve the poetry,
this is not prose.

Enter Richard alone.

Richard. I have been studying how I may compare
    This prison where I live unto the world:
    And for because the world is populous,
    And here is not a creature but myself,
    I cannot do it. Yet I'll hammer it out: 5
    My brain I'll prove the female to my soul,
    My soul the father, and these two beget
    A generation° of still°-breeding thoughts;
    And these same thoughts people this little world,
    In humors° like the people of this world,   10
    For no thought is contented. The better sort,
    As thoughts of things divine are intermixed
    With scruples,° and do set the word itself
    Against the word;° as thus: "Come, little ones";°
    And then again,   15
    "It is as hard to come as for a camel
    To thread the postern of a small needle's° eye."°
    Thoughts tending to ambition, they do plot
    Unlikely wonders: how these vain weak nails
    May tear a passage thorough the flinty ribs   20
    Of this hard world, my ragged° prison walls;
    And, for° they cannot, die in their own pride.°
    Thoughts tending to content flatter themselves
    That they are not the first of fortune's slaves,
    Nor shall not be the last, like seely° beggars   25
    Who sitting in the stocks refuge° their shame,

V.v.   **8** *generation* offspring   **8** *still* constantly   **10** *humors* psychological characteristics   **13** *scruples* doubts   **14** *word* passage of Scripture   **14** *Come, little ones* Matthew 19:14ff.   **17** *needle's* (monosyllabic)   **16-17** *It . . . eye* Matthew 19:24ff.   **21** *ragged* rugged   **22** *for* because   **22** *pride* prime   **25** *seely* (silly) simple-minded   **26** *refuge* protect themselves from

That many have, and others must, sit there;
And in this thought they find a kind of ease,
Bearing their own misfortunes on the back
30   Of such as have before endured the like.
Thus play I in one person many people,
And none contented; sometimes am I king,
Then treasons make me wish myself a beggar,
And so I am. Then crushing penury
35   Persuades me I was better when a king.
Then am I kinged again and, by and by,
Think that I am unkinged by Bolingbroke,
And straight am nothing. But whate'er I be,
Nor I, nor any man that but man is,
40   With nothing shall be pleased, till he be eased
With being nothing.°

The music plays.

Music do I hear.
Ha—ha! Keep time! How sour sweet music is
When time is broke, and no proportion° kept;
So is it in the music of men's lives:
45   And here have I the daintiness of ear
To check° time broke in a disordered°
          string,
But for the concord of my state and time,°
Had not an ear to hear my true time broke.
I wasted time,° and now doth Time° waste me:
50   For now hath Time made me his numb'ring°
          clock;
My thoughts are minutes, and with sighs they jar°
Their watches° on unto mine eyes, the outward
          watch°
Whereto my finger, like a dial's point,°
Is pointing still,° in cleansing them from tears.

39-41 *nor any man . . . nothing* i.e., man is never content until he is no
more   43 *proportion* musical time   46 *check* rebuke   46 *disordered* out
of its place, a bar wrong   47 *time* the times   49 *time* measured duration
49 *Time* Father Time   50 *numb'ring* counting hours and minutes   51 *jar*
tick (of a clock), making a discord   52 *watches* intervals of time
52 *outward watch* dial (with pun on a man keeping watch)   53 *dial's
point* hand of clock   54 *still* continually

Now, sir, the sound that tells what hour it is   55
Are clamorous groans which strike upon my
     heart,
Which is the bell. So sighs, and tears, and groans,
Show minutes, times, and hours; but my time
Runs posting on in Bolingbroke's proud joy,
While I stand fooling here, his Jack-of-the-
     clock.°   60
This music mads me: let it sound no more.
For though it have holp° madmen to their wits,
In me it seems it will make wise men mad.
Yet blessing on his heart that gives it me,
For 'tis a sign of love; and love to Richard   65
Is a strange brooch° in this all-hating world.

Enter a Groom of the stable.

Groom. Hail, royal Prince!

Richard.   Thanks, noble° peer!
The cheapest of us is ten groats too dear.
What art thou? And how comest thou hither,
Where no man never comes, but that sad dog   70
That brings me food to make misfortune live?°

Groom. I was a poor groom of thy stable, King,
When thou wert King, who, traveling towards
     York,
With much ado at length have gotten leave
To look upon my sometimes° royal master's face.   75
O, how it erned° my heart, when I beheld
In London streets, that coronation day,
When Bolingbroke rode on roan Barbary,°
That horse that thou so often hast bestrid,
That horse that I so carefully have dressed.°   80

50 *Jack-of-the-clock* mannikin to strike the hours   62 *holp* helped
56 *strange brooch* rare jewel   67 *royal . . . noble* (a royal was worth
ten shillings, a noble six shillings and eight pence; a groat, fourpence.
Richard is saying that to call him "royal" now is to price him too
high, since he is now the peer, the equal, of the groom)   71 *make misfortune live* perpetuate my unfortunate life   75 *sometimes* former
76 *erned* grieved   78 *Barbary* (here the name of the horse, as well as the
breed)   80 *dressed* groomed

Richard. Rode he on Barbary? Tell me, gentle° friend,
How went he under him?

Groom. So proudly as if he disdained the ground.

Richard. So proud that Bolingbroke was on his back!
85   That jade hath eat bread from my royal hand;
This hand hath made him proud with clapping°
    him.
Would he not stumble? Would he not fall down,
Since pride must have a fall, and break the neck
Of that proud man that did usurp his back?
90   Forgiveness, horse! Why do I rail on thee,
Since thou created to be awed by man
Wast born to bear? I was not made a horse,
And yet I bear a burden like an ass,
Spurred, galled,° and tired by jauncing° Boling-
    broke.

Enter one, [a Keeper,] to Richard with meat.

95 *Keeper.* Fellow, give place; here is no longer stay.

Richard. If thou love me, 'tis time thou wert away.

Groom. What my tongue dares not, that my heart
    shall say.   *Exit Groom.*

Keeper. My lord, wilt please you to fall to?°

Richard. Taste° of it first, as thou art wont to do.

100 *Keeper.* My lord, I dare not; Sir Pierce of Exton
Who lately came from the King, commands the
    contrary.

Richard. The devil take Henry of Lancaster, and thee!
Patience is stale, and I am weary of it.

Keeper. Help, help, help!

*The murderers [Exton and Servants]
rush in.*

---

81 *gentle* (implying groom is of gentle birth) 86 *clapping* patting
94 *galled* made sore 94 *jauncing* making the horse prance (and perhaps
himself prancing and triumphant) 98 *fall to* start eating 99 *Taste* (he
suspects poison)

Richard. How now! What means Death in this rude
    assault?°   105
  Villain, thy own hand yields thy death's instrument.

      [Snatches a weapon and kills one.]

  Go thou, and fill another room° in hell!

      *[He kills another.] Here Exton strikes
          him down.*

  That hand shall burn in never-quenching fire
  That staggers° thus my person. Exton, thy fierce
    hand
  Hath with the King's blood stained the King's own
    land.   110
  Mount, mount, my soul; thy seat is up on high,
  Whilst my gross flesh sinks downward here to die.

      [Dies.]

Exton. As full of valor as of royal blood!
  Both have I spilled. O, would the deed were good!
  For now the devil that told me I did well   115
  Says that this deed is chronicled in hell.
  This dead king to the living king I'll bear.
  Take hence the rest, and give them burial here.

      [Exeunt with the bodies.]

[Scene VI.   *Windsor Castle.*]

    *[Flourish.] Enter Bolingbroke with the
Duke of York, [other Lords and Attendants].*

Bolingbroke. Kind uncle York, the latest news we
    hear
  Is that the rebels have consumed with fire

105 *What . . . assault?* what does death mean by assaulting me so vio-
lently?   107 *room* place   109 *staggers* makes to stagger

Our town of Ciceter° in Gloucestershire,
But whether they be ta'en or slain we hear not.

Enter Northumberland.

5   Welcome, my lord; what is the news?

Northumberland. First, to thy sacred state wish I all
    happiness;
The next° news is, I have to London sent
The heads of Salisbury, Spencer, Blunt, and Kent.°
The manner of their taking may appear
10   At large discoursèd in this paper here.

Bolingbroke. We thank thee, gentle Percy, for thy
    pains,
And to thy worth will add right worthy gains.°

Enter Lord Fitzwater.

Fitzwater. My lord, I have from Oxford sent to
    London
The heads of Brocas° and Sir Bennet Seely,
15   Two of the dangerous consorted° traitors
That sought at Oxford thy dire overthrow.

Bolingbroke. Thy pains, Fitzwater, shall not be
    forgot:
Right noble is thy merit well I wot.

Enter Henry Percy [and the Bishop of Carlisle].

Percy. The grand conspirator, Abbot of Westminster,
20   With clog of conscience and sour melancholy,
Hath yielded up his body to the grave;
But here is Carlisle living, to abide
Thy kingly doom, and sentence of his pride.

Bolingbroke. Carlisle, this is your doom:
Choose out some secret place, some reverend
25   room°

V.vi. 3 *Ciceter* Cirencester 7 *next* most important 8 *Spencer, Blunt, and Kent* Lord Spencer, formerly Earl of Gloucester; Sir Thomas Blunt; Earl of Kent 12 *right worthy gains* well-deserved reward 14 *Brocas* Sir Leonard (or Bernard) Brocas 15 *consorted* associated 25 *reverend room* place of religious retirement

More than thou hast,° and with it joy° thy life.
So° as thou liv'st in peace, die free from strife;
For though mine enemy thou hast ever been,
High sparks of honor in thee have I seen.

Enter Exton with [Attendants bearing]
the coffin.

Exton. Great King, within this coffin I present   30
  Thy buried fear:° herein all breathless lies
  The mightiest of thy greatest enemies,
  Richard of Bordeaux,° by me hither brought.

Bolingbroke. Exton, I thank thee not, for thou hast
    wrought
  A deed of slander with thy fatal hand   35
  Upon my head and all this famous land.

Exton. From your own mouth, my lord, did I this deed.

Bolingbroke. They love not poison that do poison
    need,
  Nor do I thee; though I did wish him dead,
  I hate the murderer, love him murderèd.   40
  The guilt of conscience take thou for thy labor,
  But neither my good word, nor princely favor.
  With Cain go wander thorough shades of night,
  And never show thy head by day nor light.
                                                    [Exit Exton.]
  Lords, I protest, my soul is full of woe,   45
  That blood should sprinkle me to make me grow.
  Come, mourn with me for what I do lament,
  And put on sullen black incontinent.°
  I'll make a voyage to the Holy Land,
  To wash this blood off from my guilty hand.   50
  March sadly after; grace my mournings here,
  In weeping after this untimely bier.

                                                    [Exeunt.]

FINIS

26 *More than thou hast* i.e., more religious and less political   26 *joy*
enjoy   27 *So* provided that   31 *buried fear* (cf. *living fear*, V.iv.2)
33 *Bordeaux* (Richard's birthplace)   48 *incontinent* forthwith

Textual Note

Richard II was first published in 1597, after 29 August, when it was registered. The First Quarto (Q1) appeared with the following title page: "THE/ Tragedie of King Ri-/ chard the se-/ cond./ *As it hath beene publikely acted/ by the right Honourable the/ Lorde Chamberlaine his Ser-/ uants./* LONDON/ Printed by Valentine Simmes for Androw Wise, and/ are to be sold at his shop in Paules church yard at/ the signe of the Angel./ 1597."

The play is thought to have been printed from a transcript of Shakespeare's manuscript, but it may preserve some of his spelling and punctuation. Some critics (Cairncross, Brooks, Ure) think that the text is memorially contaminated in a few places (i.e., the transcriber introduced mistakes through his memory of other lines of the play and also of *Richard III*). The First Quarto forms the basis of the present edition, except for the abdication scene, which was omitted from the first three quartos and included in the Fourth (1608). The play was included in the First Folio (1623), probably from a corrected text of Q5 (1615). The Folio text (F) enables us to correct Q1 in a number of places, and it provides the best text of the abdication scene; but many of its readings are "sophistications"—unnecessary alterations—for which Shakespeare was not responsible.

The present edition modernizes spelling and punctuation, amplifies abbreviations and regularizes speech prefixes, corrects obvious typographical errors, adjusts the position of stage directions, and in a few cases alters the lineation. Q1 is not divided into acts or scenes; the present edition uses the divisions established by the Globe editors, who used those of F but who added one at V.iv. F indicates the divisions in Latin; they are translated here. Other deviations from Q1 (and for the abdication scene from F) are listed below. The adopted reading is given in italics; if it is not taken from F a note in a bracket explains that it is taken (for example) from Q5 or (again, for example) from an editor's emendation—indicated by [ed]. Next is given the original reading in roman.

I.i.118 *my scepter's* scepters 139 *But* Ah but 152 *gentlemen* Gentleman 162 *When . . . when?* When Harry? when obedience bids 192 *parle* parlee

I.ii.47 *sit* set 58 *it* is

I.iii.26 *demand of* [ed] ask 33 *comest* [Q5] comes 84 *innocency* [ed] innocence 172 *then but* but 180 *you owe* y'owe 221 *night* nightes 238 *had it* [ed] had't

I.iv.1 s.d. *Bagot* [ed] Bushie 20 *cousin, cousin* Coosens Coosin 23 *Bagot . . . Green* [Q6] [Q1] omits; F has "heere Bagot and Greene"] 53 *Bushy, what' news?* [Q1 omits, but prints the s.d. "Enter Bushie with newes"] 65 *All* [ed; Q and F omit]

II.i.18 *fond* [ed] found [the emendation to "fond" is plausible; but it is possible that "found" was an error caused by the similar endings of adjacent lines—"soundes" and "sound"—or that a line was omitted by mistake] 48 *as a* as 102 *incagèd* inraged 113 *not* [ed] not, 124 *brother* [Q2] brothers 156 *kernes* kerne 177 *the* a 232 *that that* [ed] that 257 *King's* King 280 *The . . . Arundel* [ed; Q and F omit] 283 *Thomas Ramston* [Holinshed] Iohn Ramston 284 *Quoint* Coines

II.ii.16 *eye* eyes 25 *more's* more is 31 *though* thought 53 *Henry* H 88 *cold* [ed] they are cold 112 *Th'one* Tone 137 *The . . . will* [ed] Will the hateful commons

II.iii.36 *Hereford* Herefords 98 *the lord* lord

III.ii.32 *succor* [ed] succors 38 *and* [ed] that 40 *boldly* [ed] bouldy 72 *O'erthrows* Ouerthrowes

III.iii.13 *with you to* to 17 *mis-take* [ed] mistake 30 *lord* Lords 59 *waters—on* [ed] water's on 118 *prince and* [ed] princesse

III.iv.11 *joy* [ed] griefe   21 *good.* good?   26 *pins* pines   57 *We at* [ed] at   80 *Cam'st* Canst

IV.i.22 *him* them   54 *As* [ed] As it   55 *sun to sun* [ed] sinne to sinne   76 *my bond* bond   154-319 [for this passage, here printed from F, Q1 has only "Let it be so, and loe on wednesday next, / We solemnly proclaime our Coronation, / Lords be ready all"]   182 *and on* [Q4] on   182 *yours* [Q4] thine   250 *and* [Q4] a   254 *Nor* [Q4] No, nor   275 *the* [Q4] that   284 *was* [Q4] Is   284 *that* [Q4] which   285 *And* [Q4] That   288 *a* [Q4] an   295 *manners* [Q4] manner   332 *I will* [ed] Ile

V.i.25 *stricken* throwne

V.ii.55 *prevent me* [ed] preuent   78 *life, my* [ed] life, by my   116 *And* An

V.iii.10 *While* [ed] Which   20 *but yet* [ed] yet   35 *that I* that   67 *and* an   110 *Bolingbroke* Yorke   134-35 *With . . . him* [ed] I pardon him with al my heart   143 *cousin, too* [Q6] cousin

V.iv.1s.d. *Enter* Manet

V.v.27 *sit* set   79 *bestrid* bestride

V.vi.8 *Salisbury . . . Blunt* Oxford, Salisbury, Blunt   12 s.d. *Fitzwater* [Q6] Fitzwaters   43 *thorough* [ed] through [Q] through the [F]

The Sources of Richard II

The following have been suggested as possible sources of the play:

1. *The Chronicles* of Raphael Holinshed (1587), pp. 493–540.
2. *The Union of the Two Noble and Illustrate Famelies of Lancastre and Yorke* by Edward Hall (1548).
3. *The Cronycles of Englande* by Sir John Froissart (translated by Lord Berners, 1525).
4. J. Créton's *Histoire du Roy d'Angleterre*
5. *Chronicque de la Traïson et Mort de Richart Deux*
6. Le Beau's *Chronique de Richard II depuis l'an 1377 jusques à l'an 1399.*
   (4, 5, and 6 were in manuscript until the nineteenth century)
7. *Thomas of Woodstock* (anonymous play).
8. *The First Fowre Bookes of the Civile Wars* by Samuel Daniel (1595).
9. *A Myrroure for Magistrates* (1559)
10. A lost play.

As we have seen, Professor J. Dover Wilson believes that the main source was this lost play, the author of which used Nos. 1-6 of the works listed above. The theory presupposes that this unknown dramatist displayed a historical erudition beyond Shakespeare's customary range, although there are few signs of erudition in his companion piece, *The Troublesome Reign of King John*. As it is known that Shakespeare did in other plays combine several different sources, it is easier to believe that he followed the same practice in *Richard II* than that some unknown hack writer went to the same trouble.

If, then, we are skeptical of the existence of the lost play we can examine briefly the evidence for Shakespeare's use of the remaining nine hypothetical sources. There is no doubt that he had read parts of Holinshed, Hall, and *The Mirror for Magistrates;* almost certainly he knew Berners' Froissart and Daniel's poem; and there are enough apparent echoes of *Woodstock* to make it highly probable that he knew it, probably in the theater. Whether he had read the three French manuscripts or not is much more dubious.

It is significant that Shakespeare begins his play with the quarrel between Mowbray and Bolingbroke, for this is the point at which Hall begins his story; but, apart from this, the influence of Hall is apparently very slight.

It has been argued by Professor J. Dover Wilson (following Paul Reyher) that Shakespeare's characterization of John of Gaunt was suggested by Froissart who, in his chapter on "How the Duke of Lancaster Died," speaks of his grief at his son's banishment, and at the King's misgovernment:

> For he saw well that if he long persevered and were suffered to continue, the realm was likely to be utterly lost. With these imaginations and other, the Duke fell sick, whereon he died.

Froissart also mentions Richard's joy at Gaunt's death, and in an earlier passage he makes Gaunt say:

> Our nephew, the King of England, will shame all ere he cease. He believeth too lightly evil counsel who shall destroy him; and simply, if he live long, he will

lose his realm, and that hath been gotten with much cost and travail by our predecessors and by us.

Froissart, too, but not Holinshed, mentions the rumor that Richard was not the son of the Black Prince. This is found also in *Traïson.*

Mr. A. P. Rossiter, however, thought that the character of Gaunt could have been derived from *Woodstock,* Stow, and Hall. There is no doubt that Shakespeare was acquainted with *Woodstock,* for he echoes it in a number of places, as in the accusation that Richard had become England's landlord:

> Rent out our kingdom like a pelting farm . . .
> And thou no king, but landlord now become.

It is not possible to prove that Shakespeare read the three French manuscript chronicles, but they were not entirely inaccessible. Holinshed, Hall, and Daniel all used Créton's poem, and Holinshed refers to *Traïson* as "an old French pamphlet belonging to John Stow." If Shakespeare had wished to follow up Holinshed's references, the chances are that he could have done so, although the evidence that he actually did so has not convinced many scholars.

A messenger in Créton's poem describes the way people of all ages flocked to Bolingbroke's standard:

> Then might you have beheld young and old, the feeble and the strong, make a clamor, and regarding neither right nor wrong stir themselves up with one accord . . . they began to flee towards the Duke . . . he brings young and old under subjection.

So Scroop (III.ii.112 ff.), after describing the whitebeards and boys who have joined Bolingbroke, adds "both young and old rebel." In the same scene, Richard's appeals to heaven, the use of Salisbury as a messenger of evil tidings, and the account of successive disasters—

you may be sure he was not fain to smile, for, on all
sides, one after another, came pouring in upon him
mischief and trouble—

are all to be found in the corresponding scene of the
play. The most striking parallel, however, is the comparison of Richard's betrayal and suffering to that of Christ.
In the prose section of Créton's account, he compares
the rejection of Richard by the people to the rejection of
Christ by the Jews:

> Then spake Duke Henry quite aloud to the commons of
> the said city. "Fair sirs, behold your king! consider
> what you will do with him!" And they made answer
> with a loud voice, "We will have him taken to West-
> minster." And so he delivered him unto them. At this
> hour did he remind me of Pilate, who caused our Lord
> Jesus Christ to be scourged at the stake, and after-
> wards had him brought before the multitude of the
> Jews, saying, "Fair Sirs, behold your king!" who re-
> plied, "let him be crucified!" Then Pilate washed his
> hands of it, saying, "I am innocent of the just blood."
> And so he delivered our Lord unto them. Much in
> the like manner did Duke Henry, when he gave up his
> rightful lord to the rabble of London, in order
> that, if they should put him to death, he might say,
> "I am innocent of this deed."

In *Traïson* there are several similar passages. The
author compares Northumberland to Judas; and a few
pages later Richard compares himself to Christ, who was
likewise "undeservedly sold and given into the hands of
his enemies." Although Holinshed refers to a prelate as a
Pilate, and although Shakespeare elsewhere associates
treachery with Judas, the emphasis on the Christ parallel
is to be found only in Créton, *Traïson,* and Shakespeare.
There are a few minor parallels with *Traïson.* "Daring-
hardy" (I.iii.43) may translate *hardie* in precisely the
same context, and "base court" (III.iii.175) may likewise translate *basse cour.* There seems, therefore, to be

a slight balance of probability that Shakespeare had read both Créton's poem and *Traïson,* but there is less probability that he had read Le Beau's chronicle.

About seventy parallels have been listed with Daniel's *Civil Wars.* Some of these, however, are not peculiar to Daniel's poem, and others may be explained by the fact that both poets amplified their sources independently. But enough parallels remain to convince all recent editors (Dover Wilson, Black, Ure) that Shakespeare was influenced by Daniel, especially in II.i, IV.i, V.i, and V.ii. Shakespeare and Daniel both altered the age of the Queen, making her a woman instead of a child; Shakespeare was clearly indebted to Daniel for the account of the entry of Richard and Bolingbroke into London; and there are clear echoes of Daniel in Gaunt's speech on England:

Why Neptune hast thou made us stand alone
Divided from the world, for this say they?

A place there is where proudly raised there stands
A huge aspiring rock neighboring the skies
Whose surly brow imperiously commands
The sea his bounds that at his proud feet lies:
And spurns the waves that in rebellious bands
Assault his empire and against him rise: . . .
With what contagion France didst thou infect
The land by thee made proud to disagree?

Although we have argued that Shakespeare consulted a number of different sources, there is little doubt that the great bulk of his material came from Holinshed. The only scenes that did not largely derive from the *Chronicles* are the following:

I.ii. No direct source has been discovered
II.i.1–152. Partly based on Froissart and Daniel
II.ii. Largely invention
III.iv. No source
V.i. Possibly suggested by Daniel
V.ii.1–40. Probably suggested by Daniel

It will be observed from the relevant passages from Holinshed given below that Shakespeare sometimes combines widely separated facts for a single scene, that he telescopes events, and that on occasion he rearranges the order of historical happenings.

Of telescoping perhaps the best example is II.i. Bolingbroke had been banished in September 1398; his father died in the following February; Richard left for Ireland in May; and Bolingbroke landed at Ravenspurgh in July. But in Shakespeare's scene Gaunt is dying immediately after his son's banishment—in I.iv we have a description of Bolingbroke's leave-taking and of Gaunt's illness—but before the end of the scene we are told that Bolingbroke has already sailed from Brittany. A period of nine months elapses in the course of the scene. By this telescoping Shakespeare is able to link the death of Gaunt with the banishment of Bolingbroke, to link the confiscation of his estates with the necessities of the Irish campaign, and to link the support Bolingbroke receives with Richard's conduct and with the patriotic admonitions of Gaunt. The scene is dramatically effective on the stage, in spite of the impossibilities revealed in the study; and the fact that Bolingbroke is returning to England before he can have heard of the confiscation of his estates, and yet pretends later that this was his motive for returning from exile, is an example of the deliberate ambiguity with which the character is presented.

The fourth act provides a good example of Shakespeare's rearrangement of historical facts, although there is no essential distortion of historical truth. Bagot's accusation of Aumerle took place on October 16, Fitzwater's accusation two days later; Carlisle's speech (which was not, as in the play, associated with Bolingbroke's claim of the crown) was a week later, on October 23; the abdication took place in the Tower (not in Westminster Hall) on September 29; and the Abbot of Westminster's entertainment of the conspirators was not until December 17. Although Swinburne complained that the quarrel at the beginning of the scene was "a morally chaotic introduction of incongruous causes, inexplicable

plaintiffs, and incomprehensible defendants," it reminds
us, just before the abdication, of Gloucester's death, its
ultimate cause; and it provides Aumerle with a motive
for rebellion. Carlisle's speech, one of the most significant moments in the whole tetralogy, is much more dramatic in its place as a warning to the characters in the
play and to us of the results of Bolingbroke's usurpation at the moment of its happening. It is obviously
more dramatic for Richard to go through the ritual of his
abdication in public than before the commissioners in the
Tower; and the Abbot's plot is properly introduced at a
moment when our sympathies have been fully aroused
for Richard, especially when we realize that the plot to
restore him to the throne is the direct cause of his murder. Some details of the scene may have been suggested
by other sources—Froissart, Hall, Daniel, *The Mirror for
Magistrates,* the *Homilies,* and even *Traïson.*

Finally, an example may be given of Shakespeare's
omissions. In Holinshed's account, Northumberland persuades Richard to leave Conway Castle, ambushing him
on the way to Flint, and conveying him to Flint Castle
as a prisoner. Shakespeare omits this incident, following
Froissart, who merely says that Richard rode to Flint, and
prepared to defend the castle there.

Selections from Raphael Holinshed.
Chronicles of England, Scotland, and Ireland

[Numerals in brackets refer to acts and scenes that
deal with Holinshed's material.]

It fell out that in this parliament holden at Shrews-
bury, Henry, Duke of Hereford, accused Thomas Mowbray, Duke of Norfolk, of certain words which he should
utter in talk had betwixt them, as they rode together
lately before betwixt London and Brainford, sounding
highly to the King's dishonor. And for further proof
thereof, he presented a supplication to the King, wherein
he appealed the Duke of Norfolk in field of battle for a

traitor, false and disloyal to the King and enemy unto
the realm. This supplication was read before both the
dukes in presence of the King: which done, the Duke of
Norfolk took upon him to answer it, declaring that whatsoever the Duke of Hereford had said against him other
than well, he lied falsely like an untrue knight as he was.
And when the King asked of the Duke of Hereford what
he said to it, he, taking his hood off his head, said: "My
sovereign lord, even as the supplication which I took you
importeth, right so I say for truth, that Thomas Mowbray, Duke of Norfolk, is a traitor, false and disloyal to
your royal majesty, your crown, and to all the states of
your realm."

Then the Duke of Norfolk being asked what he said to
this, he answered: "Right dear lord, with your favor that
I make answer unto your cousin here, I say (your reverence saved) that Henry of Lancaster, Duke of Hereford, like a false and disloyal traitor as he is, doth lie,
in that he hath or shall say of me otherwise than well."
"No more," said the king, "we have heard enough";
and herewith commanded the Duke of Surrey, for that
turn Marshal of England, to arrest in his name the two
dukes. The Duke of Lancaster, father to the Duke of Hereford, the Duke of York, the Duke of Aumerle, Constable of England, and the Duke of Surrey, Marshal of the
realm, undertook as pledges body for body for the Duke
of Hereford; but the Duke of Norfolk was not suffered to
put in pledges, and so under arrest was led unto Windsor
Castle and there guarded with keepers that were appointed to see him safely kept.

Now after the dissolving of the parliament at Shrews-
bury there was a day appointed six weeks after, for the
King to come unto Windsor to hear and to take some
order betwixt the two dukes, which had thus appealed
each other. There was a great scaffold erected within the
castle of Windsor for the King to sit with the lords and
prelates of his realm: and so at the day appointed, he
with the said lords and prelates being come thither and
set in their places, the Duke of Hereford, appellant, and
the Duke of Norfolk, defendant, were sent for to come

and appear before the King, sitting there in his seat of justice. And then began Sir John Bushy to speak for the King, declaring to the lords how they should understand, that where the Duke of Hereford had presented a supplication to the King, who was there set to minister justice to all men that would demand the same, as appertained to his royal majesty, he therefore would now hear what the parties could say one against other, and withal the King commanded the dukes of Aumerle and Surrey, the one being Constable, and the other Marshal, to go unto the two dukes, appellant and defendant, requiring them on his behalf to grow to some agreement: and, for his part, he would be ready to pardon all that had been said or done amiss betwixt them, touching any harm or dishonor to him or his realm: but they answered both assuredly that it was not possible to have any peace or agreement made betwixt them.

[I.i] When he heard what they had answered, he commanded that they should be brought forthwith before his presence, to hear what they would say. Herewith an herald in the King's name with loud voice commanded the dukes to come before the King, either of them to show his reason, or else to make peace together without more delay. When they were come before the King and lords, the King spake himself to them, willing them to agree, and make peace together: for it is (said he) the best way ye can take. The Duke of Norfolk with due reverence hereunto answered it could not be so brought to pass, his honor saved. Then the King asked of the Duke of Hereford what it was that he demanded of the Duke of Norfolk, and "what is the matter that ye cannot make peace together and become friends?"

Then stood forth a knight; who asking and obtaining license to speak for the Duke of Hereford, said: "Right dear and sovereign lord, here is Henry of Lancaster, Duke of Hereford and Earl of Derby, who saith, and I for him likewise say, that Thomas Mowbray, Duke of Norfolk, is a false and disloyal traitor to you and your royal majesty and to your whole realm: and likewise the Duke of Hereford saith and I for him, that Thomas Mowbray, Duke of

Norfolk, hath received eight thousand nobles to pay the soldiers that keep your town of Calais, which he hath not done as he ought; and furthermore the said Duke of Norfolk hath been the occasion of all the treason that hath been contrived in your realm for the space of these eighteen years, and by his false suggestions and malicious counsel, he hath caused to die and to be murdered your right dear uncle, the Duke of Gloucester, son to King Edward. Moreover the Duke of Hereford saith, and I for him, that he will prove this with his body against the body of the said Duke of Norfolk within lists." The King herewith waxed angry, and asked the Duke of Hereford if these were his words; who answered: "Right dear lord, they are my words; and hereof I require right, and the battle against him."

There was a knight also that asked license to speak for the Duke of Norfolk, and obtaining it, began to answer thus: "Right dear sovereign lord, here is Thomas Mowbray, Duke of Norfolk, who answereth and saith, and I for him, that all which Henry of Lancaster hath said and declared (saving the reverence due to the King and his council) is a lie; and the said Henry of Lancaster hath falsely and wickedly lied as a false and disloyal knight, and both hath been and is a traitor against you, your crown, royal majesty and realm. This will I prove and defend as becometh a loyal knight to do with my body against his. Right dear lord, I beseech you, therefore, and your council, that it may please you in your royal discretion to consider and mark what Henry of Lancaster, Duke of Hereford, such a one as he is, hath said."

The King then demanded of the Duke of Norfolk if these were his words, and whether he had any more to say. The Duke of Norfolk then answered for himself: "Right dear sir, true it is that I have received so much gold to pay your people of the town of Calais; which I have done, and I do avouch that your town of Calais is as well kept at your commandment as ever it was at any time before, and that there never hath been by any of Calais any complaint made unto you of me. Right dear and my sovereign lord, for the voyage that I made into

France about your marriage, I never received either gold or silver of you, nor yet for the voyage that the Duke of Aumerle and I made into Almaine, where we spent great treasure. Marry, true it is that once I laid an ambush to have slain the Duke of Lancaster, that there sitteth: but nevertheless he hath pardoned me thereof, and there was good peace betwixt us, for the which I yield him hearty thanks. This is that which I have to answer, and I am ready to defend myself against mine adversary; I beseech you, therefore, of right, and to have the battle against him in upright judgment."

After this, when the King had communed with his council a little, he commanded the two dukes to stand forth, that their answers might be heard. The King then caused them once again to be asked if they would agree and make peace together, but they both flatly answered that they would not: and withal the Duke of Hereford cast down his gage, and the Duke of Norfolk took it up. The King perceiving this demeanor betwixt them, sware by Saint John Baptist that he would never seek to make peace betwixt them again. And therefore Sir John Bushy in name of the King and his council declared that the King and his council had commanded and ordained that they should have a day of battle appointed them at Coventry. Here writers disagree about the day that was appointed: for some say it was upon a Monday in August; other upon Saint Lambert's day, being the seventeenth of September, other on the eleventh of September; but true it is that the King assigned them not only the day but also appointed them lists and place for the combat, and thereupon great preparation was made, as to such a matter appertained.

[I.iii] At the time appointed, the King came to Coventry, where the two dukes were ready, according to the order prescribed therein, coming thither in great array, accompanied with the lords and gentlemen of their lineages. The King caused a sumptuous scaffold or theater and royal lists there to be erected and prepared. The Sunday before they should fight, after dinner, the Duke of Hereford came to the King (being lodged about a quarter of a mile without the town in a tower that belonged to Sir William Bagot) to take his leave of him. The morrow after, being the day appointed for the combat, about the spring of the day, came the Duke of Norfolk to the court to take leave likewise of the King. The Duke of Hereford armed him in his tent, that was set up near to the lists, and the Duke of Norfolk put on his armor betwixt the gate and the barrier of the town in a beautiful house, having a fair perclois of wood towards the gate, that none might see what was done within the house.

The Duke of Aumerle that day, being High Constable of England, and the Duke of Surrey, Marshal, placed themselves betwixt them, well armed and appointed; and when they saw their time, they first entered into the lists with a great company of men appareled in silk sendall, embroidered with silver, both richly and curiously, every man having a tipped staff to keep the field in order. About the hour of prime came to the barriers of the lists the Duke of Hereford, mounted on a white courser, barded with green and blue velvet embroidered sumtuously with swans and antelopes of goldsmiths' work, armed at all points. The Constable and Marshal came to the barriers, demanding of him what he was; he answered: "I am Henry of Lancaster, Duke of Hereford, which am come hither to do mine endeavor against Thomas Mowbray, Duke of Norfolk, as a traitor untrue to God, the King, his realm, and me." Then incontinently he sware upon the holy evangelists that his quarrel was true and just, and upon that point he required to enter the lists. Then he put up his sword, which before he held naked in his hand, and putting down his visor, made a cross on his horse, and with spear in hand, entered into the lists, and descended from his horse, and set him down in a chair of green velvet at the one end of the lists, and there reposed himself, abiding the coming of his adversary.

Soon after him, entered into the field with great triumph King Richard, accompanied with all the peers of the realm. . . . When the King was set in his seat, which was richly hanged and adorned, a king-at-arms made open

proclamation, prohibiting all men in the name of the
King and of the High Constable and Marshal to enterprise or attempt to approach or touch any part of the
lists upon pain of death, except such as were appointed
to order or marshal the field. The proclamation ended,
another herald cried: "Behold here Henry of Lancaster,
Duke of Hereford, appellant, which is entered into the
lists royal to do his devoir against Thomas Mowbray,
Duke of Norfolk, defendant, upon pain to be found false
and recreant."

The Duke of Norfolk hovered on horseback at the entry of the lists, his horse being barded with crimson velvet, embroidered richly with lions of silver and mulberry
trees; and when he had made his oath before the Constable and Marshal that his quarrel was just and true, he
entered the field manfully, saying aloud: "God aid him
that hath the right." And then he departed from his
horse, and sat him down in his chair, which was of crimson velvet, curtained about with white and red damask.
The lord delivered the one spear himself to the Duke of
Hereford, and sent the other to the Duke of Norfolk by a
knight. Then the herald proclaimed that the traverses and
chairs should be removed, commanding them on the
king's behalf to mount on horseback and address themselves to the battle and combat.

The Duke of Hereford was quickly horsed, and closed
his bavier, and cast his spear into the rest, and when
he trumpet sounded set forward courageously towards
his enemy six or seven paces. The Duke of Norfolk was
not fully set forward, when the King cast down his
warder, and the heralds cried "Ho, ho!" Then the King
caused their spears to be taken from them, and commanded them to repair again to their chairs, where they
remained two long hours, while the King and his council
deliberately consulted what order was best to be had in
so weighty a cause. Finally, after they had devised and
fully determined what should be done therein, the heralds
cried silence; and Sir John Bushy, the King's secretary,
read the sentence and determination of the King and his
council in a long roll, the effect whereof was that Henry,

Duke of Hereford, should within fifteen days depart out of the realm, and not to return before the term of ten years were expired, except by the King he should be repealed again, and this upon pain of death; and that Thomas Mowbray, Duke of Norfolk, because he had sown sedition in the realm by his words, should likewise avoid the realm, and never to return again into England, nor approach the borders or confines thereof upon pain of death; and that the King would stay the profits of his lands, till he had levied thereof such sums of money as the Duke had taken up of the King's treasurer for the wages of the garrison of Calais, which were still unpaid.

When these judgments were once read, the King called before him both the parties, and made them to swear that the one should never come in place where the other was, willingly; nor keep any company together in any foreign region; which oath they both received humbly, and so went their ways. The Duke of Norfolk departed sorrowfully out of the realm into Almaine, and at the last came to Venice, where he for thought and melancholy deceased: for he was in hope (as writers record) that he should have been borne out in the matter by the King, which when it fell out otherwise, it grieved him not a little. The Duke of Hereford took his leave of the King at Eltham, who there released four years of his banishment: so he took journey over into Calais, and from thence went into France, where he remained. A wonder it was to see what number of people ran after him in every town and street where he came, before he took the sea, lamenting and bewailing his departure, as who would say, that when he departed, the only shield, defense and comfort of the commonwealth was vaded and gone.

At his coming into France, King Charles, hearing the cause of his banishment (which he esteemed to be very slight), received him gently, and him honorably entertained, insomuch that he had by favor obtained in marriage the only daughter of the Duke of Berrie, uncle to the French King, if King Richard had not been a let in that matter, who being thereof certified, [II.i.168] sent the Earl of Salisbury with all speed into France, both to surmise

by untrue suggestion heinous offenses against him, and
also to require the French King that in no wise he would
suffer his cousin to be matched in marriage with him that
was so manifest an offender. This was a pestilent kind
of proceeding against that nobleman then being in a
foreign country, having been so honorably received as he
was at his entrance into France, and upon view and good
liking of his behavior there, so forward in marriage with
a lady of noble lineage. . . .

[I.iv.48] But yet to content the King's mind, many
blank charters were devised and brought into the city,
which many of the substantial and wealthy citizens were
fain to seal, to their great charge, as in the end appeared.
And the like charters were sent abroad into all shires
within the realm, whereby great grudge and murmuring
arose among the people: for when they were so sealed,
the King's officers wrote in the same what liked them, as
well for charging the parties with payment of money, as
otherwise.

[II.i.] In this mean time, the Duke of Lancaster departed out of this life at the Bishop of Ely's place in Holborn. . . . The death of this duke gave occasion of in-
creasing more hatred in the people of this realm toward
the King, for he seized into his hands all the goods that
belonged to him, and also received all the rents and
revenues of his lands which ought to have descended
unto the Duke of Hereford by lawful inheritance, in re-
voking his letters patents, which he had granted to him
before, by virtue whereof he might make his attorneys-
general to sue livery for him, of any manner of inheri-
ances or possessions that might from thenceforth fall
unto him, and that his homage might be respited, with
making reasonable fine: whereby it was evident that the
King meant his utter undoing.

This hard dealing was much misliked of all the nobility, and cried out against of the meaner sort: but
namely the Duke of York was therewith sore moved, who
before this time had borne things with so patient a mind
as he could, though the same touched him very near, as

the death of his brother, the Duke of Gloucester, the banishment of his nephew, the said Duke of Hereford, and other moe injuries in great number, which for the slippery youth of the King he passed over for the time, and did forget as well as he might. But now perceiving that neither law, justice, nor equity could take place where the King's willful will was bent upon any wrongful purpose, he considered that the glory of the public wealth of his country must needs decay, by reason of the King his lack of wit, and want of such as would (without flattery) admonish him of his duty: and therefore he thought it the part of a wise man to get him in time to a resting place, and to leave the following of such an unadvised captain as with a leaden sword would cut his own throat. Hereupon he with the Duke of Aumerle his son went to his house at Langley, rejoicing that nothing had mishappened in the commonwealth through his device or consent. The common bruit ran that the King had set to farm the realm of England unto Sir William Scroop, Earl of Wiltshire, and then Treasurer of England, to Sir John Bushy, Sir John Bagot, and Sir Henry Green, knights.

About the same time, the Earl of Arundel's son, named Thomas, which was kept in the Duke of Exeter's house, escaped out of the realm by means of one William Scot, mercer, and went to his uncle Thomas Arundel, late Archbishop of Canterbury, as then sojourning at Cullen.

[I.iv] King Richard being destitute of treasure to furnish such a princely port as he maintained, borrowed great sums of money of many of the great lords and peers of his realm, both spiritual and temporal, and likewise of other mean persons, promising them in good earnest, by delivering to them his letters patents for assurance, that he would repay the money so borrowed at a day appointed: which notwithstanding, he never paid.

[II.iv] In this year in a manner throughout all the realm of England, old bay trees withered, and afterwards, contrary to all men's thinking, grew green again, a strange sight, and supposed to import some unknown event.

[I.iv] In this mean time the King being advertised

that the wild Irish daily wasted and destroyed the towns
and villages within the English pale, and had slain many
of the soldiers which lay there in garrison for defense of
that country, determined to make eftsoons a voyage
thither, and prepared all things necessary for his passage
now against the spring. . . .

[II.i.] The King departed toward Bristow, from
thence to pass into [II.ii] Ireland, leaving the Queen with
her train still at Windsor: he appointed for his lieutenant
general in his absence his uncle the Duke of York: and so
in the month of April, as diverse authors write, he set
forward from Windsor, and finally took shipping at Mil-
ford, and from thence with two hundred ships and a puissant power of men of arms and archers he sailed into
Ireland. . . .

Now whilst he was thus occupied in devising how to re-
duce them into subjection, and taking orders for the good
stay and quiet government of the country, divers of the
nobility, as well prelates as other, and likewise many of
the magistrates and rulers of the cities, towns, and commonalty here in England, perceiving daily how the realm
drew to utter ruin, not like to be recovered to the former
state of wealth whilst King Richard lived and reigned (as
they took it), devised with great deliberation and con-
siderate advice, to send and signify by letters unto
Duke Henry, whom they now called (as he was indeed)
Duke of Lancaster and Hereford, requiring him with all
convenient speed to convey himself into England, promising him all their aid, power, and assistance, if he, ex-
pelling King Richard, as a man not meet for the office
he bare, would take upon him the scepter, rule, and diadem of his native land and region.

[II.i] He therefore being thus called upon by mes-
sengers and letters from his friends, and chiefly through
the earnest persuasion of Thomas Arundel, late Archbishop of Canterbury, who (as before ye have heard) had
been removed from his see and banished the realm by
King Richard's means, got him down to Britaine [Brit-
any], together with the said Archbishop, where he was
joyfully received of the Duke and Duchess, and found such

friendship at the Duke's hands that there were certain ships rigged and made ready for him, at a place in base Britaine, called Le port blanc, as we find in the chronicles of Britaine: and when all his provision was made ready, he took the sea, together with the said Archbishop of Canterbury, and his nephew Thomas Arundel, son and heir to the late Earl of Arundel, beheaded at the Tower Hill, as you have heard. There were also with him Reginald, Lord Cobham, Sir Thomas Erpingham, and Sir Thomas Ramston, knights, John Norbury, Robert Waterton and Francis Coint, esquires: few else were there, for (as some write) he had not past fifteen lances, as they termed them in those days, that is to say, men of arms, furnished and appointed as the use then was. Yet other write, that the Duke of Britaine delivered unto him three thousand men of war to attend him, and that he had eight ships well furnished for the war, where Froissart yet speaketh but of three. Moreover, where Froissart and also the chronicles of Britaine avouch that he should land at Plymouth, by our English writers it seemeth otherwise: for it appeareth by their assured report, that he approaching to the shore, did not straight take land, but lay hovering aloof, and showed himself now in this place, and now in that, to see what countenance was made by the people, whether they meant enviously to resist him, or friendly to receive him.

[II.ii] When the Lord Governor, Edmund Duke of York, was advertised that the Duke of Lancaster kept still the sea and was ready to arrive (but where he meant first to set foot on land, there was not any that understood the certainty) he sent for the Lord Chancellor, Edmund Stafford, Bishop of Exeter, and for the Lord Treasurer, William Scroop, Earl of Wiltshire, and other of the King's Privy Council, as John Bushy, William Bagot, Henry Green, and John Russell, knights; of these he required to know what they thought good to be done in this matter, concerning the Duke of Lancaster being on the seas. Their advice was to depart from London unto St. Albans, and there to gather an army to resist the Duke in his landing; but to how small purpose their counsel served, the

conclusion thereof plainly declared, for the most part that
were called, when they came thither, boldly protested
that they would not fight against the Duke of Lancaster,
whom they knew to be evil dealt withal.

[II.ii] The Lord Treasurer, Bushy, Bagot and Green,
perceiving that the commons would cleave unto and take
part with the Duke, slipped away, leaving the Lord Governor of the realm and the Lord Chancellor to make what
shift they could for themselves. Bagot got him to Chester,
and so escaped into Ireland; the other fled to the castle
of Bristow, in hope there to be in safety. The Duke of
Lancaster, after he had coasted alongst the shore a certain time and had got some intelligence how the peoples'
minds were affected towards him, landed about the beginning of July in Yorkshire, at a place sometime called
Ravenspur, betwixt Hull and Bridlington, and with him
not past threescore persons, as some write: but he was
so joyfully received of the lords, knights, and gentlemen
of those parts that he found means, by their help, forthwith to assemble a great number of people that were
willing to take his part. The first that came to him were
the lords of Lincolnshire and other countries adjoining,
as the Lords Willoughby, Ross, Darcy, and Beaumont.

[II.iii] At his coming unto Doncaster, the Earl of
Northumberland and his son Sir Henry Percy, wardens
of the marches against Scotland, with the Earl of Westmoreland, came unto him, where he sware unto those
lords that he would demand no more but the lands that
were to him descended by inheritance from his father,
and in right of his wife. Moreover, he undertook to
cause the payment of taxes and tallages to be laid
down, and to bring the King to good government, and to
remove from him the Cheshire men, which were envied
of many, for that the King esteemed of them more than
of any other; happily because they were more faithful
to him than other, ready in all respects to obey his
commandments and pleasure. From Doncaster having
now got a mighty army about him, he marched forth
with all speed through the countries, coming by Evesham
unto Berkeley. Within the space of three days all the

King's castles in those parts were surrendered unto him.

The Duke of York, whom King Richard had left as governor of the realm in his absence, hearing that his nephew, the Duke of Lancaster, was thus arrived and had gathered an army, he also assembled a puissant power of men of arms and archers (as before ye have heard) but all was in vain, for there was not a man that willingly would thrust out one arrow against the Duke of Lancaster or his partakers, or in any wise offend him or his friends. The Duke of York therefore passing forth towards Wales to meet the King, at his coming forth of Ireland, was received into the castle of Berkeley, and there remained till the coming thither of the Duke of Lancaster, whom when he perceived that he was not able to resist, on the Sunday after the feast of Saint James, which as that year came about fell upon the Friday, he came forth into the church that stood without the castle, and there communed with the Duke of Lancaster. With the Duke of York were the Bishop of Norwich, the Lord Berkeley, the Lord Seymour, and other: with the Duke of Lancaster were these: Thomas Arundel, Archbishop of Canterbury that had been banished, the Abbot of Leicester, the Earls of Northumberland and Westmoreland, Thomas Arundel, son to Richard late Earl of Arundel, the Baron of Greystoke, the Lords Willoughby and Ross, with divers other lords, knights, and other people, which daily came to him from every part of the realm. Those that came not were spoiled of all they had, so as they were never able to recover themselves again, for their goods being then taken away were never restored. And thus what for love, and what for fear of loss, they came flocking unto him from every part.

At the same present there was arrested, and committed to safe custody, the Bishop of Norwich, Sir William Elmam, and Sir Walter Burley, knights, Laurence Drew and John Golofer, esquires. On the morrow after, the foresaid Dukes with their power went towards Bristow, where, at their coming, they showed themselves before the town and castle, being an huge multitude of people. There were enclosed within the castle the Lord William Scroop, Earl of Wiltshire and Treasurer of England, Sir Henry Green and Sir John Bushy, knights, who prepared to make resistance: but when it would not prevail, they were taken and brought forth bound as prisoners into the camp before the Duke of Lancaster. On the morrow next ensuing, they were arraigned before the Constable and Marshal, and found guilty of treason, for misgoverning the King and realm, and forthwith had their heads smit off. Sir John Russell was also taken there, who, feigning himself to be out of his wits, escaped their hands for a time.

It fortuned at the same time in which the Duke of Hereford or Lancaster (whe're ye list to call him) arrived thus in England, the seas were so troubled by tempests, and the winds blew so contrary for any passage to come over forth of England to the King remaining still in Ireland, that for the space of six weeks he received no advertisements from thence; yet, at length, when the seas became calm, and the wind once turned anything favorable, there came over a ship, whereby the King understood the manner of the Duke's arrival, and all his proceedings till that day in which the ship departed from the coast of England, whereupon he meant forthwith to have returned over into England, to make resistance against the Duke: but through persuasion of the Duke of Aumerle (as was thought) he stayed till he might have all his ships and other provision fully ready for his passage.

In the meantime, he sent the Earl of Salisbury over into England to gather a power together by help of the King's friends in Wales and Cheshire with all speed possible, that they might be ready to assist him against the Duke upon his arrival—for he meant himself to follow the Earl within six days after. The Earl, passing over into Wales, landed at Conway and sent forth letters to the King's friends, both in Wales and Cheshire, to levy their people and to come with all speed to assist the King, whose request with great desire and very willing minds they fulfilled, hoping to have found the King himself at Conway, insomuch that within four days' space there were to the number of forty thousand men assembled, ready to march with the King against his enemies, if he had been there himself in person.

[II.iv] But when they missed the King, there was a bruit spread amongst them that the King was surely dead, which wrought such an impression and evil disposition in the minds of the Welshmen and others that for any persuasion which the Earl of Salisbury might use, they would not go forth with him till they saw the King: only they were contented to stay fourteen days to see if he should come or not. But when he came not within that term, they would no longer abide, but scaled and departed away; whereas if the King had come before their breaking up, no doubt but they would have put the Duke of Hereford in adventure of a field. So that the King's lingering of time before his coming over gave opportunity to the Duke to bring things to pass as he could have wished, and took from the King all occasion to recover afterwards any forces sufficient to resist him.

[III.ii] At length, about eighteen days after that the King had sent from him the Earl of Salisbury, he took the sea, together with the Dukes of Aumerle, Exeter, Surrey, and divers of the nobility, with the Bishops of London, Lincoln, and Carlisle. They landed near the castle of Barclowlie in Wales, about the feast of Saint James the Apostle, and stayed awhile in the same castle, being advertised of the great forces which the Duke of Lancaster had got together against him, wherewith he was marvelously amazed, knowing certainly that those which were thus in arms with the Duke of Lancaster against him would rather die than give place, as well for the hatred as fear which they had conceived at him. Nevertheless he, departing from Barclowlie, hasted with all speed towards Conway, where he understood the Earl of Salisbury to be still remaining.

He therefore, taking with him such Cheshire men as he had with him at that present, in whom all his trust was reposed, he doubted not to revenge himself of his adversaries, and so at the first he passed with a good courage: but when he understood as he went thus forward, that all the castles, even from the borders of Scotland unto Bristow, were delivered unto the Duke of Lancaster, and that likewise the nobles and commons, as well of the south parts as the north, were fully bent to take part with the same Duke against him; and further, hearing how his trusty councilors had lost their heads at Bristow, he became so greatly discomforted that, sorrowfully lamenting his miserable state, he utterly despaired of his own safety, and calling his army together, which was not small, licensed every man to depart to his own home.

The soldiers being well bent to fight in his defense, besought him to be of good cheer, promising with an oath to stand with him against the Duke, and all his partakers, unto death: but this could not encourage him at all, so that in the night next ensuing, he stole from his army, and with the Dukes of Exeter and Surrey, the Bishop of Carlisle and Sir Stephan Scroop, and about half a score others, he got him to the castle of Conway, where he found the Earl of Salisbury, determining there to hold himself till he might see the world at some better stay, for what counsel to take to remedy the mischief thus pressing upon him he wist not. On the one part he knew his title just, true, and infallible; and his conscience clear, pure, and without spot of envy or malice; he had also no small affiance in the Welshmen and Cheshire men. On the other side, he saw the puissance of his adversaries, the sudden departing of them whom he most trusted, and all things turned upside down. He evidently saw, and manifestly perceived, that he was forsaken of them by whom in time he might have been aided and relieved, where now it was too late, and too far overpassed.

This surely is a very notable example, and not unworthy of all princes to be well weighed and diligently marked, that this Henry of Lancaster should be thus called to the Kingdom, and have the help and assistance almost of all the whole realm, which perchance never thereof thought or yet dreamed; and that King Richard should thus be left desolate, void, and in despair of all hope and comfort, in whom if there were any offense, it ought rather to be imputed to the frailty of wanton youth than to the malice of his heart: but such is the deceivable judgment of man, which not regarding things present with due consideration, thinketh ever that things to come shall have good success, with a pleasant and delightful end. But in this dejecting of the one, and advancing of the other, the providence of God is to be respected, and his secret will to be wondered at. . . .

Sir Thomas Percy, Earl of Worcester, Lord Steward of the King's house, either being so commanded by the King, or else upon displeasure (as some write) for that the King had proclaimed his brother, the Earl of Northumberland, traitor, broke his white staff, which is the representing sign and token of his office, and without delay went to Duke Henry. . . .

The King herewith sent to Beaumaris and after to Caernarvon: but finding no provision either of victuals or other things in those castles, he came back to Conway. . . . [III.iii] After this, the Duke, with advice of his council, sent the Earl of Northumberland unto the King, accompanied with four hundred lances and a thousand archers, who coming to the castle of Flint, had it delivered unto him, and from thence he hasted forth towards Conway. But before he approached near the place, he left his power behind him, hid closely in two ambushes behind a craggy mountain, beside the highway that leadeth from Flint to Conway.

This done, taking not past four or five with him, he passed forth, till he came before the town, and then sending an herald to the King, requested a safe conduct from the King, that he might come and talk with him: which the King granted, and so the Earl of Northumberland, passing the water, entered the castle, and coming to the King, declared to him, that if it might please his grace to undertake that there should be a parliament assembled, in the which justice might be had against such as were enemies to the commonwealth, and had procured the destruction of the Duke of Gloucester and other noblemen, and herewith pardon the Duke of Hereford of all things wherein he had offended him, the Duke would be ready to come to him on his knees, to crave him forgiveness, and as an humble subject to obey him in all dutiful services. The King . . . upon the Earl's oath, for assurance that the same should be performed in each condition, agreed to go with the Earl to meet the Duke, and hereupon taking their horses, they rode forth, but the Earl rode before, as it were, to prepare dinner for the King at Rutland, but coming to the place where he had left his people, he stayed there with them. . . .

[*The King is trapped in the ambush, given dinner at Rutland, and taken to Flint.*]

The King had very few about him of his friends, except only the Earl of Salisbury, the Bishop of Carlisle, the Lord Stephan Scroop, Sir Nicholas Fereby, a son also of the Countess of Salisbury, and Jenico Dartois, a Gascoigne that still ware the cognizance or device of his master, King Richard, that is to say, a white hart, and would not put it from him, neither for persuasions nor threats. . . .

King Richard being thus come unto the castle of Flint, on the Monday the eighteenth of August, and the Duke of Hereford being still advertised from hour to hour by posts how the Earl of Northumberland sped, the morrow following, being Tuesday, and the nineteenth of August, he came thither and mustered his army before the King's presence, which undoubtedly made a passing fair show, being very well ordered by the Lord Henry Percy, that was appointed general or rather (as we may call him) master of the camp, under the Duke, of the whole army. There were come already to the castle, before the approaching of the main army, the Archbishop of Canterbury, the Duke of Aumerle, the Earl of Worcester, and divers other. The Archbishop entered first, and then followed the other, coming into the first ward.

The King, that was walking aloft on the braies of the walls to behold the coming of the Duke afar off, might see that the Archbishop and the other were come, and (as he took it) to talk with him. Whereupon he forthwith came down unto them, and beholding that they did their due reverence to him on their knees, he took them up, and drawing the Archbishop aside from the residue, talked with him a good while and, as it was reported, the Archbishop willed him to be of good comfort, for he should be assured not to have any hurt as touching his person; but he prophesied not as a prelate, but as a Pilate. For, was it no hurt, think you, to his person to be spoiled of his royalty, to be deposed from his crown, to be translated from principality to prison, and to fall from honor into horror? All which befell him to his extreme heart-grief, no doubt: which to increase, means, alas, there were many; but to diminish, helps, God wot, but a few. . . .

Then the Earl of Northumberland, passing forth of the castle to the Duke, talked with him awhile in sight of the King, being again got up to the walls to take better view of the army, being now advanced within two bow-shots of the castle, to the small rejoicing, ye may be sure, of the sorrowful King. The Earl of Northumberland, returning to the castle, appointed the King to be set to dinner, for he was fasting till then, and after he had dined, the Duke came down to the castle himself, and entered the same all armed, his bassenet only excepted, and being within the first gate he stayed there, till the King came forth of the inner part of the castle unto him.

The King, accompanied with the Bishop of Carlisle, the Earl of Salisbury, and Sir Stephan Scroop, knight, who bare the sword before him, and a few other, came forth into the utter ward, and sat down in a place prepared for him. Forthwith, as the Duke got sight of the King, he showed a reverend duty as became him, in bowing his knee, and coming forward did so likewise the second and third time, till the King took him by the hand, and lift him up, saying: "Dear cousin, you are welcome." The Duke, humbly thanking him, said: "My sovereign Lord and King, the cause of my coming at this present is (your honor saved) to have again restitution of my person, my lands and heritage, through your favorable license." The King hereunto answered: "Dear cousin, I am ready to accomplish your will, so that ye may enjoy all that is yours, without exception."

Meeting thus together, they came forth of the castle, and the King there called for wine, and after they had drunk, they mounted on horseback, and rode that night to Flint, and the next day unto Chester, the third unto Nantwich . . . and so came to London.

[V.ii.] Neither was the King permitted all this while to change his apparel, but rode still through all these towns simply clothed in one suit of raiment, and yet he was in his time exceeding sumptuous in apparel. . . . And so he was brought the next way to Westminster.

As for the Duke, he was received with all the joy and pomp that might be of the Londoners, and was lodged in the Bishop's palace by Paul's church. It was a wonder to see what great concourse of people and what number of horses came to him on the way as he thus passed the countries, till his coming to London, where, upon his approach to the city, the mayor rode forth to receive him, and a great number of other citizens. Also the clergy met him with procession, and such joy appeared in the countenances of the people, uttering the same also with words, as the like not lightly been seen. For in every town and village where he passed, children rejoiced, women clapped their hands, and men cried out for joy. But to speak of the great numbers of people that flocked together in the fields and streets of London at his coming, I here omit; neither will I speak of the presents, welcomings, lauds, and gratifications made to him by the citizens and commonalty. . . .

The next day after his coming to London, the King from Westminster was had to the Tower, and there committed in safe custody. Many evil-disposed persons, assembling themselves together in great numbers, intended to have met with him, and to have taken him from such as had the conveying of him, that they might have slain him. But the mayor and aldermen gathered to them the worshipful commoners and grave citizens, by whose policy, and not without much ado, the other were revoked from their evil purpose. . . .

[IV.i.] After this was a parliament called by the Duke of Lancaster, using the name of King Richard in the writs directed forth to the lords and other states for their summons. This parliament began the thirteenth day of September, in the which many heinous points of misgovernance and injurious dealings in the administration of his kingly office were laid to the charge of this noble prince, King Richard, the which (to the end the Commons might be persuaded that he was an unprofitable prince to the commonwealth and worthy to be deposed) were ingrossed up in 33 solemn articles, heinous to the ears of all men. . . .

Then for so much as these articles and other heinous and detestable accusations were laid against him in open parliament, it was thought by the most part that he was worthy to be deposed from all kingly honor and princely government: and to bring the matter without slander the better to pass, divers of the King's servants, which by license had access to his person, comforted him (being with sorrow almost consumed and in manner half dead) in the best wise they could, exhorting him to regard his health and save his life.

And first, they advised him willingly to suffer himself to be deposed, and to resign his right of his own accord, so that the Duke of Lancaster might without murder or battle obtain the scepter and diadem, after which (they well perceived) he gaped: by mean whereof they thought he might be in perfect assurance of his life long to continue. . . . The King being now in the hands of his enemies, and utterly despairing of all comfort, was easily persuaded to renounce his crown and princely pre-eminence, so that in hope of life only he agreed to all things that were of him demanded. And so . . . he renounced and voluntarily was deposed from the royal crown and kingly dignity, the Monday being the nine and twentieth day of September and feast of St. Michael the Archangel, in the year of our Lord 1399, and in the three and twentieth year of his reign. . . .

[*Declaration of the Commissioners.*] Within the said place of the Tower . . . was rehearsed unto the King by the mouth of the foresaid Earl of Northumberland that beforetime at Conway . . . the King . . . promised . . . that he for insufficiency which he knew himself to be of to occupy so great a charge as to govern the realm of England, he would gladly leave off and renounce his right and title. . . . Upon the same afternoon the King looking for the coming of the Duke of Lancaster, at last the said Duke, with the Archbishop of Canterbury and the persons afore recited, entered the foresaid chamber, bringing with them . . . divers other. Where, after due obeisance done by them unto the King, he familiarly and with a glad countenance (as to them and us appeared) talked with the said Archbishop and Duke a good season; and that communication finished, the King, with glad countenance in presence of us and the other above rehearsed, said openly that he was ready to renounce and resign all his kingly majesty in manner and form as he before had promised . . . himself therefore read the scroll of resignation, in manner and form followeth. . . .

Now forthwith in our presence and others he subscribed the same, and after delivered it unto the Archbishop of Canterbury, saying that . . . he would that the Duke of Lancaster there present should be his successor. . . .

Upon the morrow after, being Tuesday, and the last day of September, all the lords, spiritual and temporal, with the Commons of the said parliament, assembled at Westminster where, in the presence of them, the Archbishop of York and the Bishop of Hereford, according to the King's request, showed unto them the voluntary renouncing of the King, with the favor also which he bare to his cousin of Lancaster to have him his successor. And moreover showed them the schedule or bill of renouncement, signed in King Richard's own hand, which they caused to be read· first in Latin, as it was written, and after in English. This done, the question was first asked of the Lords, if they would admit and allow that renouncement: the which, when it was of them granted and confirmed, the like question was asked of the Commons, and of them in like manner confirmed. After this, it was then declared, that notwithstanding the foresaid renouncing, so by the Lords admitted and confirmed, it was necessary, in avoiding of all suspicions and surmises of evil-disposed persons, to have in writing and registered the manifold crimes and defaults before done by King Richard, to the end that they might first be openly declared to the people, and after to remain of record amongst other of the King's records forever.

All this was done accordingly. . . . Then forsomuch as the lords of the parliament had well considered the voluntary resignation of King Richard and that it was behooveful and, as they thought, necessary for the weal of the realm to proceed unto the sentence of his deposing.

Immediately as the sentence was in this wise passed, and that by reason thereof the realm stood void without head or governor for the time, the Duke of Lancaster, rising from the place where before he sat, and standing where all those in the house might behold him, in reverend manner made a sign of the cross on his forehead and likewise on his breast.

[*Bolingbroke claims the crown and the Archbishop of Canterbury preaches on the text "Vir dominabitur in populo," saying that*] Instead of a child willfully doing his lust and pleasure without reason, now shall a man be lord and ruler, that is replenished with sapience and reason, and shall govern the people by skillful doom, setting apart all willfulness and pleasure of himself.

[*Bolingbroke is crowned on the feast of Edward the Confessor. Richard hoped to escape with his life by handing to his successor all his goods and wealth.*] But whatsoever was promised, he was deceived therein. For shortly after his resignation, he was conveyed to the castle of Leeds in Kent, and from thence to Pomfret, where he departed out of this miserable life (as after you shall hear). He was seemly of shape and favor, and of nature good enough, if the wickedness and naughty demeanor of such as were about him had not altered it.

[*Holinshed moralizes on Richard's fate.*] His chance verily was greatly infortunate. . . . He was prodigal, ambitious, and much given to the pleasure of the body. He kept the greatest port, and maintained the most plentiful house that ever any king in England did either before his time or since. For there resorted daily to his court above ten thousand persons that had meat and drink allowed them. . . . And this vanity was not only used at court in those days, but also other people abroad in the towns and countries had their garments cut far otherwise than had been accustomed before his days . . . and every day there was devising of new fashions, to the great hindrance and decay of the commonwealth. . . . Furthermore, there reigned abundantly the filthy sin of lechery and fornication, with abominable adultery, specially in the King, but most chiefly in the prelacy. . . . But if I may boldly say what I think: he was a prince the most unthankfully used of his subjects, of any one of whom ye shall lightly read. For although (through the frailty of youth) he demeaned himself more dissolutely than seemed convenient for his royal estate, and made choice of such councilors as were not favored by the people, whereby he was the less favored himself: yet in no king's days were the commons in greater wealth, if they could have perceived their happy state, neither in any other time were the nobles and gentlemen more cherished, nor churchmen less wronged. But such was their ingratitude towards their bountiful and loving sovereign that those whom he had chiefly advanced were readiest to control him; for that they might not rule all things at their will, and remove from him such as they misliked, and place in their rooms whom they thought good, and that rather by strong hand than by gentle and courteous means, which stirred such malice betwixt him and them, till at length it could not be assuaged without peril of destruction to them both.

The Duke of Gloucester, chief instrument of this mischief, to what end he came ye have heard. And although the Duke of Hereford took upon him to revenge his death, yet wanted he moderation and loyalty in his doings, for the which both he himself and his lineal race were scourged afterwards, as a due punishment unto rebellious subjects. . . . What unnaturalness, or rather, what tigerlike cruelty was this . . . wolvishly to lie in wait for the distressed creature's life, and ravenously to thirst after his blood, the spilling whereof should have touched his conscience so, as that death ought rather to have been adventured for his safety, than so savagely to have sought his life after the loss of his royalty. . . .

Thus much ado there was in this parliament, specially about them that were thought to be guilty of the Duke of Gloucester's death, and of the condemning of the other lords adjudged traitors in the foresaid late parliament holden in the said one and twentieth year of King Richard's reign. Sir [William] Bagot, knight, then prisoner in the Tower, disclosed many secrets unto the which he was privy; and being brought on a day to the bar, a bill was read in English which he had made, containing certain evil practices of King Richard; and further what great affection the same King bare to the Duke of Aumerle, insomuch that he heard him say, that if he should renounce the government of the kingdom, he wished to leave it to the said Duke, as to the most able man for wisdom and manhood of all other: for though he could like better of the Duke of Hereford, yet he said that he knew if he were once King, he would prove an extreme enemy and cruel tyrant to the church.

It was further contained in that bill, that as the same Bagot rode on a day behind the Duke of Norfolk in the Savoy street toward Westminster, the Duke asked him what he knew of the manner of the Duke of Gloucester his death, and he answered that he knew nothing at all: but the people (quoth he) do say that you have murdered him. Whereunto the Duke sware great oaths that it was untrue, and that he had saved his life, contrary to the will of the King and certain other lords, by the space of three weeks and more; affirming withal, that he was never in all his lifetime more afraid of death than he was at his coming home from Calais at that time to the King's presence, by reason he had not put the Duke to death. And then (said he) the King appointed one of his own servants, and certain other that were servants to other lords to go with him to see the said Duke of Gloucester put to death, swearing that as he should answer afore God, it was never his mind that he should have died in the fort, but only for fear of the King, and saving of his own life. Nevertheless, there was no man in the realm to whom King Richard was so much beholden as to the Duke of Aumerle: for he was the man that to fulfill his mind had set him in hand with all that was done against the said Duke and the other lords. . . . There was also contained in the said bill that Bagot had heard the Duke of Aumerle say that he had rather than twenty thousand pounds that the Duke of Hereford were dead, not for any fear he had of him, but for the trouble and mischief that he was like to procure within the realm.

After that the bill had been read and heard, the Duke of Aumerle rose up and said, that as touching the points contained in the bill concerning him, they were utterly false and untrue, which he would prove with his body in what manner soever it should be thought requisite.

On the Saturday next ensuing, Sir William Bagot and the said John Hall were brought both to the bar, and Bagot was examined of certain points and sent again to prison. The Lord Fitzwater herewith rose up, and said to the King, that where the Duke of Aumerle excuseth himself of the Duke of Gloucester's death, I say (quoth he) that he was the very cause of his death, and so he appealed him of treason, offering by throwing down his hood as a gage to prove it with his body. There were twenty other lords also that threw down their hoods, as pledges to prove the like matter against the Duke of Aumerle. The Duke of Aumerle threw down his hood to try it against the Lord Fitzwater, as against him that lied falsely in that he had charged him with, by that his appeal. These gages were delivered to the Constable and Marshal of England and the parties put under arrest.

The Duke of Surrey stood up also against the Lord Fitzwater, avouching that where he had said that the appellants were causers of the Duke of Gloucester's death, it was false, for they were constrained to sue the same appeal, in like manner as the said Lord Fitzwater was compelled to give judgment against the Duke of Gloucester and the Earl of Arundel; so that the suing of the appeal was done by constraint, and if he said contrary he lied: and therewith he threw down his hood. The Lord Fitzwater answered hereunto that he was not present in the parliament house when judgment was given against them, and all the lords bare witness thereof. Moreover, where it was alleged that the Duke of Aumerle should send two of his servants to Calais to murder the Duke of Gloucester, the said Duke of Aumerle said that if the Duke of Norfolk affirm it he lied falsely, and that he would prove with his body, throwing down another hood which he had borrowed. The same was likewise delivered to the Constable and Marshal of England, and the King licensed the Duke of Norfolk to return, that he might arraign his appeal. . . .

On Wednesday following, request was made by the Commons, that sith King Richard had resigned, and was lawfully deposed from his royal dignity, he might have judgment decreed against him, so as the realm were not troubled by him, and that the causes of his deposing might be published through the realm for satisfying of the people: which demand was granted. [IV.i.114] Whereupon the Bishop of Carlisle, a man both learned, wise, and stout of stomach, boldly showed forth his opinion concerning that demand, affirming that there was none amongst them worthy or meet to give judgment upon so noble a prince as King Richard was, whom they had taken for their sovereign and liege lord by the space of two and twenty years and more; "And I assure you" (said he) "there is not so rank a traitor, nor so errant a thief, nor yet so cruel a murderer apprehended or detained in prison for his offense, but he shall be brought before the justice to hear his judgment; and will ye proceed to the judgment of an anointed king, hearing neither his answer nor excuse? I say that the Duke of Lancaster, whom ye call king, hath more trespassed to King Richard and his realm, than King Richard hath done either to him or us; for it is manifest and well known that the Duke was banished the realm by King Richard and his council, and by the judgment of his own

father, for the space of ten years, for what cause ye
know, and yet without license of King Richard he is returned again into the realm, and (that is worse) hath
taken upon him the name, title, and pre-eminence of
King. And therefore I say, that you have done manifest
wrong to proceed in anything against King Richard, without calling him openly to his answer and defense." As
soon as the bishop had ended his tale, he was attached
by the Earl Marshal and committed to ward in the Abbey
of Saint Albans.

[*Aumerle, Surrey, and Exeter are deprived of their
titles of Dukes.*]

[IV.i.] This year Thomas Mowbray, Duke of Nor-
folk, died in exile at Venice. . . . [II.ii] The same year deceased the Duchess of Gloucester, through sorrow (as
was thought) which she conceived for the loss of her
son and heir the lord Humphrey, who being sent for forth
of Ireland . . . was taken with the pestilence, and died
by the way. . . . [IV.i.320-33] But now to speak of the
conspiracy which was contrived by the Abbot of Westminster as chief instrument thereof. Ye shall understand that this Abbot (as it is reported) upon a time
heard King Henry say, when he was but Earl of Derby
and young of years, that princes had too little, and religious men too much. He therefore doubting now lest,
if the King continued long in the estate, he would remove
the great beam that then grieved his eyes and pricked
his conscience, became an instrument to search out the
minds of the nobility and to bring them to an assembly
and council, where they might consult and commen together how to bring that to effect which they earnestly
wished and desired: that was, the destruction of King
Henry and the restoring of King Richard. For there were
divers lords that showed themselves outwardly to favor
King Henry, where they secretly wished and sought his
confusion. The Abbot, after he had felt the minds of
sundry of them, called to his house on a day in the
term time all such lords and other persons which he
either knew or thought to be as affectioned to King Richard, so envious to the prosperity of King Henry, whose

names were, John Holland, Earl of Huntington (late Duke of Exeter), Thomas Holland, Earl of Kent (late Duke of Surrey), Edward, Earl of Rutland (late Duke of Aumerle) son to the Duke of York, John Montacute, Earl of Salisbury, Hugh, Lord Spenser (late Earl of Gloucester), John, the Bishop of Carlisle, Sir Thomas Blunt, and Maudelen, a priest, one of King Richard's chapel.

The Abbot highly feasted these lords, his special friends, and when they had well dined, they withdrew into a secret chamber, where they sat down in council, and after much talk and conference had about the bringing of their purpose to pass concerning the destruction of King Henry, at length by the advice of the Earl of Huntington, it was devised that they should take upon them a solemn jousts to be enterprised between him and twenty on his part, and the Earl of Salisbury and twenty with him at Oxford; to the which triumph King Henry should be desired, and when he should be most busily marking the martial pastime, he suddenly should be slain and destroyed, and so by that means King Richard, who as yet lived, might be restored to liberty, and have his former estate and dignity. It was further appointed, who should assemble the people, the number and persons which should accomplish and put in execution their devised enterprise. Hereupon was an indenture sextipartite made, sealed with their seals, and signed with their hands, in the which each stood bound to other, to do their whole endeavor for the accomplishing of their purposed exploit. Moreover, they sware on the holy evangelists to be true and secret each to other, even to the hour and point of death.

When all things were thus appointed, the Earl of Huntington came to the King unto Windsor, earnestly requiring him that he would vouchsafe to be at Oxenford on the day appointed of their jousts, both to behold the same, and to be the discoverer and indifferent judge (if any ambiguity should rise) of their courageous acts and doings. The King, being thus instantly required of his brother-in-law, and nothing less imagining than that which was pretended, gently granted to fulfill his request. Which thing obtained, all the lords of the conspiracy departed home to their houses, as they noised it, to set armorers on work about the trimming of their armor against the jousts, and to prepare all other furniture and things ready, as to such an high and solemn triumph appertained. The Earl of Huntington came to his house and raised men on every side, and prepared horse and harness for his compassed purpose, and when he had all things ready, he departed towards Oxenford, and at his coming thither he found all his mates and confederates there, well appointed for their purpose, except the Earl of Rutland, by whose folly their practiced conspiracy was brought to light and disclosed to King Henry.

[V.ii,iii] For this Earl of Rutland, departing before from Westminster to see his father, the Duke of York, as he sat at dinner, had his counterpane of the indenture of the confederacy in his bosom. The father, espying it, would needs see what it was, and though the son humbly denied to show it, the father, being more earnest to see it, by force took it out of his bosom; and perceiving the contents thereof, in a great rage caused his horses to be saddled out of hand, and spitefully reproving his son of treason, for whom he was become surety and mainpernour for his good abearing in open parliament, he incontinently mounted on horseback to ride towards Windsor to the King, to declare unto him the malicious intent of his complices. The Earl of Rutland, seeing in what danger he stood, took his horse and rode another way to Windsor in post, so that he got thither before his father, and when he was alighted at the castle gate, he caused the gates to be shut, saying that he must needs deliver the keys to the King. When he came before the King's presence, he kneeled down on his knees, beseeching him of mercy and forgiveness, and declaring the whole matter unto him in order as everything had passed, obtained pardon. Therewith came his father, and being let in, delivered the indenture which he had taken from his son unto the King, who thereby perceiving his son's words to be true, changed his purpose for his going to Oxenford. . . .

The conspirators being at Oxenford at length perceived

by the lack of the Earl of Rutland that their enterprise was revealed to the King, and thereupon determined now openly with spear and shield to bring to pass which before they covertly attempted, and so they adorned Maudelen, a man most resembling King Richard, in royal and princely vesture, and named him to be King Richard, affirming that by favor of his keepers he was escaped out of prison.

[*The conspirators, arriving at Windsor, find Henry gone. They retire before his army and arrive at Cirencester.*]

In the night season the bailiff of the town with four score archers set on the house where the Earl of Kent and the other lay, which house was manfully assaulted and strongly defended in great space. The Earl of Huntington being in another inn with the Lord Spenser set fire on divers houses in the town, thinking that the assailants would leave the assault and rescue their goods, which thing they nothing regarded. The host lying without, hearing noise, and seeing this fire in the town, thought verily that King Henry had been come thither with his puissance, and thereupon fled without measure, every man making shift to save himself. . . .

The Earl of Huntington . . . seeing no hope of comfort, fled into Essex. The other lords which were left fighting in the town of Cirencester were wounded to death and taken, and their heads stricken off and sent to London. . . .

[*The Earl of Huntington and others are captured and beheaded.*] [V.vi] Shortly after, the Abbot of Westminster, in whose house the conspiracy was begun (as it is said) going between his monastery and mansion, for thought fell into a sudden palsy, and shortly after, without speech, ended his life.

The Bishop of Carlisle dieth through fear, or rather through grief of mind, to see the wicked prosper, as he took it.

The Bishop of Carlisle was impeached and condemned of the same conspiracy; but the King, of his merciful clemency, pardoned him of that offense, although he died shortly after, more through fear than force of sickness, as some have written.

[V.iv,v] One writer, which seemeth to have great knowledge of King Richard's doings, saith that King Henry, sitting on a day at his table, sore sighing, said: "Have I no faithful friend which will deliver me of him, whose life will be my death, and whose death will be the preservation of my life?" This saying was much noted of them which were present, and especially of one called Sir Piers of Exton. This knight incontinently departed from the court with eight strong persons in his company, and came to Pomfret, commanding the esquire, that was accustomed to sew and take the assay before King Richard, to do so no more, saying: "Let him eat now, for he shall not long eat." King Richard sat down to dinner, and was served without courtesy or assay: whereupon, much marveling at the sudden change, he demanded of the esquire why he did not his duty. "Sir" (said he) "I am otherwise commanded by Sir Piers of Exton, which is newly come from King Henry." When King Richard heard that word, he took his carving knife in his hand, and strake the esquire on the head, saying: "The devil take Henry of Lancaster and thee together!" And with that word, Sir Piers entered the chamber, well armed, with eight tall men likewise armed, every of them having a bill in his hand.

King Richard, perceiving this, put the table from him, and stepping to the foremost man, wrung the bill out of his hands, and so valiantly defended himself, that he slew four of those that came to assail him. Sir Piers, being half dismayed herewith, leaped into the chair where King Richard was wont to sit, while the other four persons fought with him, and chased him about the chamber. And in conclusion, as King Richard traversed his ground, from one side of the chamber to another, and coming by the chair where Sir Piers stood, he was felled with a stroke of a poleax which Sir Piers gave him upon the head, and therewith rid him out of life, without giving him respite once to call to God for mercy of his past offenses. It is said that Sir Piers of Exton, after he had thus slain him, wept right bitterly, as one stricken with the prick of a guilty conscience, for murdering him whom he had so long time obeyed as King.

After he was thus dead, his body was imbalmed, and cered, and covered with lead, all save the face, to the intent that all men might see him, and perceive that he was departed from this life: for as the corpse was conveyed from Pomfret to London, in all the towns and places where those that had the conveyance of it did stay with it all night, they caused *Dirige* to be sung in the evening and mass of *Requiem* in the morning; and as well after the one service as the other, his face discovered was showed to all that coveted to behold it.

Thus was the corpse first brought to the Tower, and after through the city to the cathedral church of Saint Paul, barefaced, where it lay three days together that all men might behold it. There was a solemn obsequy done for him both at Paul's, and after at Westminster, at which time both at *Dirige* overnight, and in the morning at the mass of *Requiem,* the King and the citizens of London were present. . . .

[1413] In this fourteenth and last year of King Henry's reign, a council was holden in the White Friars in London, at the which, among other things, order was taken for ships and galleys to be made ready and all other things necessary to be provided for a voyage which he meant to make into the Holy Land, there to recover the city of Jerusalem from the Infidels.

Commentaries

Walter Pater

Shakespeare's English Kings

One gracious prerogative, certainly, Shakespeare's English kings possess: they are a very eloquent company, and Richard is the most sweet-tongued of them all. In no other play perhaps is there such a flush of those gay, fresh, variegated flowers of speech—color and figure, not lightly attached to, but fused into, the very phrase itself—which Shakespeare cannot help dispensing to his characters, as in this "play of the Deposing of King Richard the Second," an exquisite poet if he is nothing else, from first to last, in light and gloom alike, able to see all things poetically, to give a poetic turn to his conduct of them, and refreshing with his golden language the tritest aspects of that ironic contrast between the pretensions of a king and the actual necessities of his destiny. What a garden of words! With him, blank verse, infinitely graceful, deliberate, musical in inflection, becomes indeed a true "verse royal," that rhyming lapse, which to the Shakespearean ear, at least in youth, came as the last touch of refinement on it, being here doubly appropriate. His eloquence blends with that fatal beauty, of which he was so frankly aware, so amiable to his friends, to his wife, of the effects of which on the people his enemies were so much afraid, on which Shakespeare himself dwells so attentively as the "royal

From *Appreciations* (1889).

blood" comes and goes in the face with his rapid changes of temper. As happens with sensitive natures, it attunes him to a congruous suavity of manners, by which anger itself became flattering: it blends with his merely youthful hopefulness and high spirits, his sympathetic love for gay people, things, apparel—"his cote of gold and stone, valued at thirty thousand marks," the novel Italian fashions he preferred, as also with those real amiabilities that made people forget the darker touches of his character, but never tire of the pathetic rehearsal of his fall, the meekness of which would have seemed merely abject in a less graceful performer.

Yet it is only fair to say that in the painstaking "revival" of *King Richard the Second,* by the late Charles Kean, those who were very young thirty years ago were afforded much more than Shakespeare's play could ever have been before—the very person of the king based on the stately old portrait in Westminster Abbey, "the earliest extant contemporary likeness of any English sovereign," the grace, the winning pathos, the sympathetic voice of the player, the tasteful archaeology confronting vulgar modern London with a scenic reproduction, for once really agreeable, of the London of Chaucer. In the hands of Kean the play became like an exquisite performance on the violin.

The long agony of one so gaily painted by nature's self, from his "tragic abdication" till the hour in which he

Sluiced out his innocent soul thro' streams of blood,

was for playwrights a subject ready to hand, and became early the theme of a popular drama, of which some have fancied surviving favorite fragments in the rhymed parts of Shakespeare's work.

> The king Richard of Yngland
> Was in his flowris then regnand:
> But his flowris efter sone
> Fadyt, and ware all undone:

says the old chronicle. Strangely enough, Shakespeare
supposes him an overconfident believer in that divine
right of kings, of which people in Shakespeare's time
were coming to hear so much; a general right, sealed to
him (so Richard is made to think) as an ineradicable
personal gift by the touch—stream rather, over head and
breast and shoulders—of the "holy oil" of his consecra-
tion at Westminster; not however, through some over-
sight, the genuine balm used at the coronation of his
successor, given, according to legend, by the Blessed
Virgin to Saint Thomas of Canterbury. Richard himself
found that, it was said, among other forgotten treasures,
at the crisis of his changing fortunes, and vainly sought
reconsecration therewith—understood, wistfully, that it
was reserved for his happier rival. And yet his coronation, by the pageantry, the amplitude, the learned care,
of its order, so lengthy that the king, then only eleven
years of age, and fasting, as a communicant at the ceremony, was carried away in a faint, fixed the type under
which it has ever since continued. And nowhere is there
so emphatic a reiteration as in *Richard the Second* of
the sentiment which those singular rites were calculated
to produce.

> Not all the water in the rough rude sea
> Can wash the balm off from an anointed king,

as supplementing another, almost supernatural, right.
"Edward's seven sons," of whom Richard's father was
one,

> Were as seven phials of his sacred blood.

But this, too, in the hands of Shakespeare, becomes for
him, like any other of those fantastic, ineffectual, easily
discredited, personal graces, as capricious in its opera-
tion on men's wills as merely physical beauty, kindling
himself to eloquence indeed, but only giving double
pathos to insults which "barbarism itself" might have

pitied—the dust in his face, as he returns, through the streets of London, a prisoner in the train of his victorious enemy.

How soon my sorrow hath destroyed my face!

he cries, in that most poetic invention of the mirror scene, which does but reinforce again that physical charm which all confessed. The sense of "divine right" in kings is found to act not to much as a secret of power over others, as of infatuation to themselves. And of all those personal gifts the one which alone never altogether fails him is just that royal utterance, his appreciation of the poetry of his own hapless lot, an eloquent self-pity, infecting others in spite of themselves, till they too become irresistibly eloquent about him.

In the Roman Pontifical, of which the order of Coronation is really a part, there is no form for the inverse process, no rite of "degradation," such as that by which an offending priest or bishop may be deprived, if not of the essential quality of "orders," yet, one by one, of its outward dignities. It is as if Shakespeare had had in mind some such inverted rite, like those old ecclesiastical or military ones, by which human hardness, or human justice, adds the last touch of unkindness to the execution of its sentences, in the scene where Richard "deposes" himself, as in some long, agonizing ceremony, reflectively drawn out, with an extraordinary refinement of intelligence and variety of piteous appeal, but also with a felicity of poetic invention, which puts these pages into a very select class, with the finest "vermeil and ivory" work of Chatterton or Keats.

Fetch hither Richard that in common view
He may surrender!

And Richard more than concurs: he throws himself into the part, realizes a type, falls gracefully as on the world's stage. Why is he sent for?

> To do that office of thine own good will
> Which tired majesty did make thee offer.—
> Now mark me! how I will undo myself.

"Hath Bolingbroke deposed thine intellect?" the Queen asks him, on his way to the Tower:

> Hath Bolingbroke
> Deposed thine intellect? hath he been in thy heart?

And in truth, but for that adventitious poetic gold, it would be only "plume-plucked Richard."

> I find myself a traitor with the rest,
> For I have given here my soul's consent
> To undeck the pompous body of a king.

He is duly reminded, indeed, how

> That which in mean men we entitle patience
> Is pale cold cowardice in noble breasts.

Yet at least within the poetic bounds of Shakespeare's play, through Shakespeare's bountiful gifts, his desire seems fulfilled.

> O! that I were as great
> As is my grief.

And his grief becomes nothing less than a central expression of all that in the revolutions of Fortune's wheel goes *down* in the world.

No! Shakespeare's kings are not, nor are meant to be, great men: rather, little or quite ordinary humanity, thrust upon greatness, with those pathetic results, the natural self-pity of the weak heightened in them into irresistible appeal to others as the net result of their royal prerogative. One after another, they seem to lie composed in Shakespeare's embalming pages, with just that touch of nature about them, making the whole world akin, which has infused into their tombs at Westminster a rare poetic grace. It is that irony of kingship, the sense that it is in its happiness child's play, in its sorrows, after all, but children's grief, which gives its finer accent to all the changeful feeling of these wonderful speeches: the great meekness of the graceful, wild creature, tamed at last.

> Give Richard leave to live till Richard die!

his somewhat abject fear of death, turning to acquiescence at moments of extreme weariness:

> My large kingdom for a little grave!
> A little little grave, an obscure grave!

his religious appeal in the last reserve, with its bold reference to the judgment of Pilate, as he thinks once more of his "anointing."

And as happens with children he attains contentment finally in the merely passive recognition of superior strength, in the naturalness of the result of the great battle as a matter of course, and experiences something of the royal prerogative of poetry to obscure, or at least to attune and soften men's griefs. As in some sweet anthem of Handel, the sufferer, who put finger to the organ under the utmost pressure of mental conflict, extracts a kind of peace at last from the mere skill with which he sets his distress to music.

> Beshrew thee, Cousin, that didst lead me forth
> Of that sweet way I was in to despair!

"With Cain go wander through the shades of night!" cries the new king to the gaoler Exton, dissimulating his share in the murder he is thought to have suggested; and in truth there is something of the murdered Abel about Shakespeare's Richard. The fact seems to be that he died of "waste and a broken heart": it was by way of

proof that his end had been a natural one that, stifling a
real fear of the face, the face of Richard, on men's
minds, with the added pleading now of all dead faces,
Henry exposed the corpse to general view; and Shakespeare, in bringing it on the stage, in the last scene of his
play, does but follow out the motive with which he has
emphasized Richard's physical beauty all through it—that
"most beauteous inn," as the Queen says quaintly, meeting him on the way to death—residence, then soon to be
deserted, of that wayward, frenzied, but withal so affec-
tionate soul. Though the body did not go to Westminster
immediately, his tomb,

> That small model of the barren earth
> Which serves as paste and cover to our bones,

the effigy clasping the hand of his youthful consort, was
already prepared there, with "rich gilding and orna-
ments," monument of poetic regret, for Queen Anne of
Bohemia, not of course the "Queen" of Shakespeare,
who however seems to have transferred to this second
wife something of Richard's wildly proclaimed affection
for the first. In this way, through the connecting link of
that sacred spot, our thoughts once more associate
Richard's two fallacious prerogatives, his personal
beauty and his "anointing."

According to Johnson, *Richard the Second* is one of
those plays which Shakespeare has "apparently revised";
and how doubly delightful Shakespeare is where he seems
to have revised! "Would that he had blotted a thousand"—a thousand hasty phrases, we may venture once
more to say with his earlier critic, now that the tire-
some German superstition has passed away which chal-
lenged us to a dogmatic faith in the plenary verbal in-
spiration of every one of Shakespeare's clowns. Like some
melodiously contending anthem of Handel's, I said, of
Richard's meek "undoing" of himself in the mirror-scene;
and, in fact, the play of *Richard the Second* does, like a
musical composition, possess a certain concentration of
all its parts, a simple continuity, an evenness in execu-

tion, which are rare in the great dramatist. With *Romeo and Juliet,* that perfect symphony (symphony of three independent poetic forms set in a grander one which it is the merit of German criticism to have detected), it belongs to a small group of plays, where, by happy birth and consistent evolution, dramatic form approaches to something like the unity of a lyrical ballad, a lyric, a song, a single strain of music. Which sort of poetry we are to account the highest, is perhaps a barren question. Yet if, in art generally, unity of impression is a note of what is perfect, then lyric poetry, which in spite of complex structure often preserves the unity of a single passionate ejaculation, would rank higher than dramatic poetry, where, especially to the reader, as distinguished from the spectator assisting at a theatrical performance, there must always be a sense of the effort necessary to keep the various parts from flying asunder, a sense of imperfect continuity, such as the older criticism vainly sought to obviate by the rule of the dramatic "unities." It follows that a play attains artistic perfection just in proportion as it approaches that unity of lyrical effect, as if a song or ballad were still lying at the root of it, all the various expression of the conflict of character and circumstance falling at last into the compass of a single melody, or musical theme. As, historically, the earliest classic drama arose out of the chorus, from which this or that person, this or that episode, detached itself, so, into the unity of a choric song the perfect drama ever tends to return, its intellectual scope deepened, complicated, enlarged, but still with an unmistakable singleness, or identity, in its impression on the mind. Just there, in that vivid single impression left on the mind when all is over, not in any mechanical limitation of time and place, is the secret of the "unities"—the true imaginative unity—of the drama.

Richard D. Altick

Symphonic Imagery in *Richard II*

Critics on occasion have remarked the peculiar unity of tone which distinguishes *Richard II* from most of Shakespeare's other plays. Walter Pater wrote that, like a musical composition, it possesses "a certain concentration of all its parts, a simple continuity, an evenness in execution, which are rare in the great dramatist. . . . It belongs to a small group of plays, where, by happy birth and consistent evolution, dramatic form approaches to something like the unity of a lyrical ballad, a lyric, a song, a single strain of music." And J. Dover Wilson, in his edition of the play, has observed that "*Richard II* possesses a unity of tone and feeling greater than that attained in many of his greater plays, a unity found, I think, to the same degree elsewhere only in *Twelfth Night, Antony and Cleopatra,* and *The Tempest.*"

How can we account for that impression of harmony, of oneness, which we receive when we read the play or listen to its lines spoken upon the stage? The secret, it seems to me, lies in an aspect of Shakespeare's genius which has oftener been condemned than praised. Critics and casual readers alike have groaned over the fine-drawn ingenuity of the Shakespearean quibble, which, as Dr. Johnson maintained, was "the fatal Cleopatra for which he lost the world, and was content to lose it."

From *PMLA,* LXII, 1947. Reprinted, with some alterations in the footnotes, by permission of the author and The Modern Language Association of America.

But it is essentially the same habit of the creative imagination—a highly sensitized associational gift—that produces iterative symbolism and imagery. Simple wordplay results from the poet's awareness of the diverse meanings of words, of which, however, he makes no better use than to demonstrate his own cleverness and to tickle for a moment the wit of the audience. These exhibitions of verbal agility are simply decorations scattered upon the surface of the poetic fabric; they can be ripped out without loss. But suppose that to the poet's associational sensitivity is added a further awareness of the multitudinous emotional overtones of words. When he puts this faculty to use he is no longer merely playing a game; instead, words have become the shells in which ideas and symbols are enclosed. Suppose, furthermore, that instead of being the occupation of a few fleeting lines of the text, certain words of multifold meanings are played upon throughout the five acts, recurring time after time like leitmotivs in music. And suppose finally that this process of repetition is applied especially to words of sensuous significance, words that evoke vivid responses in the imagination. When these things happen to certain words—when they cease to be mere vehicles for a brief indulgence of verbal fancy and, taking on a burden of serious meaning, become thematic material—the poet has crossed the borderline that separates wordplay from iterative imagery. Language has become the willing servant of structure, and what was on other occasions only a source of exuberant but undisciplined wit now is converted to the higher purpose of poetic unity.

That, briefly, is what happens in *Richard II*. The familiar wordplays of the earlier Shakespearean dramas persist: John of Gaunt puns endlessly upon his own name. But in this drama a word is not commonly taken up, rapidly revolved, so that all its various facets of meaning flash out, and then discarded. Instead, certain words are played upon throughout the drama. Far from being decorations, "gay, fresh, variegated flowers of speech," as Pater called them, they are woven deeply

into the thought-web of the play. Each word-theme symbolizes one or another of the fundamental ideas of the
story, and every time it reappears it perceptibly deepens
and enriches those meanings and at the same time
charges the atmosphere with emotional significance.

The most remarkable thing about these leitmotivs is
the way in which they are constantly mingling and coalescing, two or three of them joining to form a single new
figure, very much in the manner in which "hooked
images," as Professor Lowes called them, were formed in
the subconscious mind of Coleridge. This repeated criss-
crossing of familiar images [1] makes of the whole text one
vast arabesque of language, just as a dozen lines of *Love's
Labour's Lost* form a miniature arabesque when the poet's
quibbling mood is upon him. And since each image
motif represents one of the dominant ideas of the play
(heredity, patriotism, sycophancy, etc.) the coalescing of
these images again and again emphasizes the complex
relationship between the ideas themselves, so that the
reader is kept ever aware that all that happens in
Richard II results inevitably from the interaction of many
elements.

It is pointless to try to explain by further generaliza-
tions this subtle and exceedingly intricate weaving together of metaphor and symbol—this glorified wordplay,
if you will—which is the key to the total poetic effect of
Richard II. All I can do is to draw from the fabric, one
by one, the strands that compose it, and to suggest in
some manner the magical way in which they interact and
by association and actual fusion reciprocally deepen their
meaning.

Miss Spurgeon has pointed out how in *Antony and
Cleopatra* the cosmic grandeur of the theme is constantly emphasized by the repetition of the word *world*. In a
similar manner the symbolism of *Richard II* is dominated by the related words *earth, land,* and *ground.* In

---

[1] Throughout this paper I use the words "image" and "imagery"
in their most inclusive sense of metaphorical as well as "picture-
making" but nonfigurative language.

no other play of Shakespeare is the complex of ideas represented by these words so tirelessly dwelt upon.[2] The words are but three in number, and superficially they seem roughly synonymous; but they have many intellectual ramifications, which become more and more meaningful as the play progresses and the words are used first for one thing and then for another. As our experience of the words increases, their connotation steadily deepens. In addition to their obvious meaning in a particular context they come to stand for something larger and more undefinable—a mingling of everything they have represented earlier.

Above all, *earth* is the symbol of the English nation. It is used by Shakespeare to connote those same values which we find in the equivalent synecdoche of *soil*, as in "native soil." It sums up all the feeling inherent in the sense of pride in nation—of jealousy when the country is threatened by foreign incursion, of bitter anger when its health has been destroyed by mismanagement or greed. "This earth of majesty," John of Gaunt calls England in his famous speech, ". . . This blessed plot, this earth, this realm, this England" (II.i.41, 50). And a few lines farther on: "This land of such dear souls, this dear dear land . . ." (II.i.57). Having once appeared, so early in the play, in such lustrous context, the words *earth* and *land* forever after have richer significance. Whenever they

---

2 In *Richard II* the three words occur a total of 71 times; in *King John*, the nearest rival, 46.—I should note at this point that my identification of all the word- and image-themes to be discussed in this essay is based upon statistical study. A given word or group of related words is called a "theme" (a) if Bartlett's *Concordance* shows a definite numerical preponderance for *Richard II* or (b) if the word or group of words is so closely related to one of the fundamental ideas of the play that it is of greater importance than the comparative numerical frequency would imply. I have not included any arithmetic in this paper because all such tabulations obviously must be subjective to some degree. No two persons, doing the same counting for the same purpose, would arrive at precisely the same numerical results. But I am confident that independent tabulation would enable anyone to arrive at my general conclusions. Statistics here, as in all such critical exercises, are merely grounds upon which to base a judgment that must eventually be a subjective one.

recur, they are more meaningful, more powerful. Thus Richard's elaborate speech upon his arrival in Wales—

> As a long-parted mother with her child
> Plays fondly with her tears and smiles in meeting,
> So weeping, smiling, greet I thee, my earth,
> And do thee favors with my royal hands.
>
> . . . .
>
> Mock not my senseless conjuration, lords.
> This earth shall have a feeling, and these stones
> Prove armed soldiers, ere her native king
> Shall falter under foul rebellion's arms
>
> (III.ii.8-11, 23-26)

—undoubtedly gains in emotional splendor (as well as dramatic irony) by its reminiscences of John of Gaunt's earlier language. The two men between them make the English earth the chief verbal theme of the play.

Richard, we have just seen, speaks pridefully of "*my* earth." To him, ownership of the land is the most tangible and positive symbol of his rightful kingship. He bids Northumberland tell Bolingbroke that "every stride he makes upon my land/ Is dangerous treason" (III.iii.91-92), and as he lies dying from the stroke of Exton's sword his last thought is for his land: "Exton, thy fierce hand/ Hath with the king's blood stained the king's own land" (V.v.109-10). It is only natural, then, that *land* should be the key word in the discussions of England's sorry condition. Symbol of Englishmen's nationalistic pride and of the wealth of kings, it becomes symbol also of Englishmen's shame and kings' disgrace:

> Why, cousin, wert thou regent of the world,
> It were a shame to let this land by lease;
> But for thy world enjoying but this land,
> Is it not more than shame to shame it so?
> Landlord of England art thou now, not king.
>
> (II.i.109-13)

Northumberland's sad allusion to "this declining land"
(II.i.240), York's to "this woeful land" (II.ii.99) and
Richard's to "this revolting land" (III.iii.162) carry
on this motif.

But *earth,* while it emblematizes the foundation of
kingly pride and power, is also a familiar symbol of the
vanity of human life and of what, in the Middle Ages, was
a fascinating illustration of that vanity—the fall of
kings. "Men," Mowbray sighs, "are but gilded loam
or painted clay" (I.i.179); and Richard, luxuriating in
self-pity, often remembers it; to earth he will return.

> Ah, Richard [says Salisbury], with the eyes of
>   heavy mind
> I see thy glory like a shooting star
> Fall to the base earth from the firmament.
>
>   (II.iv.18-20)

The earth, Richard knows, is accustomed to receive the
knees of courtiers: "Fair cousin," he tells Bolingbroke
after he has given away his kingdom for the sheer joy
of listening to himself do so, "you debase your princely
knee/ To make the base earth proud with kissing it"
(III.iii.188-89). And the idea of the ground as the resting place for suppliant knees, and therefore the antith-
esis of kingly elevation, is repeated thrice in the two
scenes dealing with Aumerle's conspiracy.[3]

The irony of this association of *earth* with both kingly
glory and abasement is deepened by another role the
word has in this earth-preoccupied play. For after death,
earth receives its own; and in *Richard II* the common
notion of the grave has new meaning, because the ubiquitous symbol of *earth* embraces it too. By the beginning
of the third act, *earth* has lost its earlier joyful connota-

----

[3] The much admired little passage about the roan Barbary takes
on added poignancy when the other overtones of *ground* are
remembered:
King Richard. Rode he on Barbary? Tell me, gentle friend,
  How went he under him?
Groom. So proudly as if he disdain'd the ground.
                              (V.v.81-83)

tion to Richard, and this king, whose feverish imagination
no amount of woe can cool, eagerly picks up a hint
from Scroop:

Scroop.   Those whom you curse
    Have felt the worst of death's destroying wound
    And lie full low, grav'd in the hollow ground.
. . . .
Richard. Let's talk of graves, of worms, and epitaphs;
    Make dust our paper and with rainy eyes
    Write sorrow on the bosom of the earth.
    Let's choose executors and talk of wills;
    And yet not so; for what can we bequeath
    Save our deposed bodies to the ground?
    Our lands, our lives, and all are Bolingbroke's,
    And nothing can we call our own but death,
    And that small model of the barren earth
    Which serves as paste and cover to our bones.
    For God's sake, let us sit upon the ground
    And tell sad stories of the death of kings.
                            (III.ii.138-140, 145-56)

And later, in another ecstasy of self-pity, he conjures up
an elaborate image of making some pretty match with
shedding tears:

    As thus, to drop them still upon one place,
    Till they have fretted us a pair of graves
    Within the Earth.

                            (III.iii.165-67)

The same association occurs in the speeches of the
other characters. Surrey, casting his gage at Fitzwater's
feet, envisions his father's skull lying quietly in earth (IV.
i.66-69); a moment or two later the Bishop of Carlisle
brings news that the banished Mowbray, having fought
for Jesu Christ in glorious Christian field, "at Venice
gave/ His body to that pleasant country's earth" (IV.
i.97-98); and in the same scene Richard, having handed
over his crown to the usurper, exclaims,

Long mayst thou live in Richard's seat to sit,
And soon lie Richard in an earthy pit!
(IV.i.217-18)

A final theme in the symphonic pattern dominated by
the symbol of earth is that of the untended garden. Miss
Spurgeon has adequately emphasized the importance of
this iterated image in the history plays, and, as she
points out, it reaches its climax in *Richard II*, particularly in the allegorical scene of the Queen's garden. In
Shakespeare's imagination the misdeeds of Richard and
his followers constituted an overwhelming indignity to
the precious English earth—to a nation which, in happier days, had been a sea-wall'd garden. And thus the
play is filled with references to ripeness and the seasons,
to planting and cropping and plucking and reaping,
to furrows and plowing, and caterpillars and withered
bay trees and thorns and flowers.[4]

Among the host of garden images in the play, one
especially is unforgettable because of the insistence with
which Shakespeare thrice echoes it. It is the terrible
metaphor of the English garden being drenched by
showers of blood.

I'll use the advantage of my power
And lay the summer's dust with showers of blood
Rain'd from the wounds of slaughtered Englishmen;
(III.iii.41-43)

threatens Bolingbroke as he approaches Flint castle; and
when the King himself appears upon the walls, he casts
the figure back in Bolingbroke's face:

But ere the crown he looks for live in peace,
Ten thousand bloody crowns of mothers' sons
Shall ill become the flower of England's face,

---

[4] We must not, of course, take *garden* too literally. Shakespeare
obviously intended the term in its wider metaphorical sense of fields
and orchards.

Change the complexion of her maid-pale peace
To scarlet indignation, and bedew
Her pastures' grass with faithful English blood.
(III.iii.94–99)

The Bishop of Carlisle takes up the theme:

And if you crown him, let me prophesy,
The blood of English shall manure the ground,
And future ages groan for this foul act.
(IV.i.136-38)

And the new King—amply justifying Professor Van
Doren's remark that not only are most of the characters in this play poets, but they copy one another on
occasion—echoes it:

Lords, I protest, my soul is full of woe
That blood should sprinkle me to make me grow.
(V.vi.45-46)

This extraordinary series of four images is one of
the many examples of the manner in which the principal
symbols of *Richard II* so often chime together, bringing
the ideas they represent into momentary conjunction and
thus compounding those single emotional strains into new
and revealing harmonies. In this case the "showers of
blood" metaphor provides a recurrent nexus between the
pervasive symbol of earth and another, equally pervasive, symbol: that of blood.

Both Professor Bradley and Miss Spurgeon have
pointed out the splendid horror which Shakespeare
achieves in *Macbeth* by his repeated allusions to blood.
Curiously enough, the word *blood,* together with such
related words as *bloody* and *bleed,* occurs much less
frequently in *Macbeth* than it does in most of the history
plays. What gives the word the tremendous force it
undoubtedly possesses in *Macbeth* is not the frequency
with which it is spoken, but rather the intrinsic mag-

nificence of the passages in which it appears and the fact
that in this play it has but one significance—the literal one.
In the history plays, however, the word *blood* plays two
major roles. Often it has the same meaning it has in *Macbeth,* for these too are plays in which men's minds often
turn toward the sword:

> . . . our kingdom's earth should not be soil'd
> With that dear blood which it hath fostered
>   (I.iii.125-26)

says Richard in one more instinctive (and punning!) association of blood and earth. But *blood* in the history
plays also stands figuratively for inheritance, descent,
familial pride; and this is the chief motivating theme of
the play—the right of a monarch of unquestionably legitimate blood to his throne. The two significances constantly interplay, giving the single word a new multiple
connotation wherever it appears. The finest instance of
this merging of ideas is in the Duchess of Gloucester's
outburst to John of Gaunt. Here we have an elaborate contrapuntal metaphor, the basis of which is a figure derived from the familiar medieval genealogical symbol of
the Tree of Jesse, and which is completed by a second figure of the seven vials of blood. The imposition of the
figure involving the word *blood* (in its literal and therefore most vivid use) upon another figure which for centuries embodied the concept of family descent, thus welds
together with extraordinary tightness the word and its
symbolic significance. The occurrence of *blood* in other
senses on the borders of the metaphor (in the first and
next-to-last lines of the passage) helps to focus attention
upon the process occurring in the metaphor itself.

> Hath love in thy old blood no living fire?
> Edward's seven sons, whereof thyself art one,
> Were as seven vials of his sacred blood,
> Or seven fair branches springing from one root.
> Some of those seven are dried by nature's course,
> Some of those branches by the Destinies cut;

But Thomas, my dear lord, my life, my Gloucester,
One vial full of Edward's sacred blood,
One flourishing branch of his most royal root,
Is crack'd, and all the precious liquor spilt,
Is hack'd down, and his summer leaves all faded,
By Envy's hand and Murder's bloody axe.
Ah, Gaunt, his blood was thine!

(I.ii.10-22)

Because it has this multiple function, the word *blood* in
this play loses much of the concentrated vividness and
application it has in *Macbeth,* where it means but one unmistakable thing; but its ambiguity here gives it a new sort
of power. If it is less effective as imagery, it does serve
to underscore the basic idea of the play, that violation of
the laws of blood descent leads but to the spilling of
precious English blood. That is the meaning of the word
as it pulses from beginning to end, marking the emotional rhythm of the play.

In *Richard II,* furthermore, the word has an additional,
unique use, one which involves an especially striking symbol. It has often been remarked how Shakespeare, seiz-
ing upon a hint in his sources, plays upon Richard's ab-
normal tendency to blanch and blush. In the imagery
thus called forth, *blood* has a prominent part. How, demands the haughty king of John of Gaunt, dare thou

with thy frozen admonition
Make pale our cheek, chasing the royal blood
With fury from his native residence.

(II.i.117-19)

And when the King hears the news of the Welshmen's
defection, Aumerle steadies his quaking body:

Comfort, my liege; why looks your Grace so pale?

Richard. But now the blood of twenty thousand men
Did triumph in my face, and they are fled;
And, till so much blood thither come again,

Have I not reason to look pale and dead?

(III.ii.75-79)

This idiosyncrasy of the King is made the more vivid because the imagery of the play constantly refers to pallor, even in contexts far removed from him. The Welsh captain reports that "the pale-fac'd moon looks bloody on the earth" (II.iv.10). In another speech, the words *pale* and *blood,* though not associated in a single image, occur so close to each other that it is tempting to suspect an habitual association in Shakespeare's mind:

> Pale trembling coward, there I throw my gage,
> Disclaiming here the kindred of the King,
> And lay aside my high blood's royalty.

(I.i.69-71)

And as we have already seen, the King prophesied that "ten thousand bloody crowns of mothers' sons/ Shall . . . change the complexion of [England's] maid-pale peace" (III.iii.95-97). Elsewhere Bolingbroke speaks of "pale beggar-fear" (I.i.189); the Duchess of Gloucester accuses John of Gaunt of "pale cold cowardice" (I.ii.34); and York describes how the returned exile and his army fright England's "pale-fac'd villages" with war (II.iii.93).

The idea of pallor and blushing is linked in turn with what is perhaps the most famous image-motif of the play, that of Richard (or the fact of his kingship) emblematized by the sun. More attention probably has been paid to the sun-king theme than it is worth, for although it occurs in two very familiar passages, it contributes far less to the harmonic unity of the play than do a number of other symbol strains. In any event, the conjunction of the sun image with that of blushing provides one more evidence of the closeness with which the poetic themes of the play are knit together. In the first of the sun-king speeches, Richard compares himself, at the length to which he is addicted, with "the searching eye of heaven" (III.ii.37). Finally, after some ten lines of analogy:

> So when this thief, this traitor, Bolingbroke,
> Who all this while hath revell'd in the night
> Whilst we were wand'ring with the antipodes,
> Shall see us rising in our throne, the east,
> His treasons will sit blushing in his face. . . .
>   (III.ii.47-51)

And Bolingbroke in a later scene does him the sincere
flattery of imitation:

> See, see, King Richard doth himself appear,
> As doth the blushing discontented sun
> From out the fiery portal of the east.
>   (III.iii.61-63)

Another occurrence of the sun image provides a link
with the pervasive motif of tears. Salisbury, having en-
visioned Richard's glory falling to the base earth from the
firmament, continues:

> Thy sun sets weeping in the lowly west,
> Witnessing storms to come, woe, and unrest.
>   (II.iv.21-22)

In no other history play is the idea of tears and weeping
so insistently presented.[5] It is this element which en-
forces most strongly our impression of Richard as a
weakling, a monarch essentially feminine in nature, who
has no conception of stoic endurance or resignation
but a strong predilection for grief. This is why the play
seems so strangely devoid of the heroic; the King and
Queen are too much devoted to luxuriating in their
misery, and the other characters find a morbid delight in
at least alluding to unmanly tears. Characteristically,
Richard's first question to Aumerle, when the latter returns from bidding farewell to Bolingbroke, is, "What

---

[5] There are many more references to tears and weeping in *Titus
Andronicus*, but the obvious inferiority of the poetry and the crudity
of characterization make their presence far less remarkable.

store of parting tears were shed?" (I.iv.5). Bushy, dis-
cussing with the Queen her premonitions of disaster,
speaks at length of "sorrow's eye, glazed with blinding
tears" (II.ii.16). Richard greets the fair soil of England with mingled smiles and tears; and from that point
on, his talk is full of "rainy eyes" (III.ii.146) and of
making "foul weather with despised tears" (III.iii.160).
He counsels York,

> Uncle, give me your hands: nay, dry your eyes;
> Tears show their love, but want their remedies.
> (III.iii.200-01)

In the garden scene the Queen, rejecting her lady's offer
to sing, sadly tells her:

> 'Tis well that thou hast cause;
> But thou shouldst please me better wouldst thou weep.

Lady. I could weep, madam, would it do you good.
Queen. And I could sing, would weeping do me good,
   And never borrow any tear of thee.
> (III.iv.19-23)

And echoing that dialogue, the gardener, at the close
of the scene, looks after her and says:

> Here did she fall a tear; here in this place
> I'll set a bank of rue, sour herb of grace.
> Rue, even for ruth, here shortly shall be seen,
> In the remembrance of a weeping queen.
> (III.iv.104-07)

The theme reaches a climax in the deposition scene, in
which the agonized King, handing his crown to Bolingbroke, sees himself as the lower of the two buckets in
Fortune's well:

> ... full of tears am I,
> Drinking my griefs, whilst you mount up on high.
>
> (IV.i.187-88)

And a few lines later he merges the almost ubiquitous motif of tears with another constant theme of the play: "With mine own tears I wash away my balm" (IV.i. 206). Of the frequent association of the anointing of kings, blood, and the act of washing, I shall speak a little later.

Professor Van Doren, in his sensitive essay on *Richard II*, eloquently stresses the importance of the word *tongue* in the play. *Tongue*, he says, is the key word of the piece. I should prefer to give that distinction to *earth;* but there is no denying the effectiveness of Shakespeare's tireless repetition of the idea of speech, not only by the single word *tongue* but also by such allied words as *mouth, speech,* and *word.* A few minutes' study of Bartlett's *Concordance* will show that *Richard II* is unique in this insistence upon the concept of speech; that the word *tongue* occurs here oftener than in any other play is but one indication.

This group of associated words heavily underscores two leading ideas in the play. In the first place, it draws constant attention to the propensity for verbalizing (as Shakespeare would not have called it!) which is Richard's fatal weakness. He cannot bring himself to live in a world of hard actuality; the universe to him is real only as it is presented in packages of fine words. Aumerle tries almost roughly to recall him from his weaving of sweet, melancholy sounds to a realization of the crucial situation confronting him, but he rouses himself only momentarily and then relapses into a complacent enjoyment of the sound of his own tongue. It is of this trait that we are constantly reminded as all the characters regularly use periphrases when they must speak of what they or others have said. By making the physical act of speech, the sheer fact of language, so conspicuous, they call attention to its illusory nature—to the vast difference between what the semanticists call the intensional and extensional universes. That words are mere conventional sounds molded by the tongue, and reality is something else again, is constantly on the minds of all the characters. The initial dispute between Mowbray and Bolingbroke is "the bitter clamor of two eager tongues" (I.i.49); Mowbray threatens to cram his antagonist's lie "through the false passage of thy throat" (I.i.125); and later, in a fine cadenza, he conceives of his eternal banishment in terms of the engaoling of his tongue, whose "use is to me no more/ Than an unstringed viol or a harp," and concludes:

> What is thy sentence [then] but speechless death,
> Which robs my tongue from breathing native breath?
> (I.iii.161-62, 172-73)

Bolingbroke, for his part, marvels over the power of a single word to change the lives of men:

> How long a time lies in one little word!
> Four lagging winters and four wanton springs
> End in a word: such is the breath of kings.
> (I.iii.212-14)

Gaunt too is preoccupied with tongues and speech; and when Aumerle returns from his farewell with Bolingbroke, from tears the image theme swiftly turns to tongues:

Richard. What said our cousin when you parted with him?

Aumerle. "Farewell!"
　And, for my heart disdained that my tongue
　Should so profane the word, that taught me craft
　To counterfeit oppression of such grief
　That words seem'd buried in my sorrow's grave.
　Marry, would the word "farewell" have length'ned
　　hours

And added years to his short banishment,
He should have had a volume of farewells.

(I.iv.10-18)

And we have but reached the end of Act I; the remainder
of the play is equally preoccupied with the unsubstantiality of human language.[6]

But the unremitting stress laid upon tongues and words
in this play serves another important end: it reminds us
that Richard's fall is due not only to his preference for
his own words rather than for deeds, but also to his
blind predilection for comfortable flattery rather than
sound advice. Words not only hypnotize, suspend the
sense of reality: they can sting and corrupt. And so the
tongues of *Richard II* symbolize also the honeyed but
poisonous speech of the sycophants who surround him.
"No," replies York to Gaunt's suggestion that his dying
words might yet undeaf Richard's ear,

it is stopp'd with other flattering sounds,
As praises, of whose taste the wise are fond,
Lascivious meters, to whose venom sound
The open ear of youth doth always listen.

(II.i.17-20)

The venom to which York refers and the snake which
produces it form another theme of the imagery of this
play. The snake-venom motif closely links the idea of the
garden on the one hand (for what grossly untended garden would be without its snakes?) and the idea of the
tongue on the other. All three meet in the latter part of
Richard's speech in III.ii:

6 Another way in which Shakespeare adds to the constant tragic
sense of unsubstantiality in this play—the confusion of appearance
and reality—is the repeated use of the adjective *hollow*, especially
in connection with death: "our hollow parting" (I.iv.9), the "hollow
womb" of the grave (II.i.83), "the hollow eyes of death" (II.i.270),
a grave set in "the hollow ground" (III.ii.140), "the hollow crown"
in which Death keeps his court (III.ii.160).

> But let thy spiders, that suck up thy venom,
> And heavy-gaited toads lie in their way,
> Doing annoyance to the treacherous feet
> Which with usurping steps do trample thee
> Yield stinging nettles to mine enemies;
> And when they from thy bosom pluck a flower,
> Guard it, I pray thee, with a lurking adder
> Whose double tongue may with a mortal touch
> Throw death upon thy sovereign's enemies.
>
> (III.ii.14-22)

And the double association occurs again in the garden scene, when the Queen demands of the gardener,

> Thou, old Adam's likeness, set to dress this garden,
> How dares thy harsh rude tongue sound this unpleasing
>   news?
> What Eve, what serpent, hath suggested thee
> To make a second fall of cursed man?
>
> (III.iv.73-76)

Mowbray elsewhere speaks of "slander's venom'd spear" (I.i.171), and to Richard, the flatterers who have deserted him are, naturally enough, "villains, vipers, damn'd without redemption! . . . Snakes, in my heart-blood warm'd, that sting my heart!" (III.ii.129-31).

Although England's sorry state is most often figured in the references to the untended garden and the snakes that infest it, the situation is emphasized time and again by at least four other recurrent themes, some of which refer as well to the personal guilt of Richard. One such theme—anticipating a similar motif in *Hamlet*—involves repeated references to physical illness and injury. Richard in seeking to smooth over the quarrel between Mowbray and Bolingbroke says:

> Let's purge this choler without letting blood.
> This we prescribe, though no physician;
> Deep malice makes too deep incision.
>
> (I.i.153-55)

There are repeated allusions to the swelling caused by infection. Richard in the same scene speaks of "the swelling difference of your settled hate" (I.i.201), and much later, after he has been deposed, he predicts to Northumberland that

> The time shall not be many hours of age
> More than it is, ere foul sin gathering head
> Shall break into corruption.
>
> (V.i.57-59)

Thus too there are vivid mentions of the remedy for such festering:

> Fell Sorrow's tooth doth never rankle more
> Than when he bites, but lanceth not the sore.
>
> (I.iii.301-02)

> This fest'red joint cut off, the rest rest sound.
>
> (V.iii.84)

Plague, pestilence, and *infection* are words frequently in the mouths of the characters of this play. Aumerle, during the furious gage-casting of IV.i, cries, "May my hands rot off" if he does not seize Percy's gage (IV.i.49); and elsewhere York, speaking to the unhappy Queen, says of the King,

> Now comes the sick hour that his surfeit made;
> Now shall he try his friends that flatter'd him.
>
> (II.ii.84-85)

Indeed, the imagery which deals with bodily injury directly associates the wretchedness of the monarch and his country with the tongues of the sycophants. A verbal juxtaposition of *tongue* and *wound* occurs early in the play: "Ere my tongue/ Shall wound my honor with such feeble wrong" (I.i.190-91). Gaunt carries the association one step farther when he explicitly connects Richard's and England's illness with the presence of gross flatterers in the King's retinue:

> Thy death-bed is no lesser than thy land
> Wherein thou liest in reputation sick;
> And thou, too careless patient as thou art,
> Commit'st thy anointed body to the cure
> Of those physicians that first wounded thee.
> A thousand flatterers sit within thy crown,
> Whose compass is no bigger than thy head.
>
> (II.i.95-101)

And Richard himself completes the circuit between the tongue-wound association and his personal grief: "He does me double wrong/ That wounds me with the flatteries of his tongue" (III.ii.215-16).

Again, the evil that besets England is frequently symbolized as a dark blot upon fair parchment—an image which occurs oftener in this play than in any other. The suggestion for the image undoubtedly came from contemplation of the deeds and leases by which the king had farmed out the royal demesnes; as John of Gaunt said, England "is now bound in with shame,/ With inky blots and rotten parchment bonds" (II.i.63-64). The image recurs several times. "No, Bolingbroke," says Mowbray in I.iii, "if ever I were traitor,/ My name be blotted from the book of life" (I.iii.200-01). Richard sighs through blanched lips, "Time hath set a blot upon my pride" (III.ii.81) and later speaks of the record of Northumberland's offenses as including

> one heinous article,
> Containing the deposing of a king
> And cracking the strong warrant of an oath,
> Mark'd with a blot, damn'd in the book of heaven.
>
> (IV.i.232-35)

Carlisle and Aumerle in a duet harmonize the image with the two other motifs of gardening and generation:

Carlisle. The woe's to come; the children yet unborn
  Shall feel this day as sharp to them as thorn.

Aumerle. You holy clergymen, is there no plot
  To rid the realm of this pernicious blot?
                              (IV.i.321-24)

Aumerle's conspiracy which stems from this conversation
is itself spoken of by Bolingbroke in Aumerle's own
terms: "Thy abundant goodness shall excuse/ This
deadly blot in thy digressing son" (V.iii.64-65). The vividness of the image is increased by the presence elsewhere
of allusions to books and writing: "He should have had a
volume of farewells" (I.iv.18); "The purple testament
of bleeding war" (III.iii.93);

> Let's talk of graves, of worms, and epitaphs;
> Make dust our paper and with rainy eyes
> Write sorrow on the bosom of the earth
>   (III.ii.145-47)

(an interesting example of double association of imagery—tears, earth-grave, and writing); and in the deposition scene, when Richard calls for a mirror:

> I'll read enough,
> When I do see the very book indeed
> Where all my sins are writ, and that's myself.
>   (IV.i.272-74)

The blot image has a very direct relationship with another class of figures by which Shakespeare symbolizes
guilt or evil: that of a stain which must be washed away.
This image is most commonly associated with *Macbeth,*
because of the extraordinary vividness with which it is
used there. But the theme is much more insistent in
Richard II. Twice it is associated, as in *Macbeth,* with
blood:

> Yet, to wash your blood
> From off my hands, here in the view of men
> I will unfold some causes of your deaths.
> (III.i.5-7)

> I'll make a voyage to the Holy Land,
> To wash this blood off from my guilty hand.
> (V.vi.49-50)

Elsewhere the association is with the story of the cruci-
fixion, in a repetition of which Richard fancies he is the
sufferer:

> Nay, all of you that stand and look upon me
> Whilst that my wretchedness doth bait myself,
> Though some of you with Pilate wash your hands
> Showing an outward pity; yet you Pilates
> Have here deliver'd me to my sour cross,
> And water cannot wash away your sin.
> (IV.i.236-41)

But in this play the absolution of guilt requires not merely
the symbolic cleansing of bloody hands; it entails the
washing-off of the sacred ointment of royalty—the
ultimate expiation of kingly sin. The full measure of Richard's fall is epitomized in two further occurrences of the
metaphor, the first spoken when he is in the full flush of
arrogant confidence, the second when nemesis has over-
taken him:

> Not all the water in the rough rude sea
> Can wash the balm off from an anointed king.
> (III.ii.54-55)

> With mine own tears I wash away my balm,
> With mine own hands I give away my crown.
> (IV.i.206-07)

Whatever the exact context of the image of washing, one
suggestion certainly is present whenever it appears: a sug-

gestion of momentous change—the deposition of a monarch, the cleansing of a guilt-laden soul.

But the most unusual of all the symbols of unpleasantness which occur in *Richard II* is the use of the adjective *sour,* together with the repeated contrast of sweetness and sourness. A reader of the play understandably passes over the frequent use of *sweet* as a conventional epithet used both of persons and of things. But the word, however commonplace the specific phrases in which it occurs, has a role in the poetic design which decidedly is not commonplace, for it acts as a foil for the very unaccustomed use of its antonym. There is nothing less remarkable in Shakespeare than such phrases as "sweet Richard," "your sweet majesty," "sweet York, sweet husband," even such passages as this:

> And yet your fair discourse hath been as sugar,
> Making the hard way sweet and delectable.
> (II.iii.6-7)

But what is remarkable is the manner in which, in this play alone, mention of *sweet* so often invites mention of *sour:* "Things sweet to taste prove in digestion sour" (I.iii.235); "Speak sweetly, man, although thy looks be sour" (III.ii.193); "how sour sweet music is!" (V.v.42);

> Sweet love, I see, changing his property,
> Turns to the sourest and most deadly hate.
> (III.ii.135-36)

In addition to this repeated collocation of *sweet* and *sour,* the text of *Richard II* is notable for a persistent use, unmatched in any other play, of *sour* alone, as an adjective or verb:

> Not Gloucester's death, nor Hereford's banishment
> Not Gaunt's rebukes, nor England's private wrongs,
> . . . .
> Have ever made me sour my patient cheek.
> (II.i.165-66, 169)

"I'll set a bank of rue, sour herb of grace" (III.iv.105: this in significant collocation with the motif of tears, as the next is joined with the motif of washing)—"yet you Pilates/ Have here deliver'd me to my sour cross" (IV.i.239-40);

> The grand conspirator, Abbot of Westminster,
> With clog of conscience and sour melancholy
> Hath yielded up his body to the grave.
>
> (V.vi.19-21)

The occurrence of *sour* thus lends unmistakable irony to every occurrence of *sweet,* however unimportant the latter may be in itself. Even at a distance of a few lines, mention of one quality seems to invite mention of the other, as if Shakespeare could never forget that the sour is as frequent in life as the sweet:

Duchess. The word is short, but not so short as sweet;
  No word like "pardon" for kings' mouths so meet.

York. Speak it in French, King; say *"Pardonne moi."*

Duchess. Dost thou teach pardon pardon to destroy?
  Ah, my sour husband, my hard-hearted lord,
  That set'st the word itself against the word!

  (V.iii.116-21)

This contrapuntal use of *sweet* and *sour* is one of the most revealing instances of the artistry by which the poetry of *Richard II* is unified.[7]

Two more image themes, one of major importance, the

---

[7] The *sweet-sour* contrast occurs five times in *Richard II;* no more than twice in any other play.—Compare a similar juxtaposition in three of the sonnets:

  Such civil war is in my love and hate
    That I an accessary needs must be
  To that sweet thief which sourly robs from me.   (No. 35)

  O absence, what a torment wouldst thou prove
  Were it not thy sour leisure gave sweet leave
  To entertain the time with thoughts of love.   (No. 39)

other less conspicuous, remain to be mentioned. For one of them, we must return to the Tree of Jesse passage (I.ii.10-22) quoted above. This passage is the fountainhead of one of the chief themes of the play—the idea of legitimate succession, of hereditary kingship. We have already noticed how, largely as a result of this early elaborate metaphor, the close identification of the word *blood* with the idea of family descent deepens the symbolic significance of that word as it recurs through the play. In addition, as Miss Spurgeon has pointed out, in *Richard II* there are many other cognate images derived from the ideas of birth and generation, and of inheritance from father to son. The Tree of Jesse metaphor (whose importance Miss Spurgeon failed to note) is followed in the next scene by one involving the symbol of earth and thus suggesting the vital relationship between generation and patriotism:

> Then, England's ground, farewell; sweet soil, adieu;
> My mother, and my nurse, that bears me yet!
>
> (I.iii.305-06)

For sweetest things turn sourest by their deeds. (No. 94)

It is interesting to note that in the same two groups of sonnets in which the *sweet-sour* collocation occurs can be found another word whose use is noteworthy in *Richard II*:

> And dost him grace when clouds do blot the heaven (No. 28)

> So shall those blots that do with me remain,
> Without thy help by me be borne alone. (No. 36)

> But what's so blessed-fair that fears no blot? (No. 92)

> Where beauty's veil doth cover every blot (No. 95)

If we accept the hypothesis that at a given period in his life Shakespeare habitually thought of certain abstract ideas in terms of particular metaphors, there is a good case for dating these sonnets at the time of *Richard II*. Conventional though the sweet-sour and blot ideas may be, it is plain that Shakespeare had them constantly in mind when writing *Richard II*; they are a hallmark of the style of the play. Their occurrence in these sonnets is possibly significant.

In John of Gaunt's dying speech, earth and generation
again appear, significantly, in conjunction:

> This blessed plot, this earth, this realm, this England,
> This nurse, this teeming womb of royal kings.
>
> (II.i.50-51)

In her scene with Bagot and Bushy, the Queen dwells
constantly on the idea of birth:

> Some unborn sorrow, ripe in fortune's womb,
> Is coming towards me.
>
> . . . .
>
> Conceit is still deriv'd
> From some forefather grief; mine is not so,
> For nothing hath begot my something grief,
>
> . . . .
>
> So, Green, thou art the midwife to my woe,
> And Bolingbroke my sorrow's dismal heir.
> Now hath my soul brought forth her prodigy,
> And I, a gasping new-deliver'd mother,
> Have woe to woe, sorrow to sorrow join'd.
>
> (II.ii.10-11, 34-36, 62-66)

Richard's last soliloquy begins with the same sort of
elaborated conceit:

> My brain I'll prove the female to my soul,
> My soul the father; and these two beget
> A generation of still-breeding thoughts,
> And these same thoughts people this little world,
> In humors like the people of this world,
> For no thought is contented.
>
> (V.v.6-11)

And throughout the play, as Miss Spurgeon notes, "the
idea of inheritance from father to son . . . increases the
feeling of the inevitable and the foreordained, as also of
the unlimited consequences of action."

The word *crown* as the symbol of kingship is of course

common throughout the history plays. In *Richard II*,
however, the vividness of the image and the relevance
of its symbolism to the grand theme of the play are
heightened by several instances in which its metaphorical
function goes beyond that of a simple, conventional
metonymy:

> A thousand flatterers sit within thy crown,
> Whose compass is no bigger than thy head;
>
> (II.i.100-01)
>
>   for within the hollow crown
> That rounds the mortal temples of a king
> Keeps Death his court,
>
> (III.ii.160-62)
>
> But ere the crown he looks for live in peace,
> Ten thousand bloody crowns of mothers' sons
> Shall ill become the flower of England's face,
>
> (III.iii.94-96)
>
> Now is this golden crown like a deep well
> That owes two buckets, filling one another,
> The emptier ever dancing in the air,
> The other down, unseen, and full of water.
>
> (IV.i.183-86)

In addition, the actual image of the crown is made more
splendid by the occurrence, in the play's poetic fabric,
of several images referring to jewels:

> A jewel in a ten-times-barr'd-up chest
> Is a bold spirit in a loyal breast.
>
> (I.i.180-81)

Gaunt. The sullen passage of thy weary steps
  Esteem as foil wherein thou art to set
  The precious jewel of thy home return.

Bolingbroke. Nay, rather, every tedious stride I make
  Will but remember me what a deal of world
  I wander from the jewels that I love.

(I.iii.264-69)

And again: "I'll give my jewels for a set of beads" (III.iii.146), "This precious stone set in the silver sea" (II.i.46), and "Love to Richard/ Is a strange brooch in this all-hating world" (V.v.65-66).

Keeping in mind the leading metaphors and verbal motifs which I have reviewed—*earth-ground-land, blood,* pallor, garden, sun, tears, *tongue-speech-word, snake-venom,* physical injury and illness, *blot,* washing, *sweet-sour,* generation, and jewel-crown—it is profitable to re-read the whole play, noting especially how widely the various themes are distributed, and how frequently their strands cross to form new images. There is no extended passage of the text which is not tied in with the rest of the play by the occurrence of one or more of the familiar symbols. However, the images are not scattered with uniform evenness. As in *The Merchant of Venice,* metaphorical language tends to be concentrated at the emotional climaxes of *Richard II.* At certain crucial points in the action, a large number of the unifying image-threads appear almost simultaneously, so that our minds are virtually flooded with many diverse yet closely related ideas. The first part of II.i (the prophecy of Gaunt) offers a good instance of this rapid cumulation of symbols and the resultant heightening of emotional effect. The whole passage should be read as Shakespeare wrote it; here I list simply the phrases that reveal the various image themes, omitting a number which glance obliquely at the themes but are not directly connected with them:

line		
	5	the tongues of dying men
	7	words
	8	words
	12	the setting sun
	13	As the last taste of sweets, is sweetest last
	14	Writ in remembrance
	17	flattering sounds
	19	Lascivious meters, to whose venom sound
	23	Limps

41	This earth of majesty
44	infection
45	breed
46	This precious stone
49	less happier lands
50	This earth
51	This nurse, this teeming womb of royal kings
52	breed . . . birth
57	land . . . land
64	With inky blots and rotten parchment bonds
83	hollow womb
95	land
96	sick [followed by extended metaphor]
100	thy crown
103	thy land
104–05	thy grandsire . . . his son's son . . . his sons
110–13	this land . . . this land . . . landlord
116	ague
118	pale . . . blood
122	This tongue
126	blood
131	blood
134	To crop at once a too long withered flower
136	words
141	words
149	His tongue
153	The ripest fruit first falls
157	Which live like venom where no venom else

Thus in the first 157 lines of the scene we meet no less than twelve of the motifs of the play.

In another sort of harmonization, Shakespeare strikes a long chord containing a number of the image strains and then in the following minutes of the play echoes them separately. The "Dear earth, I do salute thee with my hand" speech at the beginning of III.ii interweaves at least six themes which shortly are unraveled into individual strands. The idea of the garden which is the framework for the whole speech (6-26) recurs in the line "To ear the land that hath some hope to grow" (212). The repeated references to weeping in the initial speech ("I weep for joy" . . . "with her tears" . . . weeping") are echoed in "as if the world were all dissolv'd to tears" (108) and "rainy eyes" (146). Richard's "Nor with thy sweets comfort his ravenous sense" (13) is recalled in Scroop's "Sweet love . . . changing his property,/ Turns to the sourest and most deadly hate" (135-36) and in Richard's "speak sweetly, man, although thy looks be sour" (193) and "that sweet way I was in to despair" (205). The lurking adder and the venom which the spiders suck up (20, 14) find their sequel in Richard's later "vipers . . . snakes . . . that sting my heart" (129-31). The double tongue (21) is succeeded by "discomfort guides my tongue" (65), "my care-tun'd tongue" (92), the tongue that "hath but a heavier tale to say" (197), and the one whose flatteries wound the King at the end of the scene (216). The initial reference to wounding ("though rebels wound thee with their horses' hoofs,") is succeeded by "death's destroying wound" (139); and the same general motif of bodily hurt is carried out by "this ague fit of fear is overblown" (190), which links the disease-theme to that of the garden. Finally, the frequent use of *earth* in Richard's first speech (6, 10, 12, 24) prepares the ear for the five-times-repeated occurrence of the idea (earth . . . ground . . . lands . . . earth . . . ground) in the "Let's talk of graves, of worms, and epitaphs" speech. This progressive analysis of the components of the original chord of images is accompanied by a succession of other images not included in the chord: an extended sun metaphor (36-50), a reference to washing (54-55), the most famous instance of the pallor-blood motif (76-81), two references to the crown (59, 115), and two allusions to writing (81, 146-47). And thus the mind is crowded with a richly overlapping series of images.

Another example of the close arraying of image patterns (without the initial chord) occurs in III.iii.84-99:

> Yet know, my master, God omnipotent,
> Is mustering in his clouds on our behalf
> Armies of pestilence; and they shall strike   (illness)
> Your children yet unborn and unbegot,   (generation)
> That lift your vassal hands against my head
> And threat the glory of my precious crown.   (crown)
> Tell Bolingbroke—for yon methinks he stands—
> That every stride he makes upon my land   (earth)
> Is dangerous treason. He is come to open
> The purple testament of bleeding war;   (books, blood)
> But ere the crown he looks for live in peace,   (crown)
> Ten thousand bloody crowns of mothers' sons
>   (blood, crown, generation)
> Shall ill become the flower of England's face,   (garden)
> Change the complexion of her maid-pale peace   (pallor)
> To scarlet indignation, and bedew
> Her pastures' grass with faithful English blood.   (blood)

Curiously, the deposition scene, though it is rich enough in individual appearances of the familiar themes, does not mesh them so closely as one might expect.

A final aspect of the use of iterative imagery in *Richard II* is the manner in which a particularly important passage is prepared for by the interweaving into the poetry, long in advance, of inconspicuous but repeated hints of the imagery which is to dominate that passage. The method is exactly analogous to that by which in a symphony a melody appears, at first tentatively, indeed almost unnoticed, first in one choir of the orchestra, then another, until ultimately it comes to its reward as the theme of a climactic section. In such a manner is the audience prepared, although unconsciously, for Richard's last grandiose speech. One takes little note of the first timid appearance of a reference to beggary or bankruptcy in Bolingbroke's "Or with pale beggar-fear impeach my height" (I.i.189). But in the second act the motif recurs:

    Be York the next that must be bankrupt so!
    Though death be poor, it ends a mortal woe,
                                (II.i.151-52)

and a hundred lines later the idea is repeated: "The
king's grown bankrupt, like a broken man" (II.i.257).
The haunting dread of destitution, then, however
obliquely alluded to, is a recurrent theme, and adds its
small but perceptible share to the whole atmosphere
of impending disaster. It forms the burden of two plaints
by Richard midway in the play:

    Let's choose executors and talk of wills;
    And yet not so; for what can we bequeath
    Save our deposed bodies to the ground?
    Our lands, our lives and all are Bolingbroke's.
                                (III.ii.148-51)

    I'll give my jewels for a set of beads,
    My gorgeous palace for a hermitage,
    My gay apparel for an almsman's gown,
    My figur'd goblets for a dish of wood,
    My scepter for a palmer's walking-staff,
    My subjects for a pair of carved saints,
    And my large kingdom for a little grave.
                                (III.iii.146-52)

But the time is not ripe for the climactic utterance of
this motif. It disappears, to return for a moment in a verbal hint in the deposition scene:

    Let it command a mirror hither straight,
    That it may show me what a face I have
    Since it is bankrupt of his majesty.
                                (IV.i.264-66)
    Being so great, I have no need to beg.
                                (IV.i.308)

The Duchess of York momentarily takes up the motif: "A

beggar begs that never begg'd before" (V.iii.77), and
Bolingbroke replies:

> Our scene is alt'red from a serious thing,
> And now chang'd to "The Beggar and the King."
>   (V.iii.78-79)

And now finally comes the climax toward which these
fleeting references have been pointing: a climax which il-
luminates the purpose and direction of the earlier talk
about beggary and bankruptcy:

> Thoughts tending to content flatter themselves
> That they are not the first of fortune's slaves,
> Nor shall not be the last; like silly beggars
> Who, sitting in the stocks, refuge their shame,
> That many have and others must sit there;
> And in this thought they find a kind of ease;
> Bearing their own misfortunes on the back
> Of such as have before endur'd the like.
> Thus play I in one person many people,
> And none contented. Sometimes am I king;
> Then treasons make me wish myself a beggar;
> And so I am. Then crushing penury
> Persuades me I was better when a king.
>
>   (V.v.23-35)

A similar process can be traced in the repetition of
the word *face,* which, besides being obviously connected with the idea of Richard's personal comeliness,
underscores the hovering sense the play contains of the
illusory quality of life, of the deceptions that men accept as if they were reality. The word occurs casually,
unremarkably, often without metaphorical intent; but its
frequent appearance not only reinforces, however subtly,
a dominant idea of the play, but also points toward a
notable climax. "Mowbray's face" (I.i.195) . . . "Nor
never look upon each other's face" (I.iii.185) . . . "the
northeast wind/ Which then blew bitterly against our

faces" (I.iv.6-7) . . . "His face thou hast, for even so look'd he" (II.i.176) . . . "Frighting her pale-fac'd villages with war" (II.iii.93) . . . "The pale-fac'd moon looks bloody on the earth" (II.iv.10) . . . "His treasons will sit blushing in his face" (III.ii.51) . . . "But now the blood of twenty thousand men/ Did triumph in my face" (III.ii.76-77) . . .

> Ten thousand bloody crowns of mothers' sons
> Shall ill become the flower of England's face.
> (III.iii.95-96)

Meanwhile Bushy has introduced the corollary idea of shadow:

> Each substance of a grief hath twenty shadows,
> Which shows like grief itself, but is not so
> (II.ii.14-15)
> Which, look'd on as it is, is nought but shadows
> Of what it is not.
> (II.ii.23-24)

The related themes merge as, in retrospect, it is plain they were destined to do, in the deposition scene:

> Was this face the face
> That every day under his household roof
> Did keep ten thousand men? Was this the face
> That, like the sun, did make beholders wink?
> Is this the face which fac'd so many follies,
> That was at last out-fac'd by Bolingbroke?
> A brittle glory shineth in this face;
> As brittle as the glory is the face,
> For there it is, crack'd in an hundred shivers.
> Mark, silent king, the moral of this sport,
> How soon my sorrow hath destroy'd my face.

Bolingbroke. The shadow of your sorrow hath destroy'd
The shadow of your face.

Richard.   Say that again.
The shadow of my sorrow! Ha! let's see.

(IV.i.280-93)

And thus from beginning to end *Richard II* is, in a double sense of which Shakespeare would have approved, a play on words. As countless writers have affirmed, it is entirely fitting that this should be so. King Richard, a poet *manqué,* loved words more dearly than he did his kingdom, and his tragedy is made the more moving by the style, half rhetorical, half lyrical, in which it is told. Splendid words, colorful metaphors, pregnant poetic symbols in this drama possess their own peculiar irony.

But the language of *Richard II,* regarded from the viewpoint I have adopted in this paper, has another significance, entirely apart from its appropriateness to theme. It suggests the existence of a vital relationship between two leading characteristics of Shakespeare's poetic style: the uncontrolled indulgence of verbal wit in the earlier plays and the use of great image-themes in the plays of his maturity. As I suggested in the beginning, wordplay and iterative imagery are but two different manifestations of a single faculty in the creative imagination—an exceedingly well-developed sense of association. In *Richard II* we see the crucial intermediate stage in the development, or perhaps more accurately the utilization, of Shakespeare's singular associative gift. In such passages as John of Gaunt's speech upon his name, we are reminded of the plays which preceded this from Shakespeare's pen. But, except on certain occasions when they contribute to the characterization of the poet-king, the brief coruscations of verbal wit which marked the earlier plays are less evident than formerly. On the other hand, when we stand back and view the play as a whole, its separate movements bound so closely together by image themes, we are enabled to anticipate the future development of Shakespeare's art. The technique that is emerging in *Richard II* is the technique that eventually will have its part in producing the poetry of *Lear* and *Mac-*

beth and *Othello*. Here we have the method: the tricks of repetition, of cumulative emotional effect, of interweaving and reciprocal coloration. What is yet to come is the full mastery of the artistic possibilities of such a technique. True, thanks to its tightly interwoven imagery *Richard II* has a poetic unity that is unsurpassed in any of the great tragedies; so far as structure is concerned, Shakespeare has levied from iterative language about all the aid that it will give. The great improvement will come in another region. Taken individually, in *Richard II* Shakespeare's images lack the qualities which they will possess in the later plays. They are, many of them, too conventional for our tastes; they are marred by diffuseness; they bear too many lingering traces of Shakespeare's affection for words for words' sake. The ultimate condensation, the compression of a universe of meaning into a single bold metaphor, remains to be achieved. But in the best imagery of *Richard II*, especially in those passages which combine several themes into a richly complex pattern of meaning, we receive abundant assurance that Shakespeare will be equal to his task. The process of welding language and thought into a single entity is well begun.

Derek Traversi

From *Shakespeare from "Richard II"*
to "Henry V"

From the moment of Richard's descent, "like glister-
ing Phaethon," into the "base court" his fate is sub-
stantially sealed. The last part of the play confirms his
fall, investing it with the tragic quality that surrounds
the misfortunes of an anointed king, and consummates
the ruthless process of his rival's rise to power. After
the short scene (III.iv), conveying the Queen's meeting
with her Gardeners, which clearly answers to a certain
"symbolic" design, using an elaborately prolonged metaphor to underline the relationship between Richard's
tragedy and the disorder of his realm, the return to the
main action (IV.i) is marked by a further access of
realism, the fitting accompaniment of the new power.
The quarrel between the lords, occasioned by Bagot's accusation of Aumerle for his part in Gloucester's death, is
both elaborate in expression and detached, realistic in
presentation. Aumerle, in spite of his defiance, is aware
of weakness; the lords who turn against him, invoking
"truth" and "honor," already have an eye to their future
good. On either side, the expression is overpitched,
strained as though conscious of its own falsity; the ring-
ing rhetoric—in which an echo, as it were, of the opening scenes can still be detected—turns into shabby inter-
change of snarl and countersnarl which only Bolingbroke

From *Shakespeare from Richard II to Henry V* by Derek Traversi.
Stanford, Calif.: Stanford University Press, 1957; London: Hollis &
Carter, Ltd., 1958. Reprinted by permission of Hollis & Carter, Ltd.

is detached enough to watch without illusion. When he intervenes, with a pacifying gesture to insinuate Mowbray's return, it is left to Carlisle to evoke the values implied in his former rival's crusading venture and—at the same time—to announce the crusader's death. The counterpart of his announcement, valid in the present, is York's proclamation of Bolingbroke as king, briefly accepted by the latter with his "In God's name, I'll ascend the regal throne."

The proclamation is immediately followed, in accordance with the main design, by Carlisle's assertion of Richard's divine right, and by his prophecy which looks forward to a future of civil war:

> And if you crown him, let me prophesy:
> The blood of English shall manure the ground,
> And future ages groan for this foul act;
> Peace shall go sleep with Turks and infidels,
> And in this seat of peace tumultuous wars
> Shall kin with kin and kind with kind confound;
> Disorder, horror, fear and mutiny
> Shall here inhabit, and this land be call'd
> The field of Golgotha, and dead men's skulls.
>
> (IV.i.136-44)

The speech presents a community of style with the patriotic utterances of Gaunt, and the culminating reference to Golgotha will shortly be echoed by Richard himself. Its careful elaboration is intended to stand out against the blunt realism of Bolingbroke, here triumphant in the very process of creating for itself the cause of future tragedy. That realism, meanwhile, takes control in Northumberland's sharp comment,

> Well have you argued, sir; and, for your pains,
> Of capital treason we arrest you here,
>
> (IV.i.150-51)

which Henry caps by summoning Richard himself and by

pointing openly to the political ground of his whole proceeding:

> Fetch hither Richard, that in common view
> He may surrender; *so we shall proceed*
> *Without suspicion.*
>
> (IV.i.155-57)

Finally, Henry's realistic estimate of his position is made
clear in his sharp admonition to the arrested lords:

> Little are we beholding to your love,
> And little look'd for at your helping hands.
>
> (IV.i.160-61)

From the first moment, the new king is shrewdly aware
of the unsure foundations upon which his power rests.

The entry of Richard, stressing the note of treachery
supremely associated, not for the first time, with the evo-
cation of Judas, is characteristically poised between
pathos and emptiness. His situation is genuinely pathetic,
and the emotion stands out, up to a point, against the
cold purposefulness that surrounds him; yet it is impossible not to feel that the comparison of the crown to
a deep well in which two buckets alternately rise and
fall is too shallow to carry the weight of feeling which
the speaker desires to lay upon it. It is no accident that
Richard's elaborate renunciation of rights already surrendered is set against his rival's plain insistence on the
end in view:

> I thought you had been willing to resign.
>
> . . . .
>
> Are you contented to resign the crown?
>
> (IV.i.189, 199)

In Richard's attitude, complex and contradictory by comparison, the germs of many later Shakespearean developments can be discerned. Pathetic and yet too self-con-

scious to be entirely tragic, sincere and yet engaged in acting his own sincerity, possessed of true feeling and elaborately artificial in expressing it, Richard is the distant predecessor of more than one hero of the mature tragedies, who suffer in acute self-consciousness and whose tragedy expresses itself in terms that clearly point to the presence of the weakness that has been, in part, its cause.

The utterances of the deposed king turn, indeed, not merely on natural grief, but on a sense of vanity—*nothingness*—which the very artificiality of its expression confirms and, paradoxically, deepens:

> Ay, no; no, ay; for I must *nothing* be;
> . . . .
> Make me, that *nothing* have, with *nothing* grieved,
> And thou with all pleased, that hast all achieved!
> Long mayst thou live in Richard's seat to sit,
> And soon lie Richard in an earthy pit!
>   (IV.i.200, 215-18)

We must feel here that the word nearest to the speaker's heart is, after all his elaborations, *nothing,* and that his mood issues in an intense craving for death; but the nothingness—it must be added—is also reflected, in the last analysis, in Bolingbroke's absorbing pursuit of power. Richard's attitude to political responsibility is, of course, extreme, in a sense self-indulgent; but it is also relevant, and not least to the usurper who is now, with little but devices of policy in his mind, replacing him on the throne. *Nothing, nothing*: in the long run any relevant political conception will have to face the challenge implied in that word, and confirmed by the behavior shown in this play. As we read these elaborate expressions of feeling, we realize that the intricate rhetorical devices of the earlier plays and of Shakespeare's contemporaries are in the process of being turned, definitely though still without complete consciousness, into an instrument for the simultaneous expression of different aspects of reality.

The accusation of Richard by Northumberland, which now follows, emphasizes the royal tragedy rather than the personal disaster. Having abdicated, he has drawn upon himself sympathy; isolated and helpless, he appears less as the self-indulgent monarch than as the victim of a betrayal which his failings cannot excuse. To his final, exhausted "What more remains?" there corresponds, however, not pity, but the remorseless persecution of the accusation against him:

> No more, but that you read
> These accusations and these grievous crimes,
>   (IV.i.221-22)

followed by an admission that the real end of this proceeding is to justify the usurper in the eyes of the world:

> That, by confessing them, the souls of men
> May deem that you are worthily deposed.
>   (IV.i.225-26)

Surrounded by this ruthless calculation, Richard's weakness becomes subsidiary to his tragedy as king deposed; his reply to Northumberland raises to a fresh level of poignancy the Christian reference which, more especially from now on, runs as a principal thread of feeling through the tragedy:

> Nay, all of you that stand and look upon,
> Whilst that my wretchedness doth bait myself,
> Though some of you with Pilate wash your hands
> Showing an outward pity; yet you Pilates
> Have here deliver'd me to my sour cross,
> And water cannot wash away your sin.
>   (IV.i.236-41)

Our reaction to this is necessarily double. Richard is still exhibiting his emotions, playing with feelings the seriousness of which we cannot, in view of his weakness and consequent responsibility for his state, fully accept; and

yet the betrayal, based on the calculation that everywhere surrounds him, is indefensible and its effect deepened by the fact that it is a king whom his subjects,
sworn to loyalty, are deserting.

Richard himself is not without insight in his misfortunes. When he says, in reply to Northumberland's piti-
less "My lord, dispatch; read o'er these articles,"

> Mine eyes are full of tears, I cannot see:
> And yet salt water blinds them not so much
> But they can see a sort of traitors here,
>   (IV.i.243-45)

the play with images cannot cover the fact that a truth is
being expressed. It is the tragedy of betrayal, as well
as that of fallen royalty, that is being enacted round his
person; and the treachery, moreover, is doubly personal
because Richard, by his past irresponsibility, has betrayed
himself before he was in turn betrayed:

> Nay, if I turn mine eyes upon myself,
> I find myself a traitor with the rest.
>   (IV.i.246-47)

Richard has betrayed the office which he has unworthily
held, and the betrayal has bred treachery around him.
Bolingbroke, in due course, will prove to be similarly divided between the political virtues that are his to a degree never possessed by Richard, and a desire for power
which is ominously shared by the court to time-serving
and ambitious lords who accompany his rise to authority.
The conception, in all its possible variety, is only
sketched and faintly indicated here; but the whole series
of following plays will be largely occupied with exploring
it.

Beneath the conventionality of Richard's expression at
this stage lies, indeed, a genuine effort to define his relation to the tragic course of events. This culminates in his
request for a looking glass, in which once more artificiality, conscious self-exhibition, and true self-explora-

tion are typically blended. Henry, now secure master of the situation, contemptuously accedes to the latest emotional trick of his victim, whilst Northumberland, as ever, ruthlessly presses the charge:

> Read o'er this paper while the glass doth come,

and stresses the political motive behind his disapproval of his master's careless concession:

> The commons will not then be satisfied.

When the mirror is at last brought, Richard contemplates his features with a kind of tragic self-analysis. This opens, as he breaks the glass, in a typically artificial statement: "How soon my sorrow hath destroy'd my face"; but the comment offered by Bolingbroke points to a deeper contrast between shadow and reality, which is not without tragic content:

> The shadow of your sorrow hath destroy'd
> The shadow of your face.
>
> (IV.i.291-92)

This in turn produces from Richard, beyond the play on the related concepts of "shadow," "sun," and "substance," an indication of the deeper roots of his tragedy:

> Say that again.
> The shadow of my sorrow! ha! let's see:
> 'Tis very true, my grief lies all within;
> And these external manners of laments
> Are merely shadows to the unseen grief
> That swells with silence in the tortured soul;
> There lies the substance.
>
> (IV.i.292-98)

One can trace in Shakespeare a process by which literary artifice, expanding in complexity and psychological correspondence, becomes an instrument of self-analysis; and the person of Richard, as revealed here, represents an important stage in this process. The outer forms of grief are "shadows" of the "substance" within, in Richard as they will later be in Hamlet; between the tragic content of the two characters there is, of course, no comparison, but a process of development may possibly be traced by which the literary artifice of the one is transformed into the true complexity of the other. Once more, the later plays in the series will throw light upon the nature of this transformation. For the moment, Richard's expression of tragedy leads to the final breakdown which accompanies his request for "leave to go"

> Whither you will, so I were from your sights,

in which the measureless bitterness of his situation is simply expressed.

By the opening of the last act, the central dramatic contrast has been fully developed, and the result, as the action moves towards its foreseen conclusion, is a certain drop in tension. To Richard in his decline, the felicity he formerly enjoyed appears as a "dream" from which he has now awakened to "the truth of what we are":

> A king of beasts, indeed; if aught but beasts,
> I had been still a happy king of men.
>
> (V.i.35-36)

These meditations are interrupted once more by the entry of stern reality, in the form of Northumberland, who arrives to convey the deposed king to Pomfret. Richard's reaction, prophetic in tone, is linked with the later development of the series:

> The time shall not be many hours of age
> More than it is, ere foul sin gathering head
> Shall break into corruption: thou shalt think,
> Though he divide the realm and give thee half,
> It is too little, helping him to all;
> And he shall think that thou, which know'st the way
> To plant unrightful kings, wilt know again,

Being ne'er so little urged, another way
To pluck him headlong from the usurped throne.

(V.i.57-65)

Here, at last, Richard penetrates to a vision of the piti-
less nature of political processes in the world of "beasts"
to which he has become, too late, alive. The action in
Henry IV—the counterplay of intrigue between powers
haunted by past guilt in the form of a trustless present—
is here foreshadowed. Henry, having taught his associates
to overthrow a king, will always fear that the lesson may
be turned against himself; and his friends, in turn, will at
once anticipate the consequences against themselves of
this fear, and crave to extend the power which they have
so precariously won. After this prophecy which Northumberland grimly accepts—"My guilt be on my head,
and there an end"—the final parting of Richard and his
queen is a thin, artificial affair which leads us, however,
further along the road of the foreseen tragedy.

The following scene, in the Duke of York's palace,
points equally to the inevitable conclusion. York's account of the contrasted entries into London of Bolingbroke and Richard stresses, on the one hand, the former's
politic submission to the populace—

he, from the one side to the other turning,
Bareheaded, lower than his proud steed's neck,
Bespake them thus: "I thank you, countrymen"

(V.ii.18-20)

—and, on the other, the desertion of Richard, on whose
"*sacred* head" dust was thrown, and in the reference to
whose "gentle sorrow," "grief and patience," we may perhaps see that echo of the Christian passion which, whilst
never applicable to the person of the victim, seems none
the less present in Shakespeare's treatment of the betrayed king. The suggestion has already been implied
in Richard's own references to Judas; but as his tragedy moves from the realm of sentiment toward a dread-
ful reality, so does it gather emotional force. We are mov-

ing into a harsh world of political realities, in which
conscience and human feeling have small place: the world
to which York refers when he says:

> But heaven hath a hand in these events,
> To whose high will we bound our calm contents.
> To Bolingbroke are we sworn subjects now.
> (V.ii.37-39)

The mood is one of fatalism rather than of acceptance,
of subjection to events rather than of a true concordance
with them; but whether the issues which "heaven" will
bring to birth are propitious or otherwise, time alone
will show. Meanwhile, the first sign of the new order, developed in a spirit that recalls the conscious formalism of
the *Henry VI* plays, is York's readiness to impeach his
son for treason to his new master. Sweeping aside his
wife's plea, and apparently unmoved by the prospect of
being left heirless, he is ready to sacrifice his own blood
for a usurper who has only used him as an instrument
and who will from now on distrust him as a possible rival.
Fear is the mainspring of his action, as it is a sign of the
new order; it is as though Richard's recent prophecy were
already on the way to becoming reality.

The reappearance of the new king (V.iii), with his suggestion that his son is a "plague" hanging over him in
punishment for sin, also introduces a theme prominent
in later plays. It is not, however, developed, nor is the
mention of the "sparks of better hope" also seen by his
father in Hal's behavior. The cynicism of the dissolute
prince's attitude to the Oxford jousts is, as Percy describes it, not without meaning:

> His answer was, he would unto the stews,
> And from the common'st creature pluck a glove,
> And wear it as a favor; and with that
> He would unhorse the lustiest challenger.
> (V.iii.16-19)

This, perhaps, is more significant than may appear. The

Prince's reaction is at once an assertion of his own degradation, and a sardonic comment on the decorative but
empty tournament world which the events of this play
have so effectively shattered. Besides the obvious show
of dissolution in Henry's son, the report implies a repu-
diation of verbal dignities in a world in which the most
venerable concepts—including that of "honor" itself—
are becoming subject to compromise: a world of chivalry
already in decay under Richard and finally killed by his
rival's accession. The Prince will, in due course, make
the best of the new order of unprejudiced realism, more
limited and less artificial than its predecessor, into
which he is born; his activities, in the next play, in the
taverns and streets of London will testify at once to the
baseness around him, in which he participates, and to the
greater breadth and firmness, when compared with Richard and even with Hotspur, of his contacts with life.

All this, however, belongs to the future, and the main
action is conducted, in the meantime, on a perfunctory
level, as in the following contest between York and his
duchess for his son's life. On this, indeed, Henry seems
to say the last word with his brief:

> Our scene is alter'd from a serious thing,
> And now chang'd to "The Beggar and the King."
> (V.iii.78-79)

where the incredible theatrical effect is surely placed.
The whole of this part of the play suggests that the
author's interest in his creation, temporarily exhausted
after the presentation of contrasted orders and personali-
ties, was now flagging.

Richard's last long speech (V.v) returns to, and in
some sense sums up, the personal tragedy now being
wound up against the growing somberness and disinte-
gration of which he has been at once the cause and the
victim. Like so much else in this play, it gives a peculiar impression of convention shading almost imper-
ceptibly into a sustained attempt at self-analysis and the
expression of true feeling. The opening parallel,

> I have been studying how I may compare
> This prison where I live unto the world,
>
> (V.v.1-2)

is thoroughly artificial; the rhythm falls to an accustomed
beat, and the succession of ideas is rather mechanical
than revealing. The reference to the Christian axioms,
which follows, though it has parallels in the play, is
scarcely less abstract; the general impression is of
aphoristic wisdom using familiar illustrations—the prisoner in the stocks, the actor on the stage—to point an
attitude which strikes us less as a tragic reflection than
as an academic exercise in poetic pessimism. Only as
the speech moves to its climax is a deeper note attained, a more felt reference to a universal human situation touched upon, when Richard returns to the idea of
nothing which has been so persistently present as a background, expressed and implied, to his thoughts:

> whate'er I be,
> Nor I nor any man that but man is
> With nothing shall be pleased, till he be eased
> With being nothing.
>
> (V.v.38-41)

Here, at least, in the balance of "any man that but man
is," followed by the echo of "pleased" and "eased," and
the opposition of "nothing" to "nothing," is a serious
attempt to make expression respond to feeling, in something like a tragic statement about life. It is noteworthy,
moreover, that this increase in depth is immediately followed, most improbably in terms of realism, by the playing of "music," in what we may consider a first dim indication of one of the mature Shakespearean symbols. The
harmony, suitably contradictory in its effects, like the
speaker's thoughts—

> how sour sweet music is,
> When time is broke and no proportion kept!
>
> (V.v.42-43)

resolves itself, in an attempt at more subtle analysis, into a complicated parallel:

> here have I the daintiness of ear
> To check time broke in a disorder'd string;
> But for the concord of my state and time
> Had not an ear to hear my true time broke.
>   (V.v.45-48)

Beneath the artificial balance of the phrasing, the speaker is at least attempting to make a valid statement of his condition, and in the observation which follows—"I wasted time, and now doth time waste me"—he almost succeeds. Even the elaborate expression has a certain justification in terms of character, as the utterance of one who has habitually *acted* on his royal stage, observed, as it were, the effect of his attitudes with an eye to public effect and personal gratification:

> Thus play I in one person many people,
> And none contented.
>   (V.v.31-32)

The devices of this speech, to be fully convincing, would need to be filled out with personal experience to a degree never here attained; but, imperfect as it is, the meditation does foreshadow later developments in the presentation of the tragic hero. Certainly, the murder which follows is, by comparison, no more than a pedestrian piece of melodramatic writing. Perhaps Richard's last individual word is spoken in the bitter comment to the Groom on the value of human titles and honors: "The cheapest of us is ten groats too dear." This is at once legitimate comment and the confirmation of a character, the evaluation of an inhuman political situation and the expression of a king who has always tended to find in an effective show of cynicism a refuge from the collapse of his self-indulgent sentiments.

The final scene (V.vi) rounds off the play in a mood of foreboding and the anticipation of thwarted purposes.

Already it is clear that Bolingbroke's crime, tacitly admitted as such, will bring neither personal nor political peace. The "latest news," announced by his own mouth, is that the "rebels"—not now his own supporters, but those who have in turn risen against his usurped power—have "consumed with fire" the town of Cicester. On all sides, executions respond to renewed civil strife; the heads of numerous "traitors"—so called by him who has just ceased to be such—are on their way to London, and the spiritual power, henceforth to be increasingly involved in political intrigues, is curtailed by the death of the Abbot of Westminster and by the banishment of Carlisle, in whom Henry himself recognizes the presence of virtue:

> High sparks of honor in thee have I seen.

Upon this catalogue of mischance and cross-purposes the murderers of Richard enter with his body, not to be commended for their "deed of slander," but yet to pin bluntly upon their master the guilt to which he himself admits:

Exton. From your own mouth, my lord, did I this deed.

Bolingbroke. They love not poison that do poison need,
  Nor do I thee: though I did wish him dead,
  I hate the murderer, love him murdered.
                                    (V.vi.37-40)

Beneath the careful balance of the phrasing, the presence of "the guilt of conscience" is firmly asserted in the new king, and his last words announce the intention, which will accompany him as an unfulfilled aspiration to his death, to redeem this "guilt" by a spiritual enterprise in "the Holy Land." This aspiration, the failure to fulfill it, and its transformation into a more limited political purpose, are the themes of the plays to follow.

Suggested References

The number of possible references is vast and grows alarmingly. (The *Shakespeare Quarterly* devotes a substantial part of one issue each year to a list of the previous year's work, and *Shakespeare Survey*—an annual publication—includes a substantial review of recent scholarship, as well as an occasional essay surveying a few decades of scholarship on a chosen topic.) Russell Fraser, the editor of the Signet Classic *King Lear*, offers this warning: "These comments may be ventured, regarding the titles listed here, and the critical selections above. First, no work of criticism, however excellent in itself, is to be taken as rivaling in importance, much less as supplanting, the thing it criticizes. The play's the thing! and not the commentaries thereon. Second, any work of criticism, and particularly to the degree that it is excellent, ought to be scrutinized with a cold eye whenever it pretends to the making of a definitive judgment. In the interpretation of Shakespeare, no comment is sacrosanct or final. Let the reader beware, therefore; and let him also take heart. 'Judgment, like other faculties, is improved by practice, and its advancement hindered by submission to dictatorial decisions, as the memory grows torpid by the use of a table book.' Thus Dr. Johnson."

1. Shakespeare's Times

Byrne, M. St. Clare. *Elizabethan Life in Town and Country*. Rev. ed. New York: Barnes & Noble, Inc., 1961. Chapters on manners, beliefs, education, etc., with illustrations.

Craig, Hardin. *The Enchanted Glass: the Elizabethan Mind in Literature*. New York and London: Oxford University Press, 1936. The Elizabethan intellectual climate.

Joseph, B. L. *Shakespeare's Eden: The Commonwealth of England 1558–1629*. New York: Barnes & Noble, Inc., 1971. An account of the social, political, economic, and cultural life of England.

Nicoll, Allardyce (ed.). *The Elizabethans*. London: Cambridge Univ. Press, 1957. An anthology of Elizabethan writings, especially valuable for its illustrations from paintings, title pages, etc.

Shakespeare's England. Oxford: Clarendon Press, 1916. 2 vols. A large collection of scholarly essays on a wide variety of topics (e.g., astrology, costume, gardening, horsemanship), with special attention to Shakespeare's references to these topics.

Tillyard, E. M. W. *The Elizabethan World Picture*. London: Chatto & Windus, 1943; New York: the Macmillan Company, 1944. A brief account of some Elizabethan ideas of the universe.

Wilson, John Dover (ed.). *Life in Shakespeare's England*. 2nd ed. New York: The Macmillan Company, 1913. An anthology of Elizabethan writings on the countryside, superstition, education, the court, etc.

2.   Shakespeare

Barnet, Sylvan. *A Short Guide to Shakespeare*. New York: Harcourt Brace Jovanovich, Inc., 1974. An introduction to all of the works and to the traditions behind them.

Bentley, Gerald E. *Shakespeare: A Biographical Handbook*. New Haven, Conn.: Yale University Press, 1961. The facts about Shakespeare, with virtually no conjecture intermingled.

Bradby, Anne (ed.). *Shakespeare Criticism, 1919–1935*. London: Oxford University Press, 1936. A small anthology of excellent essays on the plays.

Bush, Geoffrey Douglas. *Shakespeare and the Natural Condition*. Cambridge, Mass.: Harvard Univ. Press, 1956; London: Oxford University Press, 1956. A short, sensitive account of Shakespeare's view of "Nature," touching most of the works.

Chute, Marchette. *Shakespeare of London*. E. P. Dutton & Co., Inc., 1949. A readable biography fused with portraits of Stratford and London life.

Clemen, Wolfgang H. *The Development of Shakespeare's Imagery*. Cambridge, Mass.: Harvard Univ. Press, 1951. (Originally published in German, 1936.) A temperate account of a subject often abused.

Chambers, E. K. *William Shakespeare: A Study of Facts and Problems*. London: Oxford University Press, 1930. 2 vols. An invaluable, detailed reference work; not for the casual reader.

Craig, Hardin. *An Interpretation of Shakespeare*. New York: Citadel Press, 1948. A scholar's book designed for the layman. Comments on all the works.

Dean, Leonard F. (ed.). *Shakespeare: Modern Essays in Criticism*. New York: Oxford University Press, 1957. Mostly Mid-twentieth-century critical studies, covering Shakespeare's artistry.

Granville-Barker, Harley. *Prefaces to Shakespeare*. Princeton, N. J.: Princeton University Press, 1946–47. 2 vols. Essays on ten plays by a scholarly man of the theater.

Harbage, Alfred. *As They Liked It*. New York: The Macmillan Company, 1947. A sensitive, long essay on Shakespeare, morality, and the audience's expectations.

———. *William Shakespeare: A Reader's Guide*. New York: Farrar, Straus, 1963. Extensive comments, scene by scene, on fourteen plays.

Ridler, Anne Bradby (ed.). *Shakespeare Criticism. 1935–1960*. New York and London: Oxford University Press, 1963. An excellent continuation of the anthology edited earlier by Miss Bradby (see above).

Schoenbaum, S. *Shakespeare's Lives*. Oxford: Clarendon Press, 1970. A review of the evidence, and an examination of many biographies, including those by Baconians and other heretics.

————. *William Shakespeare: A Compact Documentary Life*. New York: Oxford University Press, 1977. A readable presentation of all that the documents tell us about Shakespeare.

Smith, D. Nichol (ed.). *Shakespeare Criticism*. New York: Oxford University Press, 1916. A selection of criticism from 1623 to 1840, ranging from Ben Jonson to Thomas Carlyle.

Spencer, Theodore. *Shakespeare and the Nature of Man*. New York: The Macmillan Company, 1942. Shakespeare's plays in relation to Elizabethan thought.

Stoll, Elmer Edgar. *Shakespeare and Other Masters*. Cambridge, Mass.: Harvard University Press, 1940; London: Oxford University Press, 1940. Essays on tragedy, comedy, and aspects of dramaturgy, with special reference to some of Shakespeare's plays.

Traversi, D. A. *An Approach to Shakespeare*. Rev. ed. New York: Doubleday & Co., Inc., 1956. An analysis of the plays, beginning with words, images, and themes, rather than with characters.

Van Doren, Mark. *Shakespeare*. New York: Henry Holt & Company, Inc., 1939. Brief, perceptive readings of all of the plays.

Whitaker, Virgil K. *Shakespeare's Use of Learning*. San Marino, Calif.: Huntington Lib., 1953. A study of the relation of Shakespeare's reading to his development as a dramatist.

3. Shakespeare's Theater

Adams, John Cranford. *The Globe Playhouse*. Rev. ed. New York: Barnes & Noble, Inc., 1961. A detailed conjecture about the physical characteristics of the theater Shakespeare often wrote for.

Beckerman, Bernard. *Shakespeare at the Globe, 1599–1609.* New York: The Macmillan Company, 1962. On the playhouse and on Elizabethan dramaturgy, acting, and staging.

Chambers, E. K. *The Elizabethan Stage.* New York: Oxford University Press, 1923. 4 vols. Reprinted with corrections, 1945. An indispensable reference work on theaters, theatrical companies, and staging at court.

Gurr, Andrew. *The Shakespearean Stage 1574–1642.* Cambridge: Cambridge University Press, 1970. On the acting companies, the actors, the playhouses, the stages, and the audiences.

Harbage, Alfred. *Shakespeare's Audience.* New York: Columbia University Press, 1941; London: Oxford University Press, 1941. A study of the size and nature of the theatrical public.

Hodges, C. Walter. *The Globe Restored.* London: Ernest Benn, Ltd., 1953; New York: Coward-McCann, Inc., 1954. A well-illustrated and readable attempt to reconstruct the Globe Theatre.

Nagler, A. M. *Shakespeare's Stage.* Tr. by Ralph Manheim. New Haven, Conn.: Yale University Press, 1958. An excellent brief introduction to the physical aspect of the playhouse.

Smith, Irwin. *Shakespeare's Globe Playhouse.* New York: Charles Scribner's Sons, 1957. Chiefly indebted to J. C. Adams' controversial book, with additional material and scale drawings for model-builders.

Venezky, Alice S. *Pagentry on the Shakespearean Stage.* New York: Twayne Publishers, Inc., 1951. An examination of spectacle in Elizabethan drama.

4. Miscellaneous Reference Works

Abbott, E. A. *A Shakespearean Grammar.* New edition. New York: The Macmillan Company, 1877. An examination of differences between Elizabethan and modern grammar.

Bullough, Geoffrey. *Narrative and Dramatic Sources of Shakespeare*. New York: Columbia University Press, 1957–; London: Routledge & Kegan Paul, Ltd., 1957–. 4 vols. Vols. 5 and 6 in preparation. A collection of many of the books Shakespeare drew upon.

Campbell, Oscar James, and Edward G. Quinn. *The Reader's Encyclopedia of Shakespeare*. New York: Thomas Y. Crowell Co., 1966. More than 2,700 entries, from a few sentences to a few pages on everything related to Shakespeare.

Greg, W. W. *The Shakespeare First Folio*. New York and London: Oxford University Press, 1955. A detailed yet readable history of the first collection (1623) of Shakespeare's plays.

Kökeritz, Helge. *Shakespeare's Names*. New Haven, Conn.: Yale University Press, 1959; London: Oxford University Press, 1960. A guide to the pronunciation of some 1,800 names appearing in Shakespeare.

————. *Shakespeare's Pronunciation*. New Haven, Conn.: Yale University Press, 1953; London: Oxford University Press, 1953. Contains much information about puns and rhymes.

Linthicum, Marie C. *Costume in the Drama of Shakespeare and His Contemporaries*. New York and London: Oxford University Press, 1936. On the fabrics and dress of the age, and references to them in the plays.

Muir, Kenneth. *Shakespeare's Sources*. London: Methuen & Co., Ltd., 1957. Vol. 2 in preparation. The first volume, on the comedies and tragedies, attempts to ascertain what books were Shakespeare's sources, and what use he made of them.

Onions, C. T. *A Shakespeare Glossary*. London: Oxford University Press, 1911; 2nd ed., rev., with enlarged addenda, 1953. Definitions of words (or senses of words) now obsolete.

Partridge, Eric. *Shakespeare's Bawdy*. Rev. ed. New York: E. P. Dutton & Co., Inc., 1955; London: Routledge & Kegan Paul, Ltd., 1955. A glossary of bawdy words and phrases.

Shakespeare Quarterly. See headnote to Suggested References.

Shakespeare Survey. See headnote to Suggested References.

Smith, Gordon Ross. *A Classified Shakespeare Bibliography 1936–1958*. University Park, Pa.: Pennsylvania State University Press, 1963. A list of some 20,000 items on Shakespeare.

Spevack, Marvin. *The Harvard Concordance to Shakespeare*. Cambridge, Mass.: Harvard University Press, 1973. An index to Shakespeare's words.

Wells, Stanley, ed. *Shakespeare: Select Bibliographies*. London: Oxford University Press, 1973. Seventeen essays surveying scholarship and criticism of Shakespeare's life, work, and theater.

5.   *Richard II*

Black, Matthew W. (ed.). *A New Variorum Edition of Shakespeare: The Life and Death of King Richard the Second*. Philadelphia, Pa.: J. B. Lippincott Co., for the Modern Language Association, 1956.

Bogard, Travis. "Shakespeare's Second Richard," *Publications of the Modern Language Association*, LXX (1955), 192–209.

Campbell, Lily B. *Shakespeare's Histories*. San Marino, Calif.: Henry E. Huntington Library; London: Cambridge University Press, 1947.

Dean, Leonard F. "*Richard II:* The State and the Image of the Theater," *PMLA*, LXVII (1952), 211–18.

Humphries, Arthur Raleigh. *Shakespeare: King Richard II*. London: Edward Arnold Ltd., 1967.

Ornstein, Robert. *A Kingdom for a Stage*. Cambridge, Mass.: Harvard University Press, 1972.

Palmer, John. *Political Characters of Shakespeare*. London and New York: The Macmillan Company, 1945, 1946.

Reese, Max Meredith. *The Cease of Majesty*. New York: St. Martin's Press, Incorporated, 1962; Leeds: E. J. Arnold and Son, Ltd., 1961.

Rossiter, A. P. *Angel with Horns and Other Shakespeare Lectures,* ed. Graham Storey. New York: Theatre Arts Books; London: Longmans, Green & Company, Ltd., 1961.

Stirling, Brents. *Unity in Shakespearian Tragedy*. New York: Columbia University Press; London: Oxford University Press, 1956.

Swinburne, A. C. *Three Plays of Shakespeare*. New York and London: Harper & Brothers, 1909.

Tillyard, E. M. W. *Shakespeare's History Plays*. New York: The Macmillan Company, 1946; London: Chatto & Windus, 1944.

Ure, Peter (ed.). *The Arden Edition of the Works of William Shakespeare: King Richard II*. 4th ed. rev. Cambridge, Mass.: Harvard University Press; London: Methuen & Co., Ltd., 1956.

Wilson, J. Dover (ed.). *The Works of Shakespeare: King Richard II*. New York: The Macmillan Company; London: Cambridge University Press, 1939.

Yeats, W. B. *Ideas of Good and Evil*. New York and London: The Macmillan Company, 1903.